WAIT UNTIL DARK

Carolina Moon Series, Book 3

By Christy Barritt

WAIT UNTIL DARK

CHRISTY BARRITT

CHAPTER 1

Brody Joyner gripped the steering wheel, his pale knuckles matching the overwhelming white outside. Snow beat down on his windshield. His tires slipped on the asphalt. He was all too aware that, on either side of the road, gigantic ditches waited like graves for anyone who made one wrong move.

He braved the massive snowstorm as a favor to his friend, police chief Joshua Haven. Brody normally worked for the Coast Guard, but he'd recently taken a leave of absence. Joshua had received a report about a stranded boater on the river, so Brody had gone out to see if he could help. When he arrived at the boat, he found it empty.

After securing the boat in the parking lot of a local boat ramp, Brody was headed home.

He cranked up the heat in the truck. Even the layers upon layers of clothing he'd donned didn't keep him warm right now. The biting cold was unrelenting.

As heat began to pour through the vents—finally!—he let out a breath and stared at the road ahead. Trees formed ghostly impressions. Where the street began and ended blurred together. Treacherous was an understatement for these conditions.

It was brutal outside. Absolutely brutal.

Something on the road in front of him caught his eye. He leaned closer to the windshield, trying to see through the blinding snow.

Just then, the downfall paused as if Old Man Winter drew in a long breath before releasing his next downpour. Brody saw a figure there.

A man. Lying in the road. Still moving—maybe.

He hit the brakes and held his breath, praying the truck didn't skid. As if suspended in motion, the truck slowed, slowed, slowed even more.

Stop. Please stop in time.

Tension pressed between his shoulders as he continued to glide.

The truck halted mere inches from the man.

Brody threw the gear into park and scrambled to check on the man. No sooner had he stepped out than did the snow begin to fall in a total whiteout. Flakes clung to his eyelashes and stung his cheeks. The wind swept through his clothing until his bones ached.

No one should be out in this weather. He was already wet from the rough surf that had splashed aboard his boat. He'd thought it was survivable—but that was when he assumed he'd be home to take a warm shower within fifteen minutes.

He was going to have to feel his way across the landscape—his vision was useless as precipitation fell in thick, downy sheets.

Finally, his foot bumped something, and he knelt on the slippery snow. This must be the guy he'd seen. All his other senses were useless at the moment, other than his ability to touch and feel. He had to trust that skill, as well as pure instinct.

When the snow cleared again for a few seconds, he

spotted an older gentleman with red cheeks and icy extremities. The man's face was wrinkled, his eyebrows bushy and white, and his figure, though clothed in layers, still obviously slight and wiry. A low moan escaped from the man's purple lips.

This man needed help—and soon.

"Come on. Let's get you in my truck," Brody muttered.

The man's eyes fluttered open and froze onto Brody's. "Be . . . careful." Each word seemed uttered with a scratchy rasp of pain.

Brody supposed anyone could have used that advice. But something about the way the man said it made Brody think twice. He shivered, but convinced himself it was because of the cold, not because of this situation or because of a kooky, perhaps delusional old man.

"I will be careful. Promise." Brody reached beneath the man's shoulders. "Let's get you to safety."

Brody hauled the guy to his feet. How long had this man been out here? He felt like a dead weight. As Brody grabbed the man's hand to stabilize him, Brody noticed the blood there. On his knuckles. The torn skin. The purple bruises.

That wasn't frostbite. It looked like this man had been in a fight. Just who was he? Why was he out here in the middle of the storm? There was nothing else around. Just the river behind him and woods on either side of the road.

Brody would think about that later.

He struggled through the snow, each step a battle to continue moving with the man's weight pressing into him. He felt like he was pushing against a wall and gaining very little traction. He had rescued people from twelve-foot swells in the middle of hurricanes. He could rescue this man now.

Finally, he reached the front passenger door. Despite thick gloves, his hands were almost numb as he grabbed the handle and pulled the door open. Using his last bit of strength, he helped the stranger into his truck and slammed the door.

He had to get off these roads or they would both be goners. Everything was becoming ice around them, making being outside a death trap in itself.

He released a slow breath, the air from his lungs instantly turning to frost. He kept one hand on his truck, using it as a guide as he scurried around to the driver's seat.

If he could just get to the end of this road, there was a gas station not too far down the highway. They could seek refuge there until the whiteout passed. At least it should be warm inside. Maybe the owner, Herb, would even have some coffee made. He was the type who didn't miss work for any reason—especially not weather emergencies.

Brody climbed in and slammed his door, the heat as welcoming as a kiss from a loved one. "We've got to get off this road. Everything is shut down in this area. At least crews treated Highway 17, but the snow is coming down so fast I'm not sure how much good it did."

He glanced at his passenger. The man sagged against the door, almost like he couldn't hold himself up. He needed help. Hypothermia was kicking in. But driving too fast down this road would only make things worse.

"What's your name?" Brody tried to keep the guy lucid as he started down the ice-coated street, moving more slowly than a narwhale in polar waters.

The man said nothing, only stared straight ahead.

"How'd you end up out here in this snowstorm?"

Brody continued.

Again, the man remained quiet. Brody had the strange feeling that it wasn't because of hypothermia as much as it was avoidance. He remembered the man's bruised, battered knuckles, and unrest sloshed inside him.

As a gust of wind swept over the road, his grip tightened on the wheel. They would be lucky to make it to the gas station in one piece. Being out here was just asking for trouble.

"Pastor . . ." the man finally whispered. He licked his lips, but his eyes looked glazed.

"Pastor? You want to go see your pastor?" Did the man sense the end was near and long for last rites? Or did he have something to confess?

The stranger pointed into the distance. "Please."

If Brody remembered correctly, they should be approaching a crossroad soon. It was impossible to tell how close they were. "You want me to turn right?"

"They're . . . coming."

Alarm shot through Brody. The man had gone from delusional to crazy. "Who's coming?"

"The men . . ." Just then, he sat up straight and grabbed Brody's arm. "There!"

Brody glanced in the direction he pointed. The snow cleared long enough for Brody to see a road sign. "What's down there?"

"Please." The man clutched his arm even harder.

The man sounded desperate. Brody wasn't sure why, but he turned. He was fairly certain he could take this street down a little farther and get to the highway. This road was a little broader and not quite as treacherous as the one he'd turned off.

Maybe the man lived down here. Maybe he wanted to go home. Maybe his pastor lived in this direction.

Who was Brody kidding? It would be nearly impossible to walk through this snow without freezing to death. If he were able to drop the man off, the guy would risk life and limb trying to get to the front door. Driveways down here were more likes lanes. Brody's truck wasn't equipped to plow through snow and he didn't have chains.

He glanced in his rearview mirror and squinted. Was that a car behind him? Was someone else crazy enough to be out in this weather?

Slowly, steadily, the car drew closer. No, not a car. It was a Hummer. He could barely see it through the deluge of snow. But it was clearly a vehicle, and it was clearly right on his bumper.

What in the world?

A crack cut through the air.

He glanced behind him.

His back window. It now bore a bullet hole.

That's when he heard his window splinter.

Someone was shooting at him.

You've got to be kidding me.

Brody pressed on the accelerator. He shouldn't go any faster—it was dangerous—but he didn't have much choice.

Another bullet pierced his vehicle, slipping through the shattered back glass and hitting his front windshield. It had raced by, only inches from his head—if that much.

He flinched, pitched forward maybe. It threw him off enough that—just for a moment—he lost control of his truck.

He hit a patch of ice. The truck swerved.

"Hold on!" he yelled.

He gripped the steering wheel, trying to right the vehicle. It was no use. It began spinning.

With a sickening crunch and a harsh lurch, the truck hit a tree.

And then everything went black.

***

Felicity French stared at the windowpane, which grew foggy as the cool air from the snowstorm outside met the warm air inside the drafty, old house her grandma had left for her.

She remembered sitting here as a child, in this very spot, using her breath to fog the window. Then, she'd draw hearts and smiley faces and flowers.

At the moment, she pondered what to create on the blank glass canvas. Not hearts and smiles and flowers. Drawing a frowning face seemed too solemn and dramatic. A broken heart seemed over the top.

Instead, she dragged three of her fingers over the glass, curving them until they formed a rainbow.

A rainbow. Hope in the middle of a storm. God's promises.

She wasn't so sure she believed in God's promises anymore. Her preacher had always said that everybody and everything in this world would let you down, but God never would.

That preacher had lied.

God had let her down big-time. Despite her prayers, her tears, her yearnings, everything she'd loved had been taken from her.

As she stared at the rainbow, she squinted.

All she'd seen for the past several hours was blinding whiteness outside as "Snowmegadon" hit the area. Out here in eastern North Carolina, snow wasn't that common. One inch of snow usually shut down roads and schools. Residents of the small, sleepy town of Hertford already had five inches from this storm, and the precipitation kept coming.

But there, in the distance, was a blob of black.

Felicity erased the rainbow and cleared more of the fog away in order to see better. Were her eyes playing tricks on her? What was that in the distance?

Another gust of snow blew past. She blinked, trying to focus. All she saw was white again.

Maybe that was all she'd ever seen.

She stared for a couple more minutes before convincing herself she was losing her mind, seeing some kind of winter mirage. Finally, she stood. She had to do something instead of gaze out the window.

Just because she was newly single and jobless didn't mean she had to act useless.

She walked back into the kitchen of the old plantation house. Her mom's mother had died not even a year ago, and no one else in the family wanted the rundown place. Felicity knew she needed a change after the fiasco in Raleigh, and she saw this house as the perfect opportunity for a fresh start.

She wasn't sure how her grandmother had survived out here for so long, though. Some of the wooden floorboards were so deteriorated that Felicity feared falling through when she walked across them. The flowered wallpaper peeled at the corners, water stains decorated the ceiling, and the stair railing was loose in more than one place.

The outside was lovely, though. It was plantation style with white columns and a massive wraparound porch. A solitary stained-glass window hung high above the front door, almost like a centerpiece.

Trees, now decrepit-looking with their frail

branches and moss that hung like threadbare clothing, lined the gravel driveway. At the end of the drive, toward the road, metal gates stood open. They were rusted that way, for that matter.

The place had been glorious at one time. Full of life and love and hopes and dreams. Felicity had spent many summers here as a child, and she'd delighted in the wide, open spaces.

Maybe with time, Felicity would fix up the house. Maybe she'd stay here awhile and then move on. She hadn't decided yet.

She refilled a chunky ceramic coffee mug, took a sip, and let the warmth fill her.

Her feet seemed to be on autopilot, and she found herself walking back toward that window again, her subconscious still dwelling on that black dot she'd seen in the distance.

"Felicity! Everything okay down there?"

Great-Aunt Bonny was staying with Felicity during the storm. Normally Aunt Bonny had her own residence at a local assisted-living facility, but Felicity had invited her to stay for a while.

Maybe *invited* was too strong of a word. Aunt Bonny had shown up on the doorstep with a suitcase in hand.

Bonny's sister-in-law—Felicity's grandmother—had owned this place. How could she refuse? Besides, she'd thought, the company would be nice. But in less than twenty-four hours together, her opinionated aunt was driving her crazy. The woman had ideas on everything—everything! The way Felicity wore her hair, what her next career move should be, what kind of man she should date.

Felicity might lose her mind if they were trapped inside alone for too much longer. However, she feared her aunt might be suffering from the start of dementia. It was the small things that made her think so. Repeating herself. Not remembering names. Forgetting to eat.

Felicity had her moved from an assisted-living facility down in Wilmington to one here in Hertford. Aunt Bonny hadn't objected. In fact, she'd made the move sound like fun, like a new adventure. She'd always been a free spirit, and she had no husband or children to dictate what she could or couldn't do.

"Everything's fine, Aunt Bonny," she yelled up the stairs. "I'm just looking at something outside."

"Something interesting?" Footsteps sounded on the wooden stairs.

Felicity stared out the window again, searching for the source of her curiosity. She saw nothing. "I'm not sure what it was. A dog, maybe? I could be seeing things."

"These old eyes aren't what they used to be, but let me take a look. I could use some excitement around here."

Aunt Bonny descended the stairs. Bonny might be in her seventies, but with her platinum-blonde hair, always perfect makeup, and trim figure, one would never know that. The woman lived by the motto that—not cleanliness—but being well-groomed was next to godliness. She'd even adopted popular styles most often seen on teenagers. Colorful leggings were her most recent favorite trend.

Felicity, at one time, had portrayed that image also: well-groomed and having everything together. But now that she was unemployed, she enjoyed letting her long, wavy blonde hair flow freely, falling halfway down her back.

She preferred no makeup, even though that meant people could see circles under her eyes or other blemishes that popped up. Overall, she had a good complexion.

Ricky had always liked her hair smooth, her flaws concealed, and her clothing tailored. That was just one more reason for her to revert back to her uninhibited state—the way she'd been before Ricky came into her life.

Aunt Bonny stood beside Felicity and peered through the glass. "I think it's a . . . it's a . . . a man."

Felicity leaned closer. Sure enough, the blob reappeared. In between the bursts of snow, the outline of a man came into view. Felicity's pulse quickened. "You're not crazy. But what's someone doing out in a storm like this?"

"Maybe it's the police, coming to give us a warning."

Felicity shook her head, continuing to stare. "I doubt the police can get down those roads."

"The Red Cross?"

"I think they come *after* disasters, not in the middle of them."

"The milkman?"

Felicity barely heard her. She stared at the figure outside. He was probably twenty feet from their porch. If anyone was out in a storm like this, it had to be an emergency.

That, coupled with the fact that this house was out in the middle of nowhere, only made Felicity's apprehension grow.

Something was wrong. She was certain of it.

Just then, the figure fell forward. Was it her imagination, or had the man staggered to the ground?

Elements like this could wipe anyone out. Permanently.

Felicity grabbed her coat and a scarf from the rack behind her.

"What are you doing?" Aunt Bonny put a hand over her heart, as if appalled at the very assumption that her niece might be going out in this storm.

"He needs help." She wrapped the scarf around her neck and pulled it tight. Then she pulled on a stocking cap and gloves. These wouldn't offer much protection. As soon as they got wet, they'd be useless. But they were a starting place.

"And you're going to be the one to give it to him?" She said the word "you're" with such a sour surprise that Felicity had to bite her tongue. Sure, Felicity knew she was petite at only five two and 120 pounds. But she had to do something. She didn't believe in turning her back on someone in need

"Someone's got to."

With that, she zipped up her coat and stepped into the whipping wind, into the smothering snow, and braced herself for what was to come.

CHAPTER 2

As soon as Felicity stepped off the porch, her legs sank into icy-cold snow. Her skin tightened at the burn, and her fingers instantly tingled with impending numbness.

Despite the elements, she pushed herself forward. She'd lost sight of the man. He'd fallen. Snow probably covered most of him now as the icy precipitation continued to pour from the sky, laying claim to everything it touched.

Snowflakes caught on her eyelashes. Felt like frozen papier-mâché on her cheeks. Made her lungs ache with every breath.

She knew she couldn't live with herself if she left someone out here to die while she stayed warm inside. No, she had to keep moving.

The snow suctioned each of her steps. But, slowly, surely, she continued forward.

Finally, she reached a dark spot in the snow. A patch of black.

A man, lying face down. A dusting of snow covered him already. He lay motionless. She wasn't even sure if his chest was rising and falling.

She had to act fast.

She grabbed the man's arm and tugged. He hardly

moved.

Felicity hadn't thought this far ahead. She'd reached the man, but now how would she help him?

She only had one idea. She slipped her coat off, the sharp wind assaulting the skin beneath her sweater. Working quickly, she turned the man over and looped her jacket under his arms. She grabbed the sleeves and tugged.

Movement. She had movement. It would still be slow. Painfully slow perhaps. But she'd take what she could get.

Feeling a bit like a workhorse pulling a plow, she tugged and jerked and gulped in deep breaths of air so cold it froze her insides. Her muscles burned. Her calves felt like they'd snap. Her back ached.

Keeping going. You can do it.

She tugged and pulled and heaved.

After what seemed like hours, her foot hit the bottom porch step.

She looked up and saw her aunt standing there. She stared at Felicity, a hand over her heart still, and her eyes wide as if shocked Felicity had made it this far.

"Help," Felicity rasped. The cold had frozen her vocal chords, making it hard to talk.

Her aunt stared at her another moment before sighing and crossing the porch. Aunt Bonny took one sleeve, and Felicity gripped the other. Together, they heaved the man up the steps, over the porch, and into their warm home.

The smooth floor made it easier to drag the man in front of the fireplace. When Felicity finally deposited him there, she took only a minute to gasp in air and give her muscles a break. Her work was far from being done.

Felicity stared at the man, soaking in his features as

he lay like a corpse in front of the blazing fire. He didn't look familiar. Of course, she hadn't been in town long enough to know most of the people. Neither had her Aunt Bonny, though she had come to visit her family's estate quite often.

He appeared young—twenty-something—and healthy. Except for the awful bump and cut on his forehead.

Aunt Bonny looked up at Felicity from her perch on the other side of the man. "He's going to go into hypothermia unless we get these wet clothes off and get him dry and warm."

Working as quickly as she could with her numb fingers, she unzipped his coat and slipped it off. Pieces of glass fell to the floor.

Glass?

Had he smashed into a windshield? Been in a car accident?

The white T-shirt was fairly dry beneath his coat, but his shoes and pants were soaked.

As Felicity realized what she had to do next, her cheeks heated. "I can't . . ."

Aunt Bonny stared at her. "A woman in her twenties with scruples? I thought your kind were extinct." She offered a half-laugh, half-snort. "I used to be a nurse. I can do this."

Nurse might be stretching it, Felicity thought. Rather, the woman had worked as a receptionist in a doctor's office. But Felicity wouldn't argue right now. At least she wouldn't have to face this blush-inducing dilemma.

Aunt Bonny knelt beside the man and slipped his shirt off. "Some of your father's old clothes are still in the back bedroom. Why don't you grab a shirt and sweats?"

Felicity hardly heard her. Her gaze fixated on a scar on the man's chest instead.

It looked like a . . . an old bullet wound.

"Felicity!"

She snapped back to the moment. "Yes?"

"Go get some clothes."

A weight bore down on Felicity's chest as she started down the hallway. "Will do."

Felicity scrambled up the stairs. She'd grab the things her aunt had requested. But, after seeing that scar, she was going to grab her gun as well. She was no expert, but that injury looked like a battle wound to her.

She just wasn't sure what side of the battle this man had been on. Had he been a drug dealer? An escaped inmate? Or maybe he was a police officer. But where was his uniform, then? A veteran? Possibly.

Until she knew for sure, she had to remain cautious.

Less than a minute later, she was back downstairs.

Fear pricked her heart, but the sense of urgency for this man's life propelled her on. His lips were blue as he lay by the fire, as still as death. But, reassuringly, the man's scarred chest rose and fell. If she didn't get his body temperature up, that movement might not continue.

"I have clothes," she announced.

Her aunt reached for them. "Now go get some blankets."

Relief filled her. "Got it."

She went room by room to gather as many blankets as she could find. Many of them smelled dusty and old, but they would work.

Back in the living room, she scrambled to cover him with layer upon layer of warmth. First, an old afghan her grandmother had crocheted. Then a quilt Felicity had picked up in Amish country. Then a cheap, store-bought fuchsia-colored cover.

With that done, Felicity retrieved a heating pad and some warm, wet cloths. She placed the pad under the blankets, before kneeling beside the man. Using a warm washcloth, Felicity wiped his face, trying to thaw his skin.

"You look like you're handling this just fine," Her aunt stood with a groan, keeping a hand on her lower back. "I'm going to go stir my stew before it burns."

She hoped her aunt hadn't pushed herself too hard. "Sounds good. Thanks, Aunt Bonny."

When her aunt walked away, Felicity stared at the man's face. He was handsome, with strong features. Dark hair that curled slightly at the hairline. Thick eyebrows, and eyes with impossibly long lashes. Full lips. His cheeks were scruffy, in a way that was all too appealing.

Her gaze landed on the gash near his temple. It was starting to swell. She needed to treat it. Leaving the warm cloth on his forehead, she hurried to get a first aid kit. After applying some ointment, she placed three butterfly bandages on the wound.

What had happened? Hopefully when he woke up, he could tell her.

Finished with that, she reached under the covers to clasp his hand. She worked it between her own hands, knowing she needed to get the blood moving. His hands and feet were the most likely places he'd have frostbite.

"Maybe you would make a decent nurse. You should go back to school," Bonny announced, entering the room again.

"I don't want to be a nurse, though, Aunt Bonny. I'm working on my PhD."

"There's a nursing shortage, you know."

Felicity shook her head, still rubbing the man's

fingers. "But I'm happy doing what I do."

But was she? Had she ever really been happy, or was all of it an elusion? Had she simply been trying to forget her pain and losses?

"Suit yourself then." Her aunt leaned closer, raising her eyebrows almost comically. "By the way, whoever he is, he has amazing pecks."

"Aunt Bonny!"

Her aunt shrugged. "Purely an observation. Of the medical variety. Of course. Get your mind out of the gutter."

With that, she walked off.

Felicity stared at the man another moment. She needed to call 911, but she doubted they'd come out in these conditions unless the situation was truly life-threatening. Still, she'd put in the call before she lost service.

At least that way, if something happened to them, there would be a record that the man was here. Felicity really hoped that wouldn't be the case, though.

***

Felicity gathered the stranger's wet clothing and took them into the ramshackle laundry room at the back of the house. She shivered when she walked inside. Though the heat was on in the house, the old place was drafty, and this room especially.

If she studied the walls hard enough, she would spot at least one crack where the wall and the ceiling were supposed to meet. Instead, there was a gap there and traces of the cold outside slithered inside.

It was one of the main things that needed to be done to this house to make it livable: the whole place needed to be patched up.

Her poor grandma. Felicity could only imagine her living here alone for all those years. Felicity should have come home more. Should have opened her eyes to her grandma's needs so she could help.

Instead, her grandmother had been murdered, for such senseless reasons, at that. Even though her killer now sat in jail, that fact didn't make Felicity feel better.

Would things have been different if Felicity had been there? Most likely, yes. She could have watched out for Grandma more. Kept an eye on her. Stopped the man who'd claimed to be a friend from killing her grandma in order to keep her silent.

But Felicity had been so wrapped up in her career. In her education. In Ricky. It had all been a mistake.

She grabbed the man's clothing from the floor and started to stuff it into the dryer so he would have some warm clothes to wear when he woke up.

If he woke up.

No, she couldn't think like that. Of course, he would wake up. Why wouldn't he? They'd found him early enough. She had called 911, and the operator walked her through the proper steps for dealing with hypothermia. Felicity had already done most of them. If he took a turn for the worse, they'd try to get an ambulance out here.

Her throat tightened as she checked his pockets. There was a wallet there. Brody Joyner. Hertford, North Carolina. She saw his birthdate and calculated his age to be thirty-one.

She dug deeper into his wallet, feeling nosy but casting her worries aside. He was a stranger in her home. She had to do whatever she needed in order to protect herself, her aunt, and her property. There was no question about that.

She found no credit cards. Was that because he was responsible financially? Or did he have collectors after him, and he had such bad credit he couldn't get cards?

She also found a punch card from a yogurt shop in the neighboring town of Elizabeth City.

How bad could a guy be who had a punch card from a frozen yogurt joint?

She shivered as she put his wallet on top of the washer. She quickly stuffed his clothes into the dryer. As she did, something clattered onto the floor.

She paused.

What was that?

A key, she realized.

She picked it up carefully. This wasn't any ordinary key. It was a skeleton key, the kind of key kids played with when they hunted for gold at the end of rainbows.

Why in the world did someone like Brody Joyner have this? He didn't wear a wedding ring. But that didn't mean he didn't have kids somewhere . . . kids who could be worried about their father right now.

After she turned on the dryer, she held the key with both hands to examine it.

This was heavier than most of the souvenir variety, like it was made of real metal. She squinted and looked closer. The key appeared slightly rusted, and the intricate yet imperfect design on the key's handle made her pause.

It was probably nothing. But, if she had a chance later, she wanted to examine it further. Right now, she needed to check on the stranger in her home.

CHAPTER 3

Ten minutes later, Felicity sat in front of the fire and sipped some coffee. The man lay behind her, a mountain of blankets piled on top of him. He still hadn't regained consciousness, but his chest rose and fell, indicating he was still alive.

The fire crackled in the fireplace, warming the room so much that it felt like a furnace. Why she was drinking coffee on top of all of the heat pouring into the space, she wasn't sure, except for the fact that coffee always comforted her. That, combined with the hearty aroma of her aunt's Brunswick stew on the stove, brought her a moment of consolation.

Well, all of that, and the fact that she'd retrieved her gun from her room. It currently rested on the floor in front of her. She didn't know what would happen when this man woke up, and she didn't want to take any chances. Better safe than sorry.

The snow still fell outside, making this a February to remember. The sun was beginning to sink lower and would soon be gone. In the background, the TV murmured and Aunt Bonny was using some bright-hued pencils to finish a page in an adult coloring book.

If Felicity planned on living here, she'd try to fix up

this place and help it return to its former glory. The ceiling and woodwork were remarkable, but everything was buried under years of age and neglect. As a child she'd imagined the parties that had once been held here, complete with women wearing corsets and fancy gowns and men dressed in their finest. She imagined soldiers returning from war, and residents covered in sweat and grime after working in the fields all day.

Felicity glanced back at the man once more, to make sure he was still breathing. What was he doing out in this weather? Had he been called to an emergency? Had he been running from someone? Was he simply not very wise?

"Handsome, isn't he?" Aunt Bonny looked up at her.

How long had her aunt been watching her? There was no telling.

Felicity's friends had always called her Crazy Aunt Bonny, but Felicity had never allowed herself that guilty pleasure. It seemed too disrespectful. But, since Felicity had moved to Hertford and gotten to know the woman better, she often wondered if her friends were right. Her aunt said some very strange things sometimes.

Felicity glanced at the man's face and shrugged. "I suppose."

There was no supposing about it. Of course, he was handsome, even in his unconscious state. But Felicity couldn't care less about his attractiveness or lack of attractiveness at the moment. All she cared about was that scar. She couldn't get it out of her mind.

Aunt Bonny nodded at her gun. "You ever used one of those before?"

Felicity glanced at the Glock in front of her. "No, but I took lessons."

"I reckon that's because you're a city girl."

Felicity had actually purchased it because she had transported valuables from her office to her home on more than one occasion. Right now, she was glad she had it, even if that job was long gone . . . just like her reputation. And it had all happened at the hands of a man who supposedly loved her.

"It's a good thing I've got this. Did you see that scar on his chest?" Her blood went cold when she thought about it.

Aunt Bonny wagged her eyebrows. "His very defined chest?"

"Aunt Bonny!"

She grinned before she shrugged nonchalantly. "Probably wrestled with a rooster."

Felicity stared at her aunt for a moment in bewilderment. "What?"

"Those roosters. They can tear someone up."

Felicity said nothing. Let her aunt think what she might. Felicity knew it was a bullet wound. And she didn't like the implications of that fact.

***

Brody Joyner had a whopper of a headache and an aching numbness throughout his body. Somewhere in his semiconscious state, he heard talking. He felt warmth.

Slowly, he began regaining feeling in his limbs—the pins and needles sort of feeling, but feeling nonetheless. His mind wafted from flashback to flashback.

First, he remembered being out on the river. He remembered docking his boat. Then he saw whiteness surrounding him, as if stuck in an episode of *The Twilight Zone*. Then he drifted into nothingness again.

Danger . . . the message seemed to call to him from afar.

Wake up.

In an instant, he was on alert. His eyes jerked open, and uneasiness filled him.

Fight, Brody. Fight. Your life depends on it.

Slowly, the room came into focus. A woman sat only a foot from him, her blonde hair and easy profile facing a crackling fire. His breath caught at the sight of her. She was beautiful.

And dangerous. He wasn't sure where the thought came from, but he had to trust his instincts.

She glanced at him, alarm filling her. He followed her gaze as it jerked to the floor. A gun. She had a gun.

His reflexes snapped into action. He lunged forward, catching the woman in a chokehold. The mug in her hands crashed to the floor. Liquid seeped onto the wood below him.

Leaving one arm around her neck, he quickly grabbed the gun from the floor and held it to the woman's head.

"Who are you?" he hissed.

The woman gasped. Clawed at his arms. Her body jostled as she tried to get away.

"I asked you who you were," he repeated through gritted teeth.

"Felicity French." Her voice quivered.

The scent of her shampoo—fruity and sweet— drifted upward, temporarily calming him. "Where have you taken me?"

"It's . . . this is my house. I found you out—outside in the snow. Half-frozen. I was afraid you would die."

He involuntarily loosened his grip as more questions hit him. He had no recall of how he had gotten here. "Where am I?"

"I told you—my house."

"No, I mean where exactly is your house?"

"Hertford, North Carolina."

"Who do you work for?" he demanded.

There were people who wanted him dead. Drug rings he'd busted. Modern-day pirates he'd sent to jail. Human-trafficking operations he'd shut down. He could remember those things. But not how he'd gotten here.

"I don't work for anyone. I'm . . . unemployed."

His eyes roamed his surroundings. It appeared to be an ordinary home, although outdated and slightly musty. It was large with high ceilings and ornate—though faded—woodwork.

"Is there anyone else here?" he demanded.

Just as the words left his mouth, an older woman stepped from the shadows with a rolling pin in hand. She patted it against her palm and scowled. "I am, and if you don't let her go, I'll bash your head in like bread dough that rose too high."

He almost laughed. But then he saw the serious expression on her face and decided better of it. "How'd I get here?"

"I told you," the woman he'd grabbed said through what sounded like clenched teeth. "I found you outside. In the snow. I obviously should have left you there, especially if this is the thanks I get."

"That's right. She saved your life, you ungrateful brat," the older woman muttered, smacking that rolling pin against her hand again. "What kind of idiot goes out in weather like this?"

Weather like this? What did she mean? He didn't dare look at the window for fear of being clobbered.

His muscles tensed. Saved his life? What had

happened?

He glanced at his arm. Where had the strange clothing come from? A blue flannel shirt covered his upper half. Sweats concealed his legs. Colorful blankets were tangled at his feet.

"Please," the woman whispered. "I was only trying to help. Put the gun down."

There was something about the desperation in her voice, the honesty in the emotion, that made him trust her.

He released his grip, and the woman scooted far away from him, gasping for air and touching her neck. Accusation and disgust stained her eyes.

Regret panged inside him. He'd scared her. Brody wasn't sure where his reaction had come from. He'd been certain he was in danger.

"I'm sorry," he started. "I didn't mean to hurt you."

She scowled, disdain dripping from her voice. "Could have fooled me. Who are you?"

"My name is Brody." At least he remembered that. He remembered his tiny house, his truck, his job with the Coast Guard. He recalled Bible studies, Sunday morning church services, and his favorite barbecue restaurant. But nothing about how he got here today.

"Why were you out in the storm, Sonny Boy?" The older woman had a G.I. Joe look on her face as she glared at him, ready to attack.

He opened his mouth to answer but shut it again. "I don't know."

"What do you mean you don't know?" the older woman asked.

He rubbed his temples, trying to make his thoughts come into focus. Finally, he shook his head. "I mean, I don't know. I only remember docking my boat. Everything after that is blank."

CHAPTER 4

"Don't play games with me." Felicity seethed out the words, her fear replaced with anger. No way was she letting someone come into her home and threaten her.

"I wish I were." The man rubbed his neck and rocked back. Confusion strained his gaze.

Felicity's eyebrows shot up at his words, and she approached the conversation cautiously. "What do you mean?"

He shook his head, still squinting and rubbing his neck. "I . . . I can't remember anything. I have no idea how I got here."

Felicity's shoulders sank. The perplexing look on his face caused her heart to soften, even though she willed it not to. Compassion would only equate to weakness in this situation. "What do you mean?"

The man studied her face. "Do I know you?"

"So help me, if this is all an act . . ." Her words came out as a low growl.

The agony in his eyes again softened her heart. He lowered his head into his hands, before raking his fingers through his thick hair. His eyes met hers.

"It's not an act." His voice sounded hoarse and scratchy with emotion. "And you're not a sham either, telling me you have no idea who I am?"

"I'm just as confused as you. Were you out of your mind going out in this weather?"

The light from the fire danced across his face. Felicity waited for him to continue, hoping a memory was emerging from some deep place in his mind. Maybe it would just take a minute. He did have that nasty bump on his forehead.

While he still stared at the fire, he spoke. "The last thing I remember is going out on a rescue mission. Someone was out on the river in this weather."

"Are you a marine police officer or something?"

He shook his head. "No, Coast Guard. Anyway, I didn't find him, and I had to come back to shore because of the snow." He lifted his gaze to hers. "Then I woke up here. I can't remember anything else."

Felicity's mind whirled at full-speed. No, it couldn't be. Things like this didn't happen in real life, only in the movies. Or maybe he was playing a trick on her, trying to fool her.

One look into his wide eyes and she believed him, though.

"You have short-term memory loss," she mumbled. Her gaze flickered to his forehead. "Your head wound might have something to do with it."

He gingerly touched the sore spot with his fingertips. For a moment he looked like a lost little boy and Felicity's heart went out to him.

He was ready to kill you, Felicity. Be careful.

He lowered his hand and touched the scruff on his chin. Felicity could see him absorbing each fact. She couldn't imagine what it would be like to not know how you'd ended up in a strange place.

The man cleared his throat and dropped his hand.

"How did you find me?"

"I was looking out the window. I saw you right before you went down."

"Thank goodness for that. This could have ended badly." He studied her a moment. "I'm sorry about what happened earlier. I don't know why . . ."

"It's okay." Felicity stood and started toward the kitchen. "I'm going to fix you something warm to drink. You're still not out of danger yet."

"I'll stand guard." Aunt Bonny pounded her rolling pin again.

Felicity didn't wait for a response. Instead she went to the kitchen and began a pot of coffee, desperate to compose herself.

When Brody put her in a headlock earlier, she'd been totally thrown off guard. She'd been unaware he possessed that kind of strength or energy, especially in his injured state. How much of his hostility stemmed from parts of his life he couldn't remember—parts related to that bullet wound? Even though he was Coast Guard, that didn't mean he was a good guy.

After the coffee finished perking, she poured the liquid into an oversized mug, and grabbed a small trash bag and several paper towels. When she returned to the living room, Brody sat on the couch, a far-off expression on his face. Cautiously, she handed him the drink.

"This will help warm you up."

He mumbled a thank you and took the mug. After the first sip, he coughed.

"Go slow." Felicity started to reach forward to help him, but stopped mid-motion and clasped her hands in front of her instead. "You're lucky you don't have hypothermia right now."

He said nothing. Felicity studied him, noting how

his eyes were tight at the corners and how the wrinkles on his forehead showed concentration. He was trying to remember, trying to put his mind at ease.

Felicity cleaned up her broken coffee mug, searching for any stray shards of porcelain, and soaking up the spilled liquid. She tied all the trash in the plastic bag and deposited it in the wastebasket.

When she sat down, he drank the last drop of his coffee and handed the mug to her. "If you'll just allow me to use your shower, I'll get out of your way."

Felicity's lip tugged up in a half-smile. "You're not going anywhere."

Brody raised his eyebrows. The questions in his eyes stirred Felicity's soul.

"Excuse me?" he asked.

Felicity arrowed her forehead toward the window. "It's been snowing all day, and it's not supposed to let up any time soon. The roads are impassable."

He was silent, brooding almost.

"The shower's down the hall," she stated. "You can help yourself."

He gave a tight nod and started to rise, but teetered. Felicity instinctively rose and slipped an arm around his waist. His weight pressed on her, and she wondered how she'd ever managed to get this man inside. In days past, she might have credited it to a higher power.

He didn't refuse her assistance, as she thought he might. Together, they slowly made their way down the hall to the bathroom, Brody walking like a man three times his age.

He paused at the doorway and looked down at the sweats and flannel shirt he wore. He touched the shirt as if the feel of it would stir a memory. "Is this what I had on when you found me?"

Felicity felt the heat rise to her cheeks. "No, your clothes were soaking wet."

When she finally pulled her eyes from the floor, she thought she saw a twinkle in Brody's eyes. Something about her embarrassment seemed to amuse him. She knew it was unusual for someone her age to blush over something like that, but it was like her aunt said: she had scruples. Ricky had never appreciated that fact.

She cleared her throat, determined not to let him know he'd affected her. "I'll see if they're dry and leave them outside the bathroom if they are."

"I'd appreciate that."

With her cheeks still flaming, she hurried away.

CHAPTER 5

Brody let the hot water hit him. He stretched an arm out, leaning on the shower wall to support himself.

What had happened to get him here?

His head pounded something fierce. He'd need some Advil as soon as possible. The knot on his forehead had done its job.

After letting the spray pound his body for several minutes, he cut the water and toweled off. He stepped onto the cold tile floor, rubbed the fog from the mirror, and looked at his reflection.

A nasty gash stretched across his forehead. What had happened out there exactly? Not remembering was driving him crazy.

He hadn't felt so thrown off guard since his girlfriend had disappeared when he was in high school. Those days afterward had felt so topsy-turvy and uncertain. Though it had happened well over a decade ago, he'd never been the same.

He smoothed his damp hair, and, as he did, an impending feeling of danger hit him again. It wasn't a memory. It was just a gut instinct that something was wrong.

That something was *very* wrong.

Had he really hit his head that hard?

His last memory was of docking the boat. What had happened between then and now?

There was only one thing he knew for sure: as soon as the snow melted, he wanted to get out of here. But he couldn't do that until the roads cleared.

He peeked out the door and found his clothes neatly folded there, just as promised. He pulled them inside, interested to see if they held any additional clues. He found his wallet and searched through it, but only the normal inhabitants were there: driver's license, a few dollars cash, debit card.

Did he have a phone in his pocket? Maybe his call history would give him some clues.

He reached for his shirt, but there was no phone. What had happened to it? Was it still in his truck? Speaking of which, where was his truck?

Maybe Felicity would let him use her phone. He needed to call his friend Joshua, the police chief. Maybe he could shed some light on the situation.

The image of the blonde with the crazy curls and fire-filled eyes crossed through his mind. How the slight woman had managed to pull him into the house amazed him. He should be grateful she'd found him. Instead, she set his nerves on edge. Something wasn't adding up.

He finished getting dressed and strode into the living room. Felicity folded clothes in the corner, and her aunt could be seen in the edge of the kitchen. Something flickered in Felicity's eyes when she saw him.

He'd gotten off to a rocky start with her, to say the least.

She pulled something out of her pocket and dangled it in front of her. "I found this."

He stepped closer and stared at the key in her

hands, unsure what she was getting at. "I've never seen that before."

"It was in your pocket."

He raised a shoulder. "In case you haven't noticed, I'm having a few memory issues right now. Besides, it looks like one of those keys you'd buy at a souvenir shop at the beach."

She swallowed hard—hard enough that Brody could see her throat tighten. "Is that right?"

"You have a different idea?"

She averted her gaze before shrugging. "Why would I have a different idea?"

"That's my question exactly."

When she said nothing, he decided to let the subject drop. The key was the least of his worries at the moment. He needed to fill in some of the blanks, and there was no better way of doing that than talking to Joshua.

"Could I use your phone?" he asked.

She didn't smile, just nodded toward the table by the couch. "Right over there. Hopefully, it still works."

He lumbered toward the table and dialed Joshua's number.

"Joshua," Brody started.

"Hey, man. Didn't recognize the number. You staying warm? I thought I'd hear from you a couple of hours ago. I tried calling your cell phone, but there was no answer."

He glanced across the room at Felicity. "I'm okay. For now. I have a situation . . ."

"What's going on?"

He filled his friend in on what he could remember.

"You must have hit an icy patch and been in an accident. That would make the most sense."

"I agree." That was probably the truth. But, for some reason, Brody didn't completely buy it.

"You said a woman named Felicity rescued you? I met a woman named Felicity at the grocery store a couple of weeks ago. Granddaughter of Fanny Pasture."

Fanny Pasture? That's whose house he was in? He'd always wondered what the inside of that old, grand house looked like. This wasn't the way he expected to get a glimpse.

He glanced over his shoulder again and saw that Felicity was preoccupied with laundry still. His gut told him that she was also very much paying attention. Even though Fanny had been an upstanding citizen, that didn't mean her granddaughter was.

"Know anything about her?"

"I heard she's nice. I don't really know much beyond that. Someone said she moved here from Raleigh. I think she used to work at a university there."

"I see." A university? He couldn't quite picture the woman with the wild untamed hair as the professional collegiate type. Then again, what did he know?

"I'd offer to drive by and pick you up, but the roads are closed. Not even emergency personnel can get out."

If I was just in a simple accident, then where had the key come from?

It was probably nothing, he realized. Yet his mind kept coming back to it.

Something had transpired in his missing time. But what?

***

As Brody talked on the phone, casting suspicious looks over his shoulder, Felicity slipped into the dining room and pulled the key from her pocket. Why was she so fascinated with this? It was probably nothing.

Yet something in the back of her mind beckoned her to dwell on various possibilities for a moment.

She studied the design a little more closely. This definitely wasn't mass-produced. It was iron and heavy. The edges showed signs of age, and bits of rust were still present in the grooves. She would bet there had been more rust at one time, but someone had attempted to restore it.

The bit had wards in it—places that were square—that would activate a lever within a lock. It also had a collar and throating on the stem—classic signs of keys from earlier centuries.

She brought it to her nose and smelled it. Old. It definitely smelled old.

If she had to guess, based on the design and size, this could easily be from the eighteenth century.

What would a huge key like this belong to? It reminded her of the kind she envisioned using in a treasure chest as a child—only larger.

"What do you have there?"

Felicity nearly jumped out of her skin at the sound of her aunt's voice. The key clattered to the floor, and she quickly snatched it up. "Nothing."

"It's a key. Where'd you get that?"

Felicity frowned. There was no use acting like she was avoiding the question. That would only raise red flags. She needed to make it seem like the key was no big deal. "It's nothing. A toy."

"Let me see it." Before Felicity could stop her, Aunt Bonny snatched it from her hands. Her aunt studied it several minutes, grunting as she turned it, held it close, held it far away, and felt the various grooves. "It's

Blackbeard's key."

Felicity laughed out loud. "Funny."

"I'm not laughing. Look at it. See that mark right there." Bonny pointed to a tiny branding on the handle. "That's Blackbeard's symbol."

Felicity blinked when she realized her aunt was serious. She studied the small symbol, but it was so tiny she couldn't make out any of the details. "That's not Blackbeard's symbol. In fact, I don't even think he had a symbol."

"I know he did."

"Aunt Bonny . . ." she warned. Felicity knew exactly where this conversation would go.

Her aunt didn't back down. "Rumors have circulated for years that he roamed the waters around here. We know he took up residence down in Bath, but a lot of people think he came up here to Hertford too. You know the story . . ."

Felicity frowned. "I've looked into that rumor myself, Aunt Bonny. There's no proof anywhere that Blackbeard was married to one of our relatives and we're in his lineage."

She shrugged, as if Felicity's opinion meant nothing. "He had several wives, most of them off the books. I know you don't believe me. You trust in your education more. But I'm telling you the truth. You know I was practically a historian."

"You worked at the visitor center," Felicity corrected. Her aunt had held many careers in her life—and she'd been married three times. One of those careers was in a doctor's office. She'd also traveled with a carnival for a summer.

"Only in title. I would have officially been the historian if they'd had any money to pay me." She let out a harrumph.

Felicity sighed, not liking arguing with her aunt. But she'd heard the stories from her aunt all of her life. Bonny was determined that Blackbeard had docked one of his boats in the river right outside this home, and he'd fathered children with Felicity's great-great-great-great-great-grandmother.

The idea was crazy.

Just to put the thought out of her mind, Felicity had researched her lineage for herself, and there was no proof of that. No proof at all.

"Face it—we've got rebel's blood," her aunt said in a singsong voice.

"You should say thieves' blood—if it's true."

Now her aunt had put a crazy idea in her head. Instead of thinking logically, Felicity was thinking about ancient pirates.

Great. As if she didn't have enough on her mind.

***

A few minutes later, they sat down to an awkward meal around the farm-style table in the kitchen. Aunt Bonny had been simmering the family recipe: Brunswick stew. The tomato-based dish was thick with butter beans, corn, okra, potatoes, and chicken. The scent of it always made her feel right at home. Aunt Bonny had also put some fresh bread in the oven, and the yeasty goodness of it made Felicity's stomach grumble.

It was the perfect meal for the cold day.

But Bonny was mad at Felicity; Felicity was agitated with her aunt; and neither of them trusted the stranger in their home.

Felicity remembered the scar across his chest. It

didn't matter that beneath the scar he was sculpted with noteworthy pecks, as her aunt had so graciously pointed out. Men like Brody sought power and control. She didn't have to know him to know that.

All of that lent to awkward conversation—or lack thereof. Instead, Felicity stared at her stew. Out the window at the white that continued to blanket the darkening sky. At the tiny flakes that clung to the window, forming fascinating crystal patterns.

A candle was lit on the table, and its flames flickered invitingly in the otherwise cringe-worthy mustard-yellow and pea-green kitchen. Felicity had always had an affinity for candles and lanterns and any other natural form of light. Her grandma had kept lanterns around the house, and Felicity had pulled a few out when she heard about the approaching storm.

"I didn't realize this was the home of Fanny Pasture," Brody started. "She was quite the fixture around the area. I used to see her in town, and she'd always insist on getting a kiss on the cheek."

Felicity smiled. "That sounds like Grandma."

Brody sobered. "I'm sorry for your loss."

Felicity's heart panged with grief. "Thank you."

"It was senseless what happened to her. I'm glad the man responsible is now in jail. He deserves to be there for a long time."

Her throat tightened at the memories. "He does."

He took another bite of the stew and wiped his mouth. "I don't ever remember seeing you around town before. I guess you weren't here often?"

Familiar guilt twisted inside her. "No, not so much. Grandma always insisted she was fine. I . . . I shouldn't have believed her."

"She wanted you to spread your wings," Aunt

Bonny said. "If she'd needed help, she would have asked."

A few minutes of silence passed. Felicity wished she believed her aunt's words, but she didn't. She never would.

"This stew is good, by the way," Brody finally said.

She shifted again. This was the perfect time to find out some information about the man trapped here with her. After all, information was power, right? And Brody had known her grandma. Knowing that helped her to let down some of her guard.

"Where are you from?" She sipped her water, trying not to look too interested. "You sound like a local."

He nodded. "I grew up here in Hertford."

"You've never left? Not many people can say that." He shrugged. "Only for college."

"You must really like it here." The town did have its appeal. There was a row of historic shops, all nestled next to the river. Historic homes decorated the streets, and the whole town gave off a friendly vibe that Felicity had always admired.

He shrugged. Some of the uncertainty left his eyes, but he looked tired. "It feels like home."

"You have family?" Aunt Bonny tore off a piece of bread and slathered it with some butter.

"Both of my parents are still here. And, by here, I mean they're in Florida for the winter. They still consider Hertford home."

"How long have you been with the Coast Guard?" Felicity asked.

"Seven years. It's all I ever wanted to do. When I was a boy, I was on the Outer Banks and I saw the Coast Guard save this man from rough waters. They did a helicopter rescue. It was incredible. I knew from that moment what I wanted to do."

"It's nice to find something you're good at."

"It is."

She wished she could say the same. She'd thought she was good at her career, but in the end she'd become a laughingstock. How would she ever get past that and move on? No one in his or her right mind would hire her now.

Before the conversation could go any further, the overhead lights flickered. Felicity braced herself. She'd known it was a good possibility that the electricity would go out. She'd only hoped it wouldn't.

Nearly as soon as the thought fluttered through her head, the house went dark. Only the brightness of the snow outside and the candle on the table offered any relief from the dimness.

"It's going to get cold in here pretty quickly," Brody said. "Do you have any more wood to keep the fire going?"

"We have some out back," Felicity said. "It's so wet from the nor'easter a couple of days ago I don't think it will do any good. I already used the dry stuff."

"If it's all we have, it's going to have to work. How about if I go check it out?"

She nodded, at once grateful he was here. Aunt Bonny wasn't as strong as she'd once been. The cold could bring on pneumonia, and her aunt might never bounce back.

"Let me grab my coat." He stomped across the rickety wooden floor to where they'd left his coat spread on the couch to dry.

As he pulled it on, Felicity realized it wasn't going to be enough. "Let me find you a hat, scarf, and gloves."

She hurried up to the room where her grandma had left her father's clothing. Ignoring the tinge of grief she felt, she found some winter gear and hurried downstairs to give it to Brody. "Here you go."

As he started to slip the hat on, she grabbed his arm, her gaze fixated on his forehead. "Your bandage . . . watch out."

He offered a rueful smile. "Thanks."

As soon as she realized she was touching him, she jerked her hand away. She needed to stay far away from Brody Joyner. Once the snow cleared, he would be out of her life, and she could return to her life as a hermit.

And that was exactly what she wanted for the future.

CHAPTER 6

Brody remembered the fleeting vulnerable look in Felicity's eyes—and then how quickly she'd pulled away from him like a scared rabbit. What was hiding behind that mask she wore? She was fiercely trying to protect herself and remain guarded. It was understandable in one sense. She had a strange man in her home. It was prudent to be cautious. But . . . she seemed a little too jumpy and untrusting

Whatever she was hiding, he found it fascinating—which wasn't a good thing.

Since Andrea had disappeared, he hadn't really dated. Sure, he'd casually gone out a few times. He'd just started dating someone—if five dates counted as dating—when the investigation into Andrea's disappearance had sprung up again and thrown him into a tailspin. He'd broken things off, feeling that familiar guilt in knowing he hadn't been able to help Andrea when she'd needed him the most.

Brody had known what Andrea's family life was like. He knew her struggles. Yet he'd gone away to college and left her to fend for herself. He'd figured she'd graduate soon and be able to get out on her own. They'd get married. Start a new life away from her family.

In an instant, all that had changed. Things would be different right now if he had been there to walk her home from school that day. But he hadn't been, and now she was dead because of it.

He'd carry that guilt with him every day for the rest of his life. Dating again—dating someone else—seemed a betrayal of her memory, for some reason. If he'd failed once, who was to say he wouldn't fail again? No, he didn't deserve another chance.

He stepped onto the back porch and a gust of icy wind caught him. The conditions outside were brutal—the kind where he encouraged people to stay inside. But the snow did seem to be letting up some.

Why had he been out in this? Was it like Joshua had said—was he on his way home from a rescue when he'd simply slid on the icy road? That made the most sense.

He was generally more cautious, and he couldn't help but think there must be more to the story.

He stared into the winter wonderland in front of him and prayed he'd be able to find this firewood. As he took a step toward the edge of the porch, he paused.

Was that a footprint?

Anywhere else in the yard, the snow would have covered such a thing. But here, the overhang above the back porch blocked much of the snowfall. He stomped toward the impression and bent down to view it.

It was fresh. Crisp. Small indentions through snow.

Definitely footprints, he realized. Leading right up to the house. And they weren't from a woman. These were too large.

He walked over to where the prints stopped by the window and peered inside.

From this vantage point, someone would have a perfect view of the home's interior, from the kitchen table all the way into the living room. It wouldn't make sense for either Felicity or her aunt to have left these tracks. They said they'd found him in the front yard.

His spine stiffened, and he glanced around. Was someone out there? Would someone risk traipsing through the snow in order to get to this house? If so, why? And where was the guy now?

He didn't like this. He needed to get that wood and get back inside.

He stepped off the porch into the deep snow. He hoped this storm let up soon. There were too many people in this town and in this county who weren't prepared for weather events like this. And with the roads being closed, getting help would be hard.

The wood was beside an old shed, just like Felicity had told him. He quickly grabbed an armload and hauled it back to the door. He kept his eyes open for danger as he worked, but he saw nothing, just a winter wonderland framed by the Perquimans River and empty fields where cotton had once grown.

His gut still sloshed with unrest, though, every time he thought about those footprints. He hoped his gut was wrong and that danger wasn't lurking close.

But his gut, on more than one occasion, had been the only thing to keep him alive.

CHAPTER 7

Felicity knelt next to Brody, trying to help him rekindle the fire. Though the electricity had only been off for probably fifteen or twenty minutes, coolness had already invaded the house. The place was rickety, at best. But without heat, it would soon be an icebox.

"Say, did you walk across to your back porch any since the snow started?" Brody asked as he crumpled some newspaper beneath the wood.

His voice sounded casual, but her instinct told her there was more to his words. "I stepped out once, but only for a moment. Why?"

"Did you walk over to the window?" He shoved one more piece of newspaper beneath the logs and then reached for the lighter.

His question struck her as strange. "Why would I do that? No, I just stepped outside and considered getting some wood. I decided not to. Bad choice, obviously."

He nodded slowly, igniting a flame. "Just wondering."

She rocked back on her heels and tried to figure out where he was going with this. "No, you're not. What's going on?"

He paused as the newspaper turned a glowing orange. "Do you think your aunt went outside?"

"And looked in the window? No. Why would she do

that?" Her curiosity turned into irritation. She wished he would just tell her what he was thinking and stop going in circles.

He turned toward her. Firelight made his face look warm and possibly kinder than he deserved. "There were footprints outside."

Footprints outside? That didn't make any sense. "The snow would have covered any footprints."

"Not on the porch. The snow is blowing from the opposite direction."

Her spine pinched as the implications of his words sank in. "Why would someone be on my porch in this snowstorm?"

"I was hoping you could tell me. Any neighbors who might be prowling around?"

"No, there's no one."

He poked the wood as sparks from the paper ignited it. As he did so, another cool draft swept through the house, reminding Felicity of just how cold it could get. This house was so drafty.

Her mind continued to race. "Besides, if someone had been out there, why didn't they knock or come inside? Why just peer into the window? Unless . . ."

Unless someone was simply watching her. Waiting for the perfect opportunity to strike. She shivered as she mentally finished her thought.

"I'm going to go lock the doors." She jetted to her feet and rushed toward the front of the house, turning the flimsy locks. She knew it wouldn't do much good. The doors were nice and solid, but the hinges were old and rusty.

Despite how futile it seemed, she slid and snapped and turned each of the locks in place on all three of the exterior doors. Thankfully, her aunt had gone to lie down for a few minutes so she wouldn't ask any more questions.

As she turned the last lock, she remembered the key in her pocket. Did this trouble have anything to do with it? Or was she reading too much into this?

Maybe it wasn't the key at all. Maybe it was Brody.

Feeling another rush of nerves, she quickly closed all the curtains as well. The last thing she needed was a Peeping Tom, and, until she knew more about this situation, she needed to remain cautious.

Of course, if Brody was a bad guy, that would mean no one could see into her house if she needed help. Who was to say Brody hadn't left those tracks? Maybe he made all of this up.

"Do you have any more guns in the house?" Brody stood from the fire as she walked back into the room. Thankfully, a small flame already blazed.

Guns. Brody was asking her about guns. But what if he was the one she needed protection from? She couldn't hand over her weapons to a man who might be dangerous.

"My grandpa had some old rifles, I think, for hunting. But I doubt there's any ammo. You really think we need guns?"

His steely gaze met hers. "I think we should be prepared for the worst. Something doesn't feel right in my gut. I don't know what."

She shuddered, wondering exactly what "the worst" looked like.

She didn't want to find out.

* * *

A nagging feeling remained in Brody's gut. Something was wrong. Something had happened to make him crash his truck and end up here—something more than icy roads. He was sure of it.

"How much longer are they calling for this snow?" Brody's hands went to his hips as the fire warmed his backside.

Felicity frowned. "Through the night, and then it's supposed to taper off in the morning. Who knows how long this blanket of ice will stick around, though?"

"Do you have enough food and supplies?"

She cast a dirty look his way. "I'm not totally incompetent. In fact, we were getting along fine before I dragged you inside my house."

He raised his hands. "Touché, touché. Sorry. I'm just trying to assess what's needed."

"I ran to the store when I heard a storm was coming. I think we'll be okay. If not, I found some preserves my grandma made. I don't know how old they are, however."

Great, if the cold didn't kill them, food poisoning might.

"You're really nervous about those footprints, aren't you?" Felicity crossed her arms, still standing across the room and glaring at him.

"They don't make any sense, Felicity. If someone is desperate enough to be out in this weather, then they're really desperate. They weren't coming here for help. They were coming here to scope the place out."

She visibly recoiled at his words. She sank to the floor in front of the fireplace and rubbed her hands together. "When you put it that way . . ."

"I'm sorry, Felicity."

She jerked her head toward him. "For what?"

"I hope I didn't lead trouble here. But I could have. I wish I could remember." He lowered himself beside her and warmed his hands and face in the growing flames. It just didn't make sense. Felicity had found him in the snow outside her home. He'd awoken from his blackout on full alert, feeling like danger was impending. Then there was the key. Where had it come from? Now the footprints added one more layer of mystery to an already tense situation.

His apology seemed to soften her shoulders, her eyes. "You're friends with the police chief?" she finally asked.

"Chief Haven? Yes, I am. He's a good guy. Why?"

She shrugged. "He seemed nice enough when I met him. I overheard you talking to him. You're just afraid you're stuck in a Stephen King novel, aren't you?"

The first honest smile crossed his face. "*Misery*? Only I'm not a writer. Maybe the thought crossed my mind."

"My aunt does have a little crazy in her. But not that much. At least, I hope not." She flashed a grin.

For the first time since this ordeal had started, he heard himself laugh.

Felicity cleared her throat, as if she'd caught herself having fun when she shouldn't be, and she stood. "I'm going to get some of the old oil lanterns my grandma left. We're going to need some more light around here. Being in the middle of nowhere, it gets especially dark at night."

"Do you mind if I make some coffee?"

She paused half toward the hallway. "Without electricity?"

"Just point me to some grounds, a pot, and some water."

She continued to stare.

Finally he shrugged. "What can I say? Once an Eagle scout, always an Eagle scout."

She nodded, as if that was the first explanation that made any sense to her. "It's all in the kitchen. Knock yourself out."

As Felicity wandered off to gather some lanterns and flashlights, he found what he needed. A warm drink sounded like the perfect medicine. After he put the water over the fire, he glanced around again.

It was getting dark outside. In early February the days were still short. Forecasters said that next week looked to be sunny and in the sixties. That was the way the weather around here usually worked. He should be used to it.

As he waited for Felicity to return, he walked to the window and shoved the curtain aside long enough to glance out.

He couldn't see anything, which didn't surprise him. Everything was white and dull as the snow continued to fall.

Innocent. Everything appeared innocent and clean when blanketed beneath the snow. He'd always thought so.

But right now the snow seemed like sheep's clothing covering a wolf. What was it hiding?

At once, an image flashed back to him, and he squeezed his eyes shut.

He was in his truck. The wipers were going. It was cold. So cold. Not to mention treacherous.

Suddenly, he hit the brakes.

But why?

What was it? The reason was on the edge of his consciousness. Had it been a deer? Another stopped car?

No, he remembered. It was a man.

A man had been in the road.

Brody had helped him to his feet. Put him inside his

truck. Started down the road again.

Then what? What had happened next?

"Are you okay?" A voice pulled him from the memories.

His eyes popped open and Felicity stood there, staring at him with something close to concern in her eyes. She'd put on a snug-fitting gray sweater. His throat went dry for a moment, and he forced his thoughts to focus.

He shook his head, and dropped the curtain, knowing it was too late to regain the memory now. "Yeah, I'm fine."

"You just looked like you were in pain or something. Sorry to interrupt you."

The scent of coffee hit his senses. It should almost be ready. Maybe some caffeine would perk him up. "No, it wasn't that. It was a flashback, I suppose."

Her eyes widened. "Of today?"

He rubbed his throbbing temples. "I remember leaving the docks. As I was driving, I saw a man in the road and stopped to help."

"What next?"

"I remember putting him in my truck. He was nearly frozen. But that's it. I don't know what happened after that."

"To get from the boat ramp to my house, you would have had to turn down a different road. It's not a straight shot from the docks to here . . ."

He nodded. "That's true. You think there was a reason I didn't go straight, directly to the highway?"

"That seems to be the logical conclusion."

"I wish I had answers for you."

"Me too." Her voice sounded wistful.

Just then, something crashed in the distance. Near her aunt's room.

They both took off running.

CHAPTER 8

Felicity's heart hammered into her ribcage as she thought about her aunt. If something bad happened to Aunt Bonny, she'd never forgive herself. It would be her fault for bringing this stranger into their home. What if he'd brought trouble with him?

Brody reached the room a moment before she did. He held onto the doorframe and propelled himself inside. Felicity nearly collided with his back.

She peered around him, anxious to see if her aunt was okay.

When the room came into view, she released her breath.

Felicity should have known. But she was paranoid and not thinking clearly.

Aunt Bonny stood at a little worktable in the corner, lit by one of her grandma's many lanterns. She raised her hammer again and smashed another teacup.

"What . . . ?" Brody stepped back, a wrinkle between his eyes.

"She makes mosaics out of broken china," Felicity explained, chiding herself for being so paranoid. "I think it's a stress relief for her."

"Destroying things is always relaxing." Aunt Bonny

raised her hammer again, ready to swing. "You should try it sometime."

"Aren't you cold in here, Aunt Bonny?" She'd looked so frail lately—at least when compared to the robust woman she'd once been.

"No, I feel good. When I get cold, I'll come out. You can count on that."

"I don't want you to get sick."

"Child, I'm fine. Now go on back to whatever you were doing. I'm going to bust some more cups and plates. I'm making a patio tabletop. If you're nice, I'll give it to you."

Felicity resisted, shaking her head at her aunt's antics. She should be used to them, but she wasn't.

"Is that normal?" Brody whispered as the dark hallway enveloped them.

"As normal as Aunt Bonny gets," she said quietly.

"I'm going to go check on that coffee. Do you want some?"

"A warm drink does sound nice."

Using some hot pads, he took the cast-iron pot from the fire and carried it carefully into the kitchen. Felicity watched, halfway fascinated. She'd been in the world of academia and away from anything survival related. Seeing someone using this kind of skill fascinated her.

A few minutes later, Brody offered her a cup of coffee. The mug had been one of her grandma's favorites: It had Snoopy on the front and was probably twenty years old. It was one of Felicity's favorites also.

As she took the drink, another crash sounded from her aunt's room. Life was always interesting around her aunt, that was for sure.

Felicity lowered herself into a chair by the fire. "So,

you have no idea who the man was from your flashback?"

His eyes glazed with thought for a moment. "No, I don't. Not yet."

"You took a pretty big hit on your head. There was glass inside your coat, so your windshield must have broken."

He shook his head. "I don't even remember waking up in the truck. I only remember leaving the boat ramp and then waking up here. Thank goodness you found me. Otherwise, I could have frozen to death."

"Is that your way of saying thank you?" She raised an eyebrow.

"I suppose it is."

"Then you're welcome." A teasing grin played at the corners of her lips.

As a reward, Brody flashed a smile, displaying a row of straight, white teeth and features that looked friendly instead of intrusive.

He leaned on his elbows. "Do you have any other buildings out back?"

"Buildings? Like a garage or shed?"

He nodded. "Exactly."

"There's an old shed and a barn. They're all falling apart. Why do you ask?" Even as she said that, the truth lingered in her mind. "You think someone could be hiding out there?"

He shrugged. "It's a possibility."

"Your gut is telling you there's some kind of foul play involved in all of this. Why?"

"I'm not sure. Partly the footprints. Partly the fact that I know myself, and I know that I'm careful. I want to see my truck, find out if there are any clues there."

"That won't happen until the snow clears." She parted the curtains and glanced out the window. Darkness had fallen, but she knew the snow was still coming down. They were expected to get a foot, which around here equated to a lot.

He folded his arms across his broad chest. "I'm not one to sit and wait."

"We don't have much of a choice."

"That's true."

Felicity settled back in the seat, letting her thoughts carry her away. "Could this be connected with your last rescue on the river? What happened?"

"Chief Haven got a mayday call from the Perquimans. I went to check things out, but when I found the boat, it was empty. The conditions are too dangerous to begin a search-and-rescue effort."

"You didn't do it for the Coast Guard?"

"No, I help out the chief sometimes. I'm . . . I'm taking some time off from the Coast Guard."

"Why?"

"Mostly because I never take time off. Especially not since—" He stopped himself. "Well, just because I don't. I have so much vacation time built up that my boss urged me to use some of it."

Felicity couldn't help but wonder what he was about to say. What had happened in his past to make him a workaholic? She'd been a workaholic . . . until everything fell apart. Now she had more free time on her hands than she knew what to do with.

"Did you tell him that you're related to Blackbeard?" Aunt Bonny sauntered into the room and paused in front of them.

In an instant, any of the relaxation Felicity had felt disappeared. "Aunt Bonny . . ."

Brody looked at her, curiosity in his gaze. "No, she didn't."

To him, this might as well be a campfire story to pass his time. To Felicity, this seemed like another humiliation to add to her already long list. Her aunt loved to tell stories about meeting JFK and spotting UFOs and traveling with the circus—all exaggerations. She'd actually been to a restaurant where JFK had once eaten; she'd seen lights in the sky—most likely a plane; and she'd traveled for a summer with a carnival.

"There's no story to hear," Felicity said.

"Sure, there is," Aunt Bonny said. "You're related to the infamous pirate. That's why it was so fun to say 'batten down the hatches' when this storm approached. Aye aye, matey?"

Felicity shook her head behind her aunt's back to let Brody know not to listen to her.

Her aunt sat down, settling in to tell the story she'd been telling for as long as Felicity could remember. She started, repeating about how the grand master of all pirates had docked on the shores outside this home, fallen in love with Loretta Pasture, and together they had a secret love child. Loretta was married, but her husband worked as a fisherman, and he was out to sea for weeks at a time.

"Is this a book you're talking about?" Brody asked.

Bonny shook her head. "A book? No, of course not. It's a family story that's been handed down from generation to generation. Plus, there's that." Bonny pointed to something above the fireplace.

Felicity tried not to close her eyes and show her embarrassment. "It's just a sword, Aunt Bonny."

"It's not just a sword, darling. It's *Blackbeard's* sword."

"I'm pretty sure my grandma found it at a yard sale," Felicity quickly explained. "She collected swords . . .

if you can't tell."

There were numerous swords hanging in various places on the walls.

"No, she found that one in the attic. Thank you very much." Her aunt nodded matter-of-factly.

Felicity had never taken the time to examine it herself, which was strange for someone who liked to research everything. By the time she knew her grandmother had found it, Felicity was immersed in her studies and her job.

She wished she could have come more. Why couldn't she?

Guilt clawed at her.

She'd glanced at the sword when she arrived two months ago, but she questioned her abilities too much now. Besides, what were the chances?

The disaster surrounding her career had sent her reeling into a state of professional hermitism.

Brody stood to examine the sword himself. "This was Blackbeard's?"

"That's right. You can still hear him walking around here at night sometimes. And, candles have been known to mysteriously go out."

"It's because the house is drafty," Felicity explained. "And the sounds are just mice or birds living between the walls."

Brody nodded slowly. "Still a fascinating story. I heard that parts of this area were his haunts. Like Holiday Island. Some people believe his treasure was buried there."

"Some people believe there's no treasure at all," Felicity quickly added. "Maybe good old Eddie took it all for himself, or maybe it sank to the bottom of the ocean."

"If it did, maybe they'll find it," Brody said. "I'm

sure you've probably heard they think they found the remains of the *Queen Anne's Revenge* down in Beaufort."

"That's right. I did hear that."

"A friend of mine lives down there. It's really fascinating stuff. It reminds you of a time when life was much different than it is now."

"You're Coast Guard," Aunt Bonny said. "I'm sure you still see pirates."

He nodded. "A different kind of pirate, but we have encountered some. Thankfully, I haven't had to walk the plank yet."

"I've got that gypsy spirit in me still!" Aunt Bonny stood and did a little jig. "So does Felicity. She just doesn't want to admit it."

"Aunt Bonny!" Where Felicity had too many scruples, her aunt didn't have enough.

"What? It's true. Deep down inside you're a free spirit who longs for adventure. You've just hidden it behind your stuffy persona for so long . . ."

"I'm not stuffy."

"Sure you are. Teaching at the college. Doing all of your research papers. Getting your PhD and working for that prestigious firm. That's stuffy. Not fun. You're suppressing your inner pirate."

"I was following my life's passion. That's adventurous." Why did she even feel the need to defend herself? And to defend her position on suppressing an inner pirate, at that?

"You would have done better for yourself if it wasn't for that Ricky . . ."

"Aunt Bonny . . ." Felicity's voice held warning. The last thing she wanted was to rehash the details of her failed love life with a stranger sitting here.

"Okay, okay. I've overstepped my bounds." She

picked up a wooden box of dominoes. "Chickenfoot, anyone?"

Felicity closed her eyes. Brody really was going to think they were crazy. Not that she cared what he thought. It wasn't like she'd ever have to see him again after this snow melted.

"Chickenfoot?" Brody asked.

"It's a domino game. Certainly you've heard of it."

"I thought it was a pirate game." He smiled, which delighted her aunt.

"That's the spirit." She let out a pirate-like "argh" and hooked her arm.

Felicity rolled her eyes, but Brody laughed. He was finding all of this humorous, wasn't he?

Felicity suddenly had the urge to feign being tired—only it was too early. She couldn't jump on the computer—she had no electricity. She had no presentations to prepare for, so using work as an excuse was out of the question.

She was pretty much stuck here, especially if she wanted to keep warm. The rest of the house—the extremities—would be the first to feel the brittle cruelty of the cold.

"All right, I'm in," she said, before carefully adding, "For now."

***

"They're coming . . ."

Brody sat up in the old recliner, cold sweat across his forehead, as the words echoed in his mind.

He'd had a dream. Or was it a memory?

He couldn't be sure.

But the images in his head featured the same man

from his earlier memory. Brody had rescued him from the side of the road during the snowstorm. The man had climbed into his truck, and then he'd muttered something.

What was it?

Pastor.

At least, that's what Brody had though he'd said.

But what if he'd actually said, "Pasture," as in Fanny Pasture, Felicity's grandma?

He glanced at Felicity now as she slept on one of the two couches across the room. Only her hair and part of her face were visible in the firelight, and she was dead still. Did she fit in with all of this somehow?

Was that how Brody had ended up on this road? Had the man wanted him to come here? What sense would that make? Neither Felicity nor her aunt gave any indication they were waiting for someone.

He sat up and pulled his blanket closer around his shoulders. There was a new chill in the air as the fire began to wane in its wall-ensconced cubby.

The three of them had made the decision to sleep around the warm flames tonight. The ladies had offered him a couch, but he'd refused. Aunt Bonny slept on the other one now, snoring away under a pile of blankets. He'd stretched out in an old recliner instead.

A moment of envy shot through Brody as he looked at Aunt Bonny. What he wouldn't do to sleep so well. He hadn't slept that well since Andrea . . .

He shook his head. Why did his thoughts keep going there? He'd done a good job staying busy and keeping his thoughts occupied. But now thoughts of her kept pouring into his head, unwilling to retreat.

He sighed, his gaze moving to Felicity again. In the dancing light of the fire, she also looked peaceful, though deep down inside he wondered if she was asleep at all.

She seemed too on edge to rest.

Just like he was.

Despite all of that, they'd had a fairly relaxing game of dominoes, then Uno®, and finally pick-up sticks—all Aunt Bonny's idea. It was a nice distraction from having to talk, having to face sharing any more information than he had to. With Brody's help, they'd heated some hot chocolate and cooked popcorn over the flames.

He squinted as he looked more closely at Felicity. Was that her . . . gun . . . beneath her pillow?

He crept closer. It sure was. She didn't trust him. At all. Not that he could blame her, after what he'd done when he'd come out of his unconscious state. But she really wasn't taking any chances, was she?

"Skeleton key . . ." Aunt Bonny muttered, her hand flopping toward the floor. She was obviously dreaming.

He couldn't help but smile. Her pirate stories sure were interesting. As a kid growing up around here, he'd wanted to believe that Blackbeard's treasure was stashed in this area. Every kid had. It was part of the intrigue of living in a coastal community like Hertford, and all of eastern North Carolina, for that matter.

He looked up at the sword. Wouldn't that be something if Blackbeard really had owned that? What were the chances? A house like this had to have a rich history. As the old saying went . . . if these walls could speak. They'd have incredible stories to tell.

Just then he heard a creak, and his instincts went on alert.

CHAPTER 9

Brody's muscles tightened. What was that? The house settling? The wind?

His gut told him no.

His pumping adrenaline propelled him forward, urging him to action.

Quickly, he slid the gun out from beneath Felicity's pillow. She might hate him for it, but he had no choice.

He stayed close to the wall as he neared the kitchen. He felt nearly certain that was where the sound was coming from.

He peered around the corner. Sure enough, a man stood outside at the door. Playing with the lock. Trying to get inside.

He rushed toward Felicity and shook her. Her eyes fluttered open, and when she spotted him, she scowled before drawing back.

"Someone's outside," Brody rushed. "Get your aunt and go to a bedroom. Lock yourself in until I give you word to come out."

Instantly, she threw her legs over the edge and reached for her gun. "My . . ." Her gaze met his and she scowled. "You have my gun?"

"I don't have time for this now. Someone's trying

to get inside."

With one more dirty look, she darted toward her aunt. Once they were on their way down the hallway, Brody started back toward the kitchen.

He peered around the corner in time to see the man push the door open and step inside.

Brody scanned him quickly. At his waist was a gun. But it wasn't in his hand. Not yet.

Holding Felicity's Glock, Brody stepped from the shadows. "I'll shoot first and ask questions later."

The man's head jerked up. He wore a black mask over his face. But, even with the mask, Brody saw his eyes widen in surprise.

Brody raised his gun and held his breath, waiting for the man's reaction. Fight or flight?

A tense moment stretched between them, every second that passed crackling with indecision.

Then, the man ran.

***

"Was it Blackbeard's ghost?" Aunt Bonny asked as she huddled in the corner of a spare bedroom with Felicity.

Felicity kept her arm around her aunt, hoping she wouldn't do anything impulsive or irresponsible. "No, not a ghost. Brody thinks someone was trying to break in."

"It's a good thing he was here then."

Was it? Or was the man trying to get in because Brody had brought trouble with him?

The thought left her unsettled.

She could hardly breathe. Tension pressed on her chest. What was happening out there? How had a simple bad weather situation turned into this? What if she'd never seen Brody outside?

No, she couldn't think like that. She was glad she'd found him when she did. She just wished all this trouble hadn't ensued.

"Your parents would be proud of you, you know," Aunt Bonny muttered.

Where had that thought come from? Here they were in the middle of this situation and now she brought this up?

"Thank you, Aunt Bonny." She nudged the blanket up higher around her aunt's shoulders.

"My heart broke after what happened to them."

"Mine too," Felicity said.

She tried to push away the memories, but they flooded her mind anyway. Suddenly, she felt like she was back in time, ten years earlier. It was a month before she left for college, and she was living in Wilmington with her parents.

Her mom and dad had gone on a mission trip with the church and were on their way home. They'd headed back a day earlier so they could spend a week at the beach with Felicity. It had been a late graduation/going-away-to-college gift. Their plane had crashed, killing all 258 passengers on board.

Her life hadn't been the same since.

Someone rapped on the door and pulled her from the memories.

"Stay here," she whispered to her aunt.

She grabbed a heavy vase from the dresser and held it like a baseball bat as she approached the door. She hesitated as she stood in front of it.

"Who is it?" she asked, unwilling to take any chances.

"It's Brody."

She released her breath, but refused to throw

caution to the wind. She kept the vase raised, just in case. She turned the lock, and her hand twisted the knob and pulled the door toward her until a crack appeared.

She saw Brody's face there.

Without invitation, he slipped inside and closed the door behind him.

She quickly soaked him in. His breathing was rapid. His shoes had bits of snow on them. The gun was still in his hand.

If he'd fired, she would have heard it.

"He ran away," he said. "Any idea who it might have been?"

"The same person who left the footprints earlier," she guessed.

"Whoever he was, he doesn't want to announce his presence. Why?"

She shoved a finger into her chest. "You think I know?"

He stared at her a moment before shaking his head. "No, I'm just thinking out loud. Nothing is making sense."

"Have you remembered anything else?"

He shook his head. "No, nothing."

She shivered involuntarily. "I don't even feel safe here anymore."

"I'll stand guard for the rest of the night so you and your aunt can get some rest."

"You don't have to do that."

"No, let him. He should earn his keep!" Aunt Bonny chirped in the background.

Felicity let out a quick breath—almost a chuckle, but not quite.

"She's right," Brody said. "I've intruded on your plans, your house, and your sense of peace. The least I can do is make sure all of this isn't my fault."

She stared at him a moment before nodding. "Fine then. Have it your way."

She hoped she didn't regret this, because he still had her gun.

CHAPTER 10

As the early morning sun peaked through the slits in the curtains, Felicity rose and pulled on a sweatshirt to ward off the cold. Apparently her aunt was already awake because the smell of bacon wafted through the house. The power must be back on.

She rubbed her eyes, trying to get the cobwebs out of her brain. The events of yesterday flashed back to her. Had that been real? Or was it all just a nightmare?

When she glanced across the room and saw blankets on both the couch and the recliner, she knew everything really had happened.

Brody Joyner was in her house.

Everything had been crazy in the past twenty-four hours, turning her life upside down. No, she thought. If that were the case, then her life would finally be right side up. It had been upside down for a long time now.

"Breakfast is on!" her aunt called.

Where had Brody gone?

When she walked into the kitchen, she spotted him sitting at the table, chatting with her aunt as if they were old friends.

She gave her aunt the eye. *Traitor*.

She sat down and stared across the breakfast table

at him. He looked even more rugged this morning. His five o'clock shadow had become thicker and more pronounced. His eyes were somehow more shaded. The overall effect gave him a rugged, bad-boy look—a very appealing bad-boy look.

"After last night, I'm not sure how safe you're going to be staying here." Brody glanced out the window. "The snow has stopped, but I'm estimating we got more than six inches. It's going to take a while for that to melt."

"They're saying it's going to start raining. You know what the weather's like around here." Aunt Bonny wiped down the stovetop. "Sunny and eighty one minute, and thirty and snowing the next."

Felicity wanted to argue with her, but she couldn't. It was true. The weather changed faster than her ex-boyfriend's moods, it seemed. It kept life interesting, to say the least.

"When is your leave up with the Coast Guard?" Felicity took another bite of eggs.

"I still have three weeks." His jaw hardened as he said the words.

Her spine clenched. What wasn't he telling her? Had he been disciplined by the Coast Guard for unscrupulous actions? Was that why he'd supposedly taken leave? Had he had a mental breakdown?

Maybe she'd been too hard on him and should give him the benefit of the doubt. He'd proven to be helpful in his time here. Her paranoid instincts may have been working overtime since she'd been here in Hertford.

"I'd like to trek out to my truck today and see what I can find there." Brody wiped his mouth with a paper towel from the center of the table.

All at once, she had a vision of what it might be like to sit here every morning. To have coffee and breakfast and read the newspaper with someone. With someone like Brody.

Her cheeks heated. Where had that thought come from? She quickly pushed the idea aside. She couldn't even trust the man. There was no need to start imagining a future with him.

She cleared her throat. "It's going to be a cold walk."

"I'll be okay. I've been through worse."

"Come see this, guys," Aunt Bonny said.

They both stood from their bacon and eggs and went into the living area. The tinny sound of the TV filled the room, and her aunt stood in front of the screen.

"We got only six inches of snow instead of the twelve they were calling for. Plus, the weather service is saying it will rain and warm up pretty quickly. That's the good news," Aunt Bonny said. "In other words, Sonny Boy here might not be stuck with us for too much longer."

She gave a pointed look to Brody. Her aunt's feelings about the man seemed to match Felicity's own—skeptical one minute, wanting to believe the best the next. But that did *not* mean she and her aunt were anything alike.

Felicity felt like she should apologize for her aunt's rudeness, but she couldn't. She felt the same way, even though she might not have worded it quite that way.

"Now listen to this." She turned up the volume.

A picture of a white-haired man appeared on the screen. The news reporter talked in the background, "The body of an unidentified man has been found in Hertford. A state trooper discovered him this morning off Highway 17. The medical examiner has not yet determined a cause of death. If you have information . . ."

"Poor man," Felicity muttered. "I hope he didn't

freeze to death out in those elements."

When Brody didn't respond, she glanced back at him and noticed that he'd gone pale.

***

Brody's mind reeled.

That was the man from the side of the road. Images of picking him up filled his thoughts. Each memory felt like a punch in the gut.

What had happened to the man?

Brody felt certain he hadn't died of natural causes. Or had he? If only he could remember everything.

"Brody? Brody?"

He snapped back to the present and saw Felicity staring at him.

"Everything okay?" she asked.

He nodded, knowing he couldn't share his thoughts. She already suspected he was up to no good. This might only confirm that in her mind. "Yeah, everything's fine. I'm going to head out to my truck before the rain starts."

She shrugged. "Suit yourself."

He bundled up, using everything he could find to keep him warm. It didn't matter if he was cold. Nothing was going to stop him now. After muttering something to Felicity and Aunt Bonny, he stepped into the white, damp outdoors.

Despite the fact that it wasn't snowing anymore, the cold still felt extreme. His legs sank into the snow, completely covering his boots. The sky overhead was gray, as if promising more precipitation.

Without the curtain of snow coming down, he could clearly see his truck in the distance. Before he ventured to it, he checked the backyard for evidence of the intruder. He easily saw where the man had come to the back door last night and then retreated. Where had he gone?

He'd check that in a moment. Right now, he had to see his truck. He needed answers as to what had happened to him. Then he'd figure out the rest.

Walking through the snow expended four times the energy of normal walking. Each step required fighting with the thick wall at his feet. He finally reached his truck, a gray 2005 Ford F150. It was the first vehicle he'd bought, right out of high school.

And it was wrapped around a tree.

He'd call his friend Ryan Shields, who owned a garage in town, and see if he could send a tow truck out to retrieve it after the snow cleared.

He looked behind him. There was a good distance between the truck and the house. Somehow he'd managed to sludge through the thick snow and make it far enough that Felicity had found him. He must have seen the house in the distance and gone for help.

As he glanced through the side window, he sucked in a breath. There was a bullet hole. Bullet *holes*.

One went through his windshield. Another pierced his shattered back window.

Someone had been shooting at him.

He'd run off the side of the road. Hit a tree. That must have knocked him out.

Then the old man he'd picked up had either been grabbed or escaped on foot. Who had been shooting at them? Had that person grabbed the man and run? Maybe the shooter thought Brody was dead.

He opened the door and peered inside his truck.

Blood had frozen on the steering wheel and some

had dripped onto the dashboard. He touched his head. That had to be from his head wound.

Brody had obviously gotten mixed up in . . . something. But what? Figuring that out was the key to discovering who the man was at the door last night.

Whatever was going on, it wasn't good.

Just as he took a step back, he heard a click behind him.

A gun. Being cocked.

CHAPTER 11

As soon as Felicity saw the bullet holes, she knew that Brody Joyner was trouble. This only confirmed it. There was something he wasn't telling her, and she wanted to know what.

First, there was his reaction to the man on TV. He'd gone pale. Then he'd hurried out to his truck like a man on a mission. She'd seen the bullet holes. Seen the blood.

Maybe this whole temporary amnesia thing was a scam.

She was not going to welcome a criminal in her home.

"What are you doing, Felicity?" Brody's back was still toward her, but every muscle visibly tight.

Had he seen her coming? Had he known she'd come after him? "How'd you know it was me?"

"I can see you in the side-view mirror."

Her jaw clenched, and she wished she had more training for this type of thing. She wished she could ignore the way her nose tingled from the cold and the snow melted into the edges of her boots.

He raised his hands. "Don't do something stupid, Felicity."

Her eyes narrowed with irritation. "I should say the

same thing to you. It looks like there's more to the story than you're telling me."

"Can I turn around?"

"Slowly."

"I blacked out, Felicity. I'm telling you the truth. There's a one- or two-hour period that I can't remember. Bits and pieces keep coming back.

The gun trembled in her hand, partly because of her surging anxiety and partly because of the cold that nipped at her. "Like the man on TV?"

He pressed his lips together before nodding. "I didn't know who he was. When I saw his picture, I had a flashback."

"Did you kill him?" She held her breath as she waited for his response.

His eyes widened. "Kill him? Who do you think I am?"

"I have no idea who you are."

"You heard me talking to the police chief. He can verify who I am. Now, why don't you put the gun down before you do something stupid?"

"What if *you* did something stupid and now you're hiding out here?" Her mind raced. She should have never given him the benefit of doubt.

"I promise you—that's not true."

"Explain those bullet holes."

"I can't. I must have hit this tree and smashed my head. That's why I'm having trouble remembering."

"I don't know what to believe." Every bit of conflicting logic warred within her. She couldn't afford to be naïve again. The first time her professional reputation had been on the line. This time it was her life and her aunt's life.

Brody stepped closer, his voice calm and pleading,

much like a negotiator. "I believe you're in danger. I don't know if that danger followed me here or not. I just know that a man tried to break in last night. I don't know where he came from or where he is. I believe something dangerous is going on. I wish I knew my connection with it."

His *connection*. He was admitting there was one. That settled it in her mind. "You need to leave as soon as the road clears," she said.

"I'll be happy to get out of your hair. You've been generous enough as it is."

"If I find out you've been lying to me, I won't hesitate to take action." Her voice sounded stronger than she felt. Inside she was a quivering mess. But she never wanted to be a victim again. Never.

"I understand." He stepped closer and lowered his eyes, his voice. "Now, please, put the gun down, Felicity."

She stared at him a moment, trying to measure her actions. If he'd wanted to hurt her, he could have done that already. And there was blood on the driver's seat, so his story could very well be true.

Hesitantly, she lowered her gun. "Don't make me regret this."

Her shoulders seemed to relax. "You won't."

She stuck the gun in the back of her jeans and licked her lips, already dry and parched from the cold. "What are you doing now?"

"Just looking for any clues as to what happened. Unfortunately, the snow covered any footprints." He looked down the road. It wasn't one he'd taken very many times. He'd never had any reason to. "How much farther does this road go?"

"About four miles until you reach the highway. Why?"

"The man was found not far from here, but I doubt he could have walked that far in the snow."

She let his words sink in a moment. "You think someone grabbed him?"

A shadow passed over his face. "Maybe. Is there any reason that man would have wanted to come to your place? Did you recognize his picture?"

"No. Why? I know no one here. I'm not working. I've pretty much been reclusive. Why would you ask?"

"He said Pasture. I remember that much. I thought he was talking about a minister or something."

She blinked as she processed the new information. "The man—the one who's now dead—said *my* grandma's last name while he was in *your* truck?"

Brody nodded, watching her every action and reaction. "Any idea why?"

"I have no idea." She shivered, suddenly even colder. "I don't like this. As soon as the roads clear, I need to take my aunt back to her assisted-living facility. I don't think she's safe here with me."

"Not a bad idea. Is there anyone you can stay with?"

She just stared at him a moment. They'd been over this. She'd made no effort to meet people since she'd been in town. She'd had no reason to. "I'll be fine here by myself. I took a shooting class once."

"Your safety was on."

"What?"

He nodded toward her gun. "You wouldn't have been able to shoot anyone."

Her cheeks heated. "Regardless, I'll be fine."

"I'm not so sure about that." He reached under his front seat and found his gun and cell phone. He tucked them into his jeans. "Now I need to go check out your backyard."

She stumbled through the snow behind him, struggling to keep up with his long strides. "I'm going with you."

"You don't have to do that. I'll tell you what I find."

"I want to go." No way would she give him the opportunity to deceive her. She had every right to know what was going on.

Ricky had liked to keep her in the dark—then he used that to his advantage. Never again.

"Suit yourself." He threw her earlier words back on her.

With every step, she struggled behind him. Her legs were considerably shorter and not nearly as muscular as Brody's. But she didn't want to give any hints that she was struggling. She was going to keep up with him if it was the last thing she did—and it very well might be.

Her lungs burned as she heaved in the icy cold air. The snow had seeped through her clothes, and now her jeans were wet and frozen. Frost had found its way through the opening between her socks and jeans and stung her skin.

One foot in front of the other, Felicity. You can do it!

She nearly collided with Brody when he stopped in front of her. Thankfully, she caught herself in time.

"What is it?" She tried to peer around his shoulder, but he was too broad. She had to reserve any extra energy for the walk back to the house.

"Tracks. It looks like they lead to that building out there." Brody turned slightly—enough for her to see around him—and pointed.

She followed the trail. "To the old barn?"

He nodded. "The old barn. Let's go check it out."

She wasn't sure she could make it that far, but she refused to let him know that. Instead, through labored breaths, she followed after him, trying to step only in his tracks. She would need a warm bath after this. And coffee. And maybe a pat on the back.

He glanced over his shoulder. "You okay?"

"I'm fine." Her deep, desperate breaths betrayed her words.

"I don't know what we'll find in there."

"I have a gun." She remembered his observation about the safety earlier and felt her cheeks warm. They were the only part of her that was warm.

"I would bet your fingers are too frozen right now to use it."

She wanted to argue, but she couldn't. She couldn't feel her fingers, now that he mentioned it. "Let me guess: you're still a good shot—even with ice cubes for fingers."

"I have been trained. If I wasn't, I wouldn't be a very good coastie."

Coast Guard. She kept forgetting. Her mind kept going to dark places—places where he was a criminal. Where he had secrets he wasn't sharing. Secrets that could destroy people. Destroy her.

But maybe he was noble. Maybe he had a good reason for all this.

They finally reached the barn, and he motioned for Felicity to stay behind him. He peered into the doorway and then nodded. "Looks clear."

Felicity had only been out to the barn once since she'd come back, and that was when she was looking for a lawn mower—which she hadn't found. The red barn had held old bales of hay, some old farm equipment, and mice. Lots of mice.

She hated mice. She hadn't entered it since then.

But right now, she stepped inside.

Even though the barn was cool, it was like the desert compared to the breezy outdoors. The flimsy walls at least blocked some of the breeze, and snow didn't trap her feet here.

Her gaze went to the little camp that had been set up on the floor there. There was a blanket and a coffee mug—an expensive looking one—and the dirt looked plenty scuffled.

Brody squatted down and examined the footprints on the ground. "Someone's definitely been here. He must have left after his failed attempt to get into the house."

"Look at this." Felicity pointed to some tire tracks on the other side of the barn, near the two huge doors that opened up to a field behind it.

"He must have stowed his vehicle here for a quick getaway."

He glanced outside. "As soon as it's safe, I'd like to ask the chief to come out and see if there's any evidence that might tell us who this man was. I'd say I'd take it to him myself, but since my truck is wrapped around a tree . . ."

"My aunt has a car here you might be able to use." Now why had she offered that? She knew: because it would get him away from her. Then she could return to being a hermit and nursing her wounds.

Brody looked at her a moment as if her words had surprised him. "That sounds great. Check the news for more information on road conditions. In the meantime, I need to check in with Joshua."

"Makes sense."

"You ready to trudge back through that snow?" he asked.

She nodded, even though she felt anything but ready. "Let's go."

***

Once she was back inside her house, she escaped to her room for a moment, feigning needing to get some rest. Then she turned on the light and held the key from Brody's shirt under the illumination.

What if the man from the truck had put this key into Brody's shirt? What if all this danger somehow circled back to this piece of metal?

But why? What would that be the case?

She squinted at what Aunt Bonny had called "Blackbeard's symbol." What was that? She almost needed a magnifying glass to say for sure. But it looked like letters were embedded in the middle of the miniscule design.

With the right equipment, she could scan this and blow it up. But she didn't have any of that with her now. Despite that, she took a few pictures with her cell phone.

If someone wanted this key badly enough that they'd run Brody off the road . . . that they'd hidden it away in his clothes . . . that they'd tried to break in last night to retrieve it—then it must have some significance.

A familiar longing began in her gut. What if this key was what she needed to clear her name and prove that she wasn't a fraud? If this key did have significance, she needed to figure out what it was.

It was going to be hard to do that when she considered this key wasn't hers.

Maybe her aunt was right. Maybe Felicity needed to tap into her inner pirate. She'd been composed and done what was expected of her for so long. Too long.

Just then, a knock sounded at her door. She jumped up, dropping the key. It clattered to the floor, seeming louder than it probably was.

"Coming." Sweat broke out across her forehead.

She grabbed the key, shoved it into her jeans pocket, and then walked to the door.

She knew it wasn't her aunt—her aunt wouldn't knock. It had to be Brody.

She tried to compose herself before jerking the door open. But as soon as she spotted Brody on the other side, any composure she'd felt disappeared faster than snow in the tropics. His hulking frame made her feel like a dwarf. He'd showered and changed back into his tight-fitting jeans.

He was handsome. She'd known that the first moment she saw him. But right now he took her breath away as a rush of attraction welled in her.

She mentally chided herself for even feeling anything.

She pushed a hair behind her ear. "Can I help you?"

His gaze seemed smoldering as it met hers. "I thought I'd let you know that the roads seem to be clearing faster than expected. Snowplows have been clearing the main roads all morning. I talked to my friend Joshua, and he said streets are slick but drivable if necessary. That said, I'd like to collect some of the evidence from the barn and take it to the police station."

"Of course."

"I cleared away the sidewalk and driveway the best I could. Is it still okay if I borrow your aunt's car? Do I need to ask her?"

"You know—you just take mine. I'll use my aunt's when I drive her back to her home. Like I said earlier, I need to do this sooner rather than later."

"I agree." His eyes continued to smolder. "I also think you shouldn't be staying here alone. That man—whoever he was—knows you're here."

"I have nowhere else to go." *And no money.* She didn't add that last part. "I should be fine."

His lips parted like he wanted to say something, but then he stopped and nodded. "Okay."

He took a step away and paused. "Oh, and do you still have that key?"

She swallowed hard, trying to think fast but failing to do so. She settled on, "The key?"

He lowered his gaze and squinted, as if not buying her confusion. "The one you said you found in my shirt."

"Oh, that key. What about it?" Great. She sounded over the top now. She'd never been a good liar. She shoved a hair behind her ear, hoping she looked more relaxed than she felt.

"I thought I should probably show Joshua—Chief Haven. Just in case it has any significance."

She nodded. "Of course. I'll go get it."

"Thanks."

Her heart slammed into her ribcage after Brody shut the door. She couldn't give up that key. Not now. It could contain all the answers she'd been searching for. She had to figure out a way to keep it . . . even if it met deceiving the stranger who'd taken shelter in her home.

***

As Aunt Bonny returned to her habit of smashing porcelain, Brody folded the last blanket and placed it on the couch. He'd officially cleaned up after himself the best he could.

"Here." Felicity emerged from the hallway and

handed him a cloth bag. "I put the key in there. I thought it might preserve any fingerprints that weren't already smudged."

Brody took it from her and shoved it in the pocket of his thick coat. "Thanks. Smart thinking."

A little strange and unexpected but thoughtful nonetheless. Why did Felicity look so nervous? Was she really this uncomfortable with him?

"I think I'm going to go ahead and take Aunt Bonny back to her home," Felicity said. "You said the roads weren't that bad?"

"It's raining, and the temperatures are climbing. I didn't say it was safe, but it's better than it was. Do you want me to drive you?"

Her eyes widened, as if the very thought alarmed her. "No, we'll be okay."

He felt like he should say something more. Like he should beg her to find somewhere else to stay. But they were practically strangers. And she was a grown woman, capable of making her own choices.

Still, a smidgen of concern wouldn't let him go. He really didn't think it was safe here.

He shifted. "You know, I have a couple of friends I could speak with. I'm sure they wouldn't mind if you camped out at their place until this passes over . . ."

She shook her head, leaving no room for question. "No, I'll be fine. But thank you."

Hesitantly, he took a step back. "Okay then. Well, I'll be in touch about returning the car. Thanks for letting me stay here. For pulling me inside and from certain death."

"No problem. I would love an update on what's going on, if you hear anything."

"The chief will probably come out here himself and

ask you some questions. It wouldn't surprise me. And as soon as a tow truck is available, I'll send someone out here to get my truck."

"Of course."

With one more hesitant nod, he stepped back. "Okay, then. I'll be going."

He told Aunt Bonny goodbye and then climbed into Felicity's neat sedan. A torn piece of newspaper was balled up on the floor. Out of curiosity, he picked it up and unfolded it.

The paper showed a headline reading: **Leading NC Antiquarian Discredited**.

Interesting. There was nothing else to read; the rest of the article was missing. Why would Felicity have torn this off? It didn't matter. It was the least of his concerns at the moment.

The snow had turned to slush. The road was still slick but not nearly as treacherous. Even with these conditions, it took him thirty minutes to get to the police station.

He stomped off his feet at the door before walking back to Joshua's office. Surprisingly, his friend was there, standing over stacks of paperwork.

Joshua had become a good friend during the past year. He was engaged to be married to Andrea's best friend, Charity. At first, it had been hard to see Joshua because he would inevitably see Charity, which brought back memories of Andrea. But God was working on him and helping him to deal with his past mistakes.

Joshua looked up. The man was lean with light brown hair and wise, kind eyes. He'd just recently been named chief after the former chief had taken a job in a different city.

Joshua turned toward Brody and leaned against the

table behind him. "Hey, Brody. You made it."

"Surprised you're here." Brody walked over to him.

"You just caught me. I've been running around all morning helping people who were stranded on the road during the storm, and now I have to catch up on paperwork. What do you have for me?"

Brody set his items on the table and explained each of them to Joshua. He brought a bullet, photos of the tire tracks in the barn, as well as pictures of the footprints left on the porch.

Finally, he got to the part of his story involving the key. He pulled the bag from his jacket pocket and opened the string at the top.

"And I believe the man put this in my pocket." He turned the bag over and a key dropped onto Joshua's desk.

Brody squinted. That was *not* the same key he'd seen earlier. This one was the same basic style, but it wasn't nearly as ornate.

"What's wrong?" Joshua asked.

His jaw hardened as he realized the truth. "Felicity switched keys."

"Felicity? The woman whose place you were staying at?"

Brody nodded. Why would she do that? Unless she knew something he didn't.

Brody stood. "I've got to go find her. Now."

***

Felicity's hands trembled as she rested them on the table that served as a desk and eating space for her aunt in her small, one-room apartment. Felicity wasn't the kind of girl who was normally deceitful, and it was getting to her.

She'd never been so jittery.

"You okay? You're jumpier than a grasshopper on a trampoline." Aunt Bonny cast a glance over her shoulder as she deposited her bag on the bed.

"I'm fine. The drive was just a little stressful." The roads had been worse than Felicity anticipated, and she'd nearly slid into a ditch. She wasn't looking forward to driving back. Not at all.

But her aunt should be safe here at the assisted-living facility she'd called home for the past two months.

Felicity didn't like the idea of staying at that old house by herself, but she had little choice at this point. At least she had her gun. If anyone came after her, she could protect herself. She'd remember to take the safety off next time.

Her hands trembled even more just thinking about what she'd done.

She'd had no choice but take that key and give Brody a fake one—one that fit into an armoire in her bedroom. She'd stuck it inside a velvety bag one of her bracelets had come in. That other key—the real one—held the power of redemption for her. She had to figure out what it unlocked, and she needed more time in order to do that.

She felt the first spark of hope and excitement in her life that she had in a long time.

That key could be the answer she'd been searching for. It could give her life back to her. Maybe she'd even be able to return to Raleigh.

"Well, you just going to stand there all day?" Aunt Bonny put her hands on her hips and stared at her. "I'll be fine. Now go on home. Besides, Bingo starts in ten minutes. I don't want to miss it."

Felicity nodded and stepped out the door of her

aunt's little apartment.

Nervous energy consumed her with each step. She had the key, but certainly Brody would discover that information soon. That meant she had to act fast. But she wasn't sure where to start.

What could the key possibly belong to? Did the letters on it have something to do with it? And why had the man who'd ended up dead said her grandma's last name? How was she connected with all of this?

Felicity needed to find out and fast.

She stepped outside and hurried to her car. But what she saw made her stop in her tracks.

Brody Joyner.

He leaned against her aunt's car with his arms crossed and a scowl on his face.

CHAPTER 12

Felicity slowed her steps, delaying the inevitable act of reaching Brody. There was no need to run. With his long legs and athletic ability, Brody would certainly catch her. There was also no need to deny what she'd done. Certainly, he already knew.

On the bright side, at least there was a break in the rain. Despite that, the gray sky overhead seemed to echo her situation: daunting.

"Where's the key, Felicity?" Brody's jaw flexed.

She licked her lips before drawing in a deep breath as she maneuvered over the snowy sidewalk—now gritty with salt crystals. "Not here."

He narrowed his eyes at her. "Why'd you switch it? What do you know that I don't?"

"Nothing." She attempted to breeze past him and climb into the driver's seat, but he grabbed her arm. Her skin rose at his touch.

He released her arm, only to put his hands on his hips. "You and I both know that's not true, Felicity. What's going on?"

She wanted to fight. To deny. To dig her heels in. But what good would that do?

"I couldn't let you turn that key over to the police,"

she finally said. "Not when it could have significant historical implications."

He squinted. "Why would you say that?"

"It's an antique—I'm guessing at least two hundred years old. Maybe more. There's some connection to it that someone thinks is worth killing over."

"Exactly. That's why I need to give it to Chief Haven. It's evidence."

She held her chin up higher, knowing he wouldn't understand. "I just need to study it a little more."

"You do? Why you?"

She frowned, questioning how much she should divulge. As little as possible, she decided, but enough to get his attention. "I'm a researcher. This is in my wheelhouse. I have a better chance of finding the answers than small-town cops."

"That could be construed as insulting."

"I don't mean it that way. I just mean I have *experience*." Just like she thought—he wouldn't understand how important this was to her.

He continued to stare at her. "Why do you care?"

She couldn't tell him the truth. Couldn't tell him about her failure. Her embarrassment and humiliation. He'd never trust her competence. Just like no one else would. "Because I'm connected to this somehow. That man said my family's name. Maybe he was headed to my house. I need to know why."

Brody's jaw flexed. "I want the key back, Felicity. I'm not going to impede a police investigation."

Desperation tugged inside her. Her need for redemption trumped her logic at the moment. It wasn't a good place to be in, but she had to fight her way through this. "Please, just give me a little time. When I have more answers, I'll turn the key over."

"I can't do that. I need the key." He held his hand out, as if expecting her to plop it there.

Her shoulders tightened as determination took over. "Well, I'm not driving home and then driving back out here to give it to you. You'll have to wait until the snow melts. I almost went into the ditch on the way here."

Something flickered in his gaze. He wasn't about to be walked on, she realized.

"I'll drive you home," he said. He looked formidable as he stood against the car with his hands on his hips. His jaw was thick and strong. His eyes were too observant for her comfort. His mouth was set in a firm line.

She hadn't expected his offer to drive her home and tried to quickly think of a counter. She finally settled on, "You don't have to do that."

She knew it sounded weak, but comebacks had never been her strong suit.

Satisfaction lined his gaze. "I want to. I insist. I'll get the chief to pick me up. He wants to come check out my truck anyway."

She tried to think of an excuse, but none came to mind.

"Let's take your car," he said. "And leave your aunt's here with her. Makes more sense, right?"

Before she could stop him, he led her across the parking lot to her sedan. Next thing she knew, she was snug in the passenger seat with the door closed, heat blaring, and Brody was behind the wheel. He eased out of the parking space and started down the road before she could object.

She expected to feel fear—fear because of Brody, because of the roads, because of the situation. But there was something steady about his grip on the steering wheel, about his gaze on the road, about his control of the vehicle.

For some strange reason, she felt safe.

For a moment, at least.

"I didn't take you as the type to pull a stunt like this," he finally said. "I knew you didn't trust me. All along, I guess I shouldn't have trusted you."

Ouch. That didn't feel good.

"You wouldn't understand," she muttered.

"You might be surprised."

Should she tell him? Tell him how she failed? How she was professionally humiliated? How her peers had laughed at her?

She opened her mouth but then shut it again. No. She couldn't share that. Not right now.

"I'll give you the key back," she said instead, crossing her arms. She realized she probably looked like a five-year-old, but it was too late to undo what had been done.

"Good."

Silence stretched between them: uncomfortable, unwelcome, unbecoming.

Finally, her house came into sight. It appeared just like they'd left it, but the snow was beginning to melt.

He pulled to a stop and said nothing for a moment. Then he looked at her with a touch of annoyance in his eyes. "You ready?"

She wasn't ready. She didn't want to give up the key. But she wasn't willing to go too far for what could be nothing. Part of her wanted to fight for it. To raise a ruckus. To figure out a way to keep it.

But that would be foolish. She had to be wise here.

"Yes, let's go."

"Watch your step. It looks like it might be slick on

the sidewalk."

She bit back a "harrumph." He actually sounded, for a minute, like he didn't hate her. But, just as he said the words, her feet hit an icy patch, and she felt them sliding out from underneath her. She was sure she was going to hit the ground with an embarrassing and painful thud when a strong hand grabbed her elbow. She fell into Brody instead.

"You okay?"

She nodded, pulling herself together and mentally scolding herself for the way her cheeks flushed at his nearness. As the strength in his grip made her crave more. As the scent of spearmint and leather made her heart flutter. "Yes, I'm fine. Thank you."

She straightened and brushed off some snow, desperate to keep herself occupied so he wouldn't see how awkward she felt. If only it was that easy. It was probably written all over her face.

She'd never been sly or demure or graceful. Those had been the girls she'd admired in high school. They'd gotten all the dates while she'd gotten the good grades. Her mother and grandmother both had been stunning— the kind of women who turned heads in their younger days. Felicity used to envy them for it.

Brody kept a hand on her elbow as she climbed the steps. She wanted to shoo him away, but she knew she'd only further embarrass herself by falling again. It was better to grin and bear it.

Finally, her clumsy, frozen fingers managed to unlock the door, and she stepped into the warmth of the house. "One minute," she told him.

The key was in her room, and she didn't want him following her there. Things already felt awkward enough between them. She hurried away before he could stop her.

She stepped into her room and started to shut the door.

By the time she heard the floor creak beside her, it was too late.

CHAPTER 13

"Don't turn toward me," the man growled into her ear. He pressed something into her side with one hand. The other hand locked her arms behind her back.

Felicity froze, fear coursing through her veins. There was a man in her house. In her room. And he had a gun.

She had no choice but to listen to him.

"Where's the key? I know you have it."

"Key? What key?" She wasn't sure feigning ignorance was the best choice, but maybe he'd buy it.

Her senses went on full alert. She soaked in the smell of his expensive cologne. The fancy ring on his finger. The thick gold bracelet at his wrist. Blond hair peaked out from his sleeves. And he had an accent. Australian.

"Don't play dumb with me. Give me the key."

"I don't know—"

Before she could finish her statement, the man jammed the gun into her ribcage with enough force to leave a bruise. She let out a yelp.

"Felicity, are you—" Just as Brody appeared in the doorway, the man shoved the gun to her temple.

"One step closer and she dies."

Brody's eyes widened, and he stepped back, hands

in the air. "Okay, okay. Don't hurt her."

"I just want the key," the man growled.

Felicity was all too aware of the gun. That one slip of the man's finger could mean the end of her life. That her next breath could be her last.

Sweat sprinkled across her forehead.

Who was this man? What was so important about that key? This only confirmed her theory that it was in some way valuable or significant.

She didn't have time to think about it now.

"Where is it?" The man's other hand tightened around her arm, cutting off her blood flow until her fingers began to tingle.

Brody's eyes met hers, and he seemed to silently urge her to remain calm. But she could tell by his body language that he was edgy. His actions were quick, yet his responses hesitant. His voice sounded placating—something she didn't think was possible.

"I can get it for you." Her words hardly registered in her own ears. "But I can't do that with a gun to my head."

"One wrong move, and you die. Understand?"

She wanted to nod, but couldn't bring herself to do it. She needed to remain still. Instead, she muttered, "Yes, I understand."

"You too," the man barked.

"Just don't hurt her," Brody said.

He slowly lowered the gun from her temple, but she was all too aware of how close it still remained. It hovered at her ribs.

"Now, move!" The man shoved her away.

She nearly lost her balance but caught herself on the edge of the dresser.

She had to get the key. She had no choice.

Slowly, she walked toward her nightstand and lifted the jewelry box there. She'd stashed the key inside, figuring it was safer than keeping it on her.

She glanced in the mirror and saw the man. He wore a black ski mask. Seeing him caused a new jolt of fear to spring through her. It made the situation all too real.

Her fingers trembled as she grabbed the key. As soon as she grasped it, the man snatched it from her hands.

"This is rightfully mine." He stared at the key for a moment before shoving it into his pocket.

"You've got the key. Now you can leave," Brody said. He sounded like a negotiator with his gentle, pleading tones. But would they work?

"If only it was that easy." The man grabbed Felicity's arm again and tugged her toward the door. "You're coming with me."

"That's not necessary," Brody said, alarm heightening his voice and causing his body to visibly tense even more.

"Really. I won't tell anyone." Felicity didn't bother to hide her desperation. "Take the key. I don't even know what it's for anyway."

The man paused in front of Brody. "Why'd you come here? Did that man tell you something?"

Brody blinked before giving the man a hard stare. "What do you mean, tell me something? What man? The one in my truck? You were the one who ran us off the road, weren't you?"

"He had something that belonged to me. Now I'm the one asking the questions. What did he say to you?" He shoved the gun into Felicity's side again. "Tell me or she dies."

Brody raised his hands again. "I promise you—he

didn't tell me anything. He was barely conscious when I found him."

"He gave you the key."

"He must have stuck it in my pocket after I passed out. I didn't even know it was there."

She could feel the man staring at Brody from over her shoulder. He finally let out a grunt and began dragging her into the hall. He never left his back exposed to Brody, though.

Desperation began to claw at her. She couldn't go with the man. She knew the statistics. She knew what would happen and how her chances of dying increased exponentially.

"Please, don't take her," Brody said. "Take me instead."

Her heart stuttered in her chest. He'd really offer up himself for her? He didn't even know her.

Warmth spread through her in a swift heat wave. It was more like a ball of fire that erupted quickly and disappeared even more quickly. This wasn't personal—it was simply noble. Maybe even ingrained in him from his job.

"No way. I know how this operates. She's coming with me."

"Don't hurt her." Brody took a step closer, a new plea in his voice.

"Stay right there," the man said. "One more step, and she dies. Do you understand? Any quick moves, and she dies. Understand? You do anything, she dies."

"Understood," Brody said.

"In the closet." The man pointed to a door with his gun.

Brody looked behind him. "In there?"

The man nodded. "That's right. Stop asking

questions. Get in."

"Fine, fine. I'm going." Brody pulled the hall closet door open. Coats and brooms and blankets atop the shelf waited there.

"Get in."

Brody's eyes met Felicity's, some kind of silent message being conveyed. He didn't want to do this. But she could tell also that he couldn't go all Rambo and try to save her right now. The man had a gun. Pointed at her. One wrong move, and she was dead.

As soon as Brody was in the closet, the man slammed the door. "Go get a chair," he ordered Felicity.

With jittery motions and steps, she hurried across the creaky wooden floor and grabbed a dining-room chair. The man jammed it under the knob, preventing Brody from escaping. For a while, at least. Long enough for the man to get away. Most likely with Felicity.

Apparently satisfied with his work, the man jerked Felicity toward the kitchen and opened the back door. Another burst of frigid wind swept inside.

He pulled her into the cold, and she struggled to keep up as he dragged her toward the old barn. That was when she saw the tire tracks leading behind the structure. But the tracks led from across the field. Had he really come here the back way? Apparently.

He shoved her into the barn. A Hummer was parked there.

He opened the driver's-side door and shoved her inside. "One wrong move and you're dead. Have I made myself clear?"

She swallowed hard. "Deadly."

***

Brody threw his shoulder into the door for the third time. His bones ached. His muscles ached. Even his jaw had begun to ache—probably from gritting his teeth.

But he had to get out of here. He couldn't let that man leave with Felicity.

Visions of Andrea filled his mind. He wouldn't let someone else disappear on his watch. It didn't matter that he hardly knew Felicity. He felt such a strong instinct to protect her. Concern and guilt collided inside him.

He backed all the way to the back wall. It wasn't far. There was no way to get much momentum. But he had to do everything he could.

He propelled himself forward, and his shoulder connected with the door again. This time it cracked.

Finally!

He was making some progress. A couple more shoves, and he'd be out of this closet.

A moment later, the door splintered from its hinges. He propelled himself across the floor and ran toward the back of the house. He thought he'd heard them leave this way.

Immediately he spotted the footprints in the snow. Two sets. Leading to the barn.

He darted that direction.

Empty. It was empty.

That was when he saw the tire tracks leading through the field.

There was no way Felicity's car could follow them through an open field. He'd get stuck in no time.

He ran toward Felicity's sedan and hopped inside. He had a Plan B.

That field followed the river, and this road followed parallel to the river for a considerable distance. Maybe he could track them this way. The driver had to exit the field sometime.

How could this have happened? Brody should have checked the house before Felicity walked to her bedroom. But he hadn't thought anyone would be here, and Felicity had rushed off before he could stop her. He should have known better.

Just what was so special about that key? He needed to find out—after he found Felicity.

He grabbed his phone and dialed Joshua's office. He told his friend what had happened, and Joshua promised to put everyone on the search. He would call in the State Police and police from the surrounding communities as well.

Brody came to another road that cut through toward the river and turned there. He followed the lane, trying to move quickly but carefully on the slick surface.

His angst deepened with every tire rotation. This road was even farther from the state- and county-maintained highway, and it wasn't anywhere close to being cleared.

His heart pounded in his ears, and his grip tightened on the wheel. This had to be where the gunman had gone with Felicity.

Dear Lord, watch over her. Protect her. Don't let that man harm her.

Like Andrea.

He didn't purposefully add that part to his prayer, though he was sure God heard him anyway.

Memories tried to attack him, to consume him, but he couldn't let them. He had to stay focused.

Where exactly did this road lead?

As if to answer him, it turned by the river and began following alongside it.

Ahead, he spotted a clearing. Was that . . . the

highway?

He let out a deep sigh and barely resisted jamming his hand into the steering wheel.

It was the highway.

That meant that whoever had snatched Felicity could be anywhere by now.

***

Felicity's hands continued to tremble. Where was this man taking her? What was he planning to do with her?

All she could think about was the gun that he kept pointed at her. That meant he was driving in these conditions with only one hand on the steering wheel. She wasn't sure which made her more nervous. Actually, she was. It was the gun. That gun had the capacity to claim her life.

The thought wouldn't leave her.

If only she hadn't dropped her purse when he grabbed her. Her own gun had been inside.

She needed to use this time wisely. Maybe see what information she could get out of him. See if she could figure out where he was taking her. After all, her cell phone was still shoved into her back pocket. If she was able to get away, she could use it. Call for help.

Call Brody for help?

No. She mentally shook her head. She didn't have his number. And just because he'd tried to save her once didn't make him a savior.

She had to rely on her instincts and intelligence right now. For a moment—and just a moment—she wished she had a higher power to call on.

She wished she could trust God, just as her parents had. They'd had such a deep faith.

And look where it had gotten them. They'd died a tragic death.

She was better off relying on herself.

Okay, Felicity, what do you know at this point? The man was wealthy, based on his jewelry. He was also educated, based on his college ring. His solid build made her think he took care of himself. His accent revealed he was from Australia. His tan indicated he liked to be in the sun.

"Where are you taking me?" Her words squeaked out, making her fear evident.

"Wouldn't you like to know?"

"What's so important about the key?"

He glanced at her. "You really don't know, do you?"

"Why would I?"

He let out a half-snortle/half-laugh. "I'll let you figure it out."

She glanced down and saw a bag at her feet. Files full of papers scattered from it. There were maps, as well as pages and pages of handwritten notes, a laptop computer, and a metal detector.

"Okay, what does the key go to?" Her fingers dug into the armrest as the countryside blurred past her. "Can you tell me that?"

How was Brody? Was he still locked up? What if no one found him and he starved to death?

She tried to cast the thought aside. After all, she had bigger worries to focus on right now. Like her own survival. If she got out of this, then she could go back and help Brody.

"For someone who's supposedly so brilliant, you're not very smart," the man said.

His comment stung. It came too close to the truth.

What good was it to be intelligent if that very intelligence failed you when you needed it the most? Like right now. Like three months ago.

"I really have no idea what's going on here. I just moved here a couple of months ago."

"You don't know who you are, do you?"

She fought a sigh. Why did he keep going in circles?

"I'm Felicity French. My parents were both teachers. I'm an only child. My family has roots in this area."

"Now you're getting somewhere. What kind of roots?"

"The normal kind. Plantation owners, at one point in our history. Grew tobacco and cotton. I think my grandpa owned a market of some sort. Nothing remarkable."

He only grunted.

"Maybe we can work on this together," she said, the idea suddenly hitting her. This could be her way of saving herself. Of course, she'd never want to really align herself with this man. But if it could buy her some time . . .

"You really think you can help me?" He turned off the main highway onto another street, this one much more secluded, with trees on either side. She preferred the highway. Though there weren't a lot of people around because of the weather, at least there had been some others. Out here, there were only so many possibilities. So many *bad* possibilities.

Did she think she could help him? "I don't know. I got the key, didn't I?"

He was quiet a moment before chuckling. "Someone as pretty as you . . . I wish you could help. But unfortunately, sweetheart, this isn't a job for someone like you."

"What are the maps for?"

His chuckle quickly faded. In fact, it died on the spot. "That's not for you to know."

He grabbed the bag and tossed it into the back seat before she could see anything. It was too late. Her mind was already working and formulating.

"You're looking for something," she muttered. "Something that that key fits into. Most likely something valuable."

"What if I am?"

"It's probably in this area. And it's old. There are quite a few old buildings around. The Newbold-White house, plus a few others. Of course, if you thought that key fit into anything there, you would have most likely just tried to bulldoze your way into it. You wouldn't have waited to do it nicely."

The man's mood grew darker by the moment. He obviously didn't appreciate her deductions, yet she couldn't seem to stop herself.

"So I'm going to venture to say that whatever you're looking for is hidden. You don't know where it is. That's why you have those maps—some of which are old."

"You need to stop." His words held a menacing growl that silenced her.

Her brain kept on going, though.

What was he looking for?

She swallowed hard. He was a relic hunter, wasn't he?

Brody had said he'd been on the river right before this storm hit the area. Could that have been connected with this madness? Was someone with only money in his or her gaze stupid enough to go out into the water in weather like that? If he thought the prize at the end was valuable enough, he might.

But what kind of relic?

She glanced down again, moving only her eyes. There was still one folder down there, sticking out from under the seat. What was in that folder? Finding out might be her only chance of surviving this.

She moved her foot and shuffled some of the papers. A picture slid from the pile.

She glanced at the man beside her and noticed he was focused on the road and not on her.

Moving carefully, she used her foot to pull the paper out some more. Her throat went dry.

It was a copy of a diary of some sort. She couldn't make out the words, but it looked old.

Before she could snoop anymore, something hard came down on her head. The last thing she remembered hearing was the man muttering, "What do you think you're doing?"

CHAPTER 14

When Felicity woke up, white surrounded her and bitter cold seeped into her bones.

She sat up with a start.

Where was she?

Her breathing instantly became labored, but the chill in the area burned her lungs with every intake of air.

Her hand hit the ground, and ice made her fingers tingle.

Snow.

She was in the snow.

In a snowdrift left by the plows that had pushed down the street.

She looked up.

She was outside. There were no buildings around. Only a pine tree not terribly far away. A gentle rain melted the landscape and soaked her to the bone.

Her head throbbed something terrible.

That's right. The man hit me.

He must have shoved her out of the car and into this snowbank.

She looked in the distance. The sun was beginning to sink. Soon it would be dark. And she'd never survive out here in the cold all night. The moisture had already invaded her clothing.

Her phone! She still had her phone.

But who could she call? Maybe her aunt was right. She should have gotten to know some people in town. Could she even get a signal to call 911?

Her fingers, once tingly, now felt numb. She managed to tug her phone out. As she did, she climbed—or fell—over the snowdrift. A small road waited on the other side. At least that was what she would guess based on the pattern of the snow. There were hardly any tread prints there, which made her believe no one probably used this very often.

She took another step, and her leg slipped into icy-cold water.

A ditch, she realized. She'd stepped into a ditch. It must be warm enough that the frozen water had melted enough for her to sink through.

She managed to pull her leg out, but her foot tingled with impending numbness.

Her hope of someone driving past and finding her shouldn't be fed. As night fell, fewer and fewer people would venture out because they'd fear the roads freezing again.

She managed to get her cell phone screen on. It took several tries because her cold fingers weren't registering on her touch screen. When she finally got it open, she saw that she didn't have a signal.

Her heart fell.

No!

She sucked on her lip a moment and realized she needed to start moving. It was the only way she was going to get out of this alive.

How long had the man driven down this road before he'd knocked her out? She tried to remember, but everything felt like a blur. Maybe ten minutes? But ten minutes of driving was entirely different than ten minutes of walking. That same distance would put her out well after the sun set. Her legs were already numb. She couldn't feel her nose or ears.

But the longer she stood here thinking about it, the less traction she was going to get on this. She'd walk until she found a signal. She had no other choice.

Her feet sank into the snow on the road. As soon as they sank, they slid, going in opposite directions. This time, Brody wasn't here to catch her.

It was just as well. She needed to learn to depend only on herself. Depending on other people had gotten her into trouble before. She didn't want that to happen again.

Yet there was a part of her that longed for it. That longed to be connected. To have community. To have people to watch her back—to really watch her back, not just pretend like they were.

Ricky.

Had he ruined her for the rest of her life? She didn't want to believe that. Yet he had made her more cautious, maybe to an extreme.

He'd stabbed her in the back after months of a tumultuous relationship. She should have seen the writing on the wall.

They'd met through her job at Cupperdine University in Raleigh. He was a guest lecturer for one of the classes, and, boy, was he a charmer, not only with his polished good looks but also with his intelligence.

She'd rushed to talk to him afterward, and he'd surprised her by asking her out. Two months later she was working for him. A week after that, they were dating.

She shook her head to clear the memories. Each step felt like she was slogging through quicksand. But she was making progress.

She paused and looked back at the pine tree.

That couldn't be right.

She hadn't even passed it yet.

It didn't matter. She'd keep moving.

She held up her cell phone again.

Still no signal.

Maybe she should rest beneath that pine tree until someone found her. The idea danced around in her mind, playing with her, teasing her, tantalizing her.

It seemed like such a nice alternative to walking through this ice-cold snow. Maybe she could curl into a ball and keep warm. Maybe, even if someone found her in the morning, it would be okay. Maybe she could survive out here at night.

No, get a hold of yourself, Felicity. You know that's not true. You need to find help. Now. You don't have any time to waste. Stay out here all night, and you'll get hypothermia and probably die. Your aunt will be the only one who comes to your funeral.

Her breath came out in frosty sheets in front of her. She had to keep moving. Every step she took felt like she was lifting a hundred pounds. While walking through sludge. In a freezer.

Dear God, I wish I still believed You could help. That You cared. But You took my parents from me.

She raised her cell phone in the air, checking for a signal.

She had service! There was only one bar, but it was better than nothing.

She blew on her fingers a moment, trying to warm them, before hitting the button to call her aunt.

Please, Aunt Bonny. Don't be crazy. Just answer. And listen to me. And get help. Please.

Her aunt answered on the first ring. "You calling to check on me? You wanna play chickenfoot again, don't you?"

"Aunt Bonny, I need your help. I'm in the middle of nowhere. I'm going to freeze to death if you don't send someone."

"What are you talking about? You been drinking?"

"Aunt Bonny, you know I don't drink. Now, please . . ."

The tease left her voice. "You are serious, aren't you? Where are you?"

"I don't know. We went down the Highway 17 and then turned a couple of miles past the barbecue place you're always talking about."

"The Bulkhead? Left or right?"

She closed her eyes a moment. "Left."

"Do you see anything?"

"Nothing except a pine tree."

"Well, how am I going to send help your way?" Her screechy voice grated on Felicity's ears. "You don't even know where you are."

"Please, Aunt Bonny. I have no idea. I just need help. Please. I'll keep walking toward the highway."

"Don't hang up. I'm going to run next door and use Margie's phone. Stay on the line."

"Yes, Aunt Bonny."

Felicity took another step. Then another. Tried to hold onto the phone.

Her head still hurt. Pounded. Warmth was a distant memory. Something that couldn't be obtained. Even her bones ached. Her bones ached *so* badly.

She had to wait for her aunt.

Wait.

She took another step.

The phone fell from her fingers, she realized.

She couldn't feel her hands.

Her legs buckled.

And she disappeared into blackness.

**

"Brody, Bonny Pasture just called." Joshua's voice blurred across the line. "Said Felicity called her. She's out somewhere a few miles past Bulkhead Barbecue. On the left. By a big pine tree."

Brody's back went ramrod straight. After borrowing a truck from Joshua, Brody had been driving on back roads for the past two hours, praying for a clue as to where they might have gone. But he'd come up with nothing. Nothing.

"Thanks." Brody carefully turned the truck around on the icy road. Rain had started again—fat, juicy drops that were helping to melt the snow. That would help make the streets safer, but it could ice up again tonight when temperatures fell again.

"I'm sending some men out that way," Joshua said.

"I'll help you look too. I'm on my way there now."

"It's getting dark. She can't stay out there all night."

"I know." Brody had thought of that. The good news was that she wasn't with the man anymore, but Aunt Bonny hadn't said what kind of condition Felicity was in. Had she been shot? Hurt in anyway? Or had the man simply dumped her somewhere?

He didn't really like any of the possibilities. But she was alive. He had to hold onto that.

Using the directions Joshua had given him, he started in her direction. There were several streets that could fit the description, though. Which one was Felicity down?

He didn't like the idea of her being out there in the snow.

She had mentioned an old pine tree? There was a tree out there that had claimed more than cars in accidents as they'd sped around the corner. Could that be the place? He remembered it well because his friend had totaled his car in high school.

He wanted to speed down the road, but he stopped himself. Conditions were getting tricky again. The road was slick. It was hard to see, and hardly any street lamps illuminated this area.

Something dark was in the middle of the road. He gently pressed his brakes and watched as the object grew closer and closer.

Finally, the truck came to a stop.

He quickly climbed out and scrambled toward the object.

No, not an object.

It was a woman.

It was Felicity!

He shook her, concerned at her stillness. Her skin was freezing. Her nose was red. A thin layer of ice had formed across her face.

This wasn't good.

Quickly, he gathered her in his arms and carried her to the truck. He tucked her in before climbing in himself and blasting the heat. He had to get her to the hospital.

There was no time to waste.

CHAPTER 15

Felicity awoke to coldness.

Whiteness.

Brightness.

The snow, she realized with a start.

She tried to sit up as an instant sense of panic kicked in. But she couldn't move. Couldn't. Something held her down. Chains? No. More like a wire. *Wires*.

And what was that beeping sound?

She forced her eyes open as her heart rate surged.

A white room came into view.

She was indoors, she realized.

It was cold . . . but not blizzard cold. Chilly in a sterile manner—like a hospital.

In an instant, Brody appeared at her side.

At the sight of his handsome face, her throat went dry. Why did he have to have that effect on her? He'd seen her at her worst. At her weakest. Most vulnerable.

She never wanted a man to see her like that again.

"How are you?" His voice sounded husky and anxious. His eyes were laced with surprising concern. The man hardly knew her, yet he'd gone out of his way to help her. He'd stuck around, even after her key-stealing shenanigan. He should get some kind of bonus points for that.

"I'm . . . I'm okay . . . I think." She paused. "How did I get here?"

The last thing she remembered was talking to her aunt as she walked along the desolate road. Then everything had gone black.

"I found you on the road. In the snow. The man snatched you from your house. Do you remember?" His eyes crinkled at the corners as he studied her.

She closed her eyes as the memories flooded back. That was right. There was that man with the gun who'd forced her into his vehicle. He'd dumped her on the side of the road. She'd tried to walk to safety, but she hadn't made it.

Her cheeks flushed as she wondered what had played out during those missing moments. Was that what Brody had felt like after his accident? A new surge of compassion rose in her.

"I do remember that man. I can't believe you found me. I thought for sure I was going to die out there." Her voice caught as the memories pounded her.

Had God heard her prayers?

Brody seemed to sense her distress and squeezed her hand. "Your aunt called and told Chief Haven what you'd told her. Honestly, it was only by God's grace I found you when I did."

"God's grace, huh?" She wanted to snicker, but she couldn't bring herself to do so. The man had saved her life, so she could at least show some respect. But she'd given up on believing in God a long time ago.

"God's grace has carried me through some of my darkest moments," Brody said, his voice growing raspy. Suddenly he straightened, as if pulling himself together. "I'm glad you're okay. You gave us all a good scare."

She glanced around the hospital room, trying to get a sense of time. "How long have I been here?"

"About five hours."

She peered out the window and saw it was dark outside. That made sense. If Brody hadn't found her when he did . . . she'd probably be dead right now.

"Your aunt wanted to be here, but the roads have iced up again as the temperatures fell," Brody continued. "I didn't think it was safe."

His concern for her aunt caused warmth to spread in her belly. "You actually managed to convince her to listen to you?"

He shrugged nonchalantly. "Some people say I have a way with women."

Her eyebrows flinched up as she tried to read his tongue-in-cheek expression. "I'm sure you do."

"It was a joke."

Her shoulders relaxed, and she willed the rest of her body to do the same. She'd felt so uptight lately. Even more since she'd moved back here. She hadn't been like this as a child. No, something had changed in her over the past few years. Since her parents died, for that matter.

"Sorry. I'm on edge," she finally said.

"Do you really feel okay?"

At his question, she did a mental evaluation before nodding. "I think so. I can move my toes and fingers. That's a good sign."

He smiled. "Yes, it is."

"How long do I have to stay here?"

He shrugged. "I'm not sure, but I'd guess at least until morning. I'm sure the doctor will want to keep an eye on you. Besides, it's not safe for anyone to leave right now. Not even me."

She swallowed hard. "I just wanted to say thank

you. You didn't have to go out of your way for me."

"You saved me. I guess we're even now."

She nodded resolutely, shifting her thoughts from Brody's care and concern—things she most definitely should not think about—to the key that was stolen from her . . . er, from Brody.

"Did they catch the man who did this?" she asked.

Brody pressed his lips into a grim line. "Not yet. Joshua is looking into it."

"Any idea who he is?"

Brody again shook his head. "No, I don't think so. I'm sure Joshua will want to talk to you."

She pushed herself up higher in bed, careful to keep her unflattering gown around her shoulders amid her IV and heart monitor. She could only imagine what she looked like, even though that was the least of her concerns at the moment. Snippets of her conversation with the man came back to her.

"I think he's a relic hunter, Brody."

Brody squinted. "A relic hunter? Why would you think that?"

"Just from our conversation. He kept saying things that led me to believe that he thought I should know more about what was going on. I assure you, I have no idea. But he also had maps, and he had photocopies of something that looked like an old journal entry."

"And that made you think he was a relic hunter?"

She licked her lips, realizing just how crazy she was going to sound. "I think he's searching for whatever that key goes to. I think it's valuable."

"You mean like treasure?"

"Aunt Bonny would say Blackbeard's."

Brody stared at her a moment before letting out a laugh. "You're joking, right?"

She shook her head. "I know how that sounds. But that key he had . . . it's an antique. Plus the maps he was toting around were not modern-day maps. Well, a couple of them appeared to be. But there were several that were old, as well."

"Blackbeard's treasure is just local lore, Felicity."

"Not for everyone. There are lots of people out there who believe he really did hide his treasure away. You know that. You've lived around here. Certainly you've heard stories."

"About people who are related to pirates? Yeah, I've heard them."

"My aunt believes we have pirate blood in our family."

His eyebrows flickered upward, but he said nothing.

"At least you can put all of this behind you now," he finally said. "After all, the police are on the case."

She nodded. But there was no way she was letting this drop. She didn't have a job. She had nothing to lose.

She was going to get that key also, and figure out exactly what was going on here. But she'd have to plan her moves carefully.

**

Brody saw the fire flash in Felicity's eyes. Exactly what was she thinking? Certainly, she didn't have any kind of fantasies about going after that guy herself, did she?

No, she was a smart girl. She could see how incredibly stupid it would be to try and find that guy. After all, he had murdered that man.

Yes, murdered. Joshua had told him the autopsy results had come back in. The man had died from a fatal blow to the head. And he'd been tortured first. It appeared his teeth had been pulled, one by one.

"You should get some rest," he told her. "I'll wait around the hospital, just to make sure trouble doesn't come find you."

"Oh, come on. Let's be truthful: it's because the roads are too dangerous." She smiled, and he realized she was teasing.

If she only knew that there was something that was keeping him here beyond mere obligation. He didn't know what—or he didn't want to acknowledge what, at least. Felicity had stirred something inside him he'd thought was long dormant.

"Get some rest. It will do your body good," he finally said.

Nearly before he finished his sentence, her eyes began to droop. The doctors had probably given her some type of medicine that would knock her out.

He stepped into the hallway and called Joshua to give him an update. Then he sat down in a chair outside the room and began to mentally rehash everything Felicity had told him.

Blackbeard's treasure? Until the past two days, he hadn't given it a thought in years. Years. Since he was a boy.

Sure, this area was rich with folklore about the pirate. But if that treasure hadn't been found in more than two hundred years, he doubted it ever would be.

However, long-lost treasure fit in with the man being a relic hunter. Brody had encountered some in his time with the Coast Guard. Most of them searched for sunken treasure off the coast and tried to salvage any valuables. He knew the most successful were rich—some were filthy rich.

What if what Felicity had told him had merit?

Had this guy found some type of clue he thought would lead to this treasure?

Out of curiosity, he called a friend of his who was stationed with the Coast Guard at Fort Macon.

"Hey, man," Tim Chavers said. "What's going on?"

"Quick question," Brody started. "You know anything about the excavation of the *Queen Anne's Revenge* down there?"

"I know we have a lot of gawkers. People hoping to get a piece of the pie, so to speak. Why are you asking?"

Brody filled him in on some of the developments as of late.

"It all started with an old key, you said?"

"That's right. You know anything about that?"

"Maybe you could talk with the guys from Project Teach. They're the ones who record and document every find."

"Good idea. Maybe I'll do that. Speaking of that, have you had any problems with any relic hunters?"

Tim paused for a moment. "Not that I can think of. I did hear something rather interesting the other day, though. Just scuttlebutt around town."

Brody straightened. "What was that?"

"I've gone out with a girl who works at Project Teach. She told me that one of the researchers working on the project disappeared a couple of days ago. They're trying to keep it on the down-low at the moment before they bring in the authorities."

He leaned back in the chair, letting that factoid sink in. "Really."

"Yeah. His boss has been trying to call him, but hasn't been able to get in touch."

As much as Brody wanted to believe that this could

be something, there could very well be a logical explanation. "We did just have a major snowstorm. Phone lines could be down. Roads closed. He could be checking on relatives. Maybe it's not that unusual."

"When you consider that there are three different maps missing, I'd say so."

Fire heated Brody's blood. Maps? Now this was getting interesting.

"Any chance you could send me the name and a picture of this guy?" Brody asked.

"I'll see what I can do."

***

Twenty minutes later, Brody had the picture. Apparently the man's name was Archibald Campbell. Brody did an Internet search on him, but nothing came up.

Strange. Everyone left some kind of digital footprint. He needed to look further into this man. It was too bad they hadn't seen the intruder's face.

He felt certain it was the man who'd been in Felicity's house. He must have discovered something through his research that made him believe he could get rich, and he'd gone rogue.

Maybe the man Brody had picked up had found the key, and somehow this other guy—the one who'd abducted Felicity—had discovered that information.

Just then, Joshua showed up. His skin still looked rosy from the cold outside as he pulled off his gloves and stopped by Brody.

"You made it. I thought the roads might be too bad."

"The main highways aren't too bad, thankfully." He glanced at Felicity's door. "Any changes?"

"She should be released in the morning," Brody insisted. "Any updates on your end?"

"We're still searching for the man who grabbed her. Nothing yet. I came to get her statement."

Brody stopped his friend before he went into Felicity's room. "Hey, did you ever find out the name of the man who was found dead during the snowstorm?"

"Sure did. His name was Ivan Bordinski. From Hatteras. Despite the name, he was born and raised right here in North Carolina."

"Know anything else about him?"

Joshua shook his head. "Not yet. But we're working on it."

"I know you are. Thanks for the information."

Joshua nodded toward Felicity's door. "I'd love to talk more. But my workload has tripled since the storm. I don't have much time for anything but work."

"Understood." That was fine with Brody. He had enough to think about for the time being.

CHAPTER 16

"Pasture . . ." the man muttered.

Just then, a bullet pierced the back window. Brody glanced in the rearview mirror and spotted a Hummer behind them, gaining speed by the moment.

He sat up with a start, and his eyes darted around him.

"Are you okay, sir?" A nurse stopped and examined him a moment.

He leaned back in the plastic seat perched outside Felicity's hospital room and nodded. It was a flashback, he realized. More memories of what had happened during those lost hours.

"I'm fine," he insisted. He ran a hand over his face and realized he was sweating. His heart raced. It was like he was there again.

That had to be what had happened when he'd awoken from his blackout the first time. His mind and body were telling him he was back in the life-or-death situation on the road. Felicity had just happened to be there, and she'd taken the brunt of it.

He swallowed hard, the memory still feeling fresh.

He'd picked up the stranded man. That guy must have been chasing Bordinski. But why?

He glanced at his watch. It was just past eight a.m. He was surprised that he'd slept as long as he had.

He peeked into Felicity's room and saw that she was still sleeping. Good. She needed to rest.

Knowing that, he picked up his cell phone and began to look into Ivan Bordinski. He'd started the online search last night, but exhaustion had gotten the best of him.

The wonders of the Internet allowed him to quickly pull up several results.

This had to be the same man.

He clicked a couple of links, which brought up a picture.

Yes! This was the man he'd picked up on the side of the road.

Brody quickly gathered all the information he could about the guy. Ivan was in his late sixties, and he'd spent most of his life as a boat captain, based out of Cape Hatteras. He'd primarily done fishing charters.

His boat was a thirty-six-foot Carolina Custom Carman Sportfish.

That was the same kind of boat Brody had found out in the Perquimans during his search in the snowstorm. That boat had been Ivan's. What had happened?

He found phone numbers for a few other captains who launched from the same marina as Ivan. On impulse, he called one.

The first didn't answer. The second number went to voice mail. Finally, the third captain he tried picked up.

"I'm Brody Joyner with the Coast Guard. Did you know Ivan Bordinski?"

"Ivan? Yeah, I know Ivan. Why you asking?"

Did the man not know Ivan was dead? He needed to handle this carefully. "I have a few questions for you. Is this a good time?"

"I leave for a charter in ten minutes. You have five. Is Ivan okay? I noticed his boat wasn't in the slip this morning."

"I'm sorry to tell you that he's dead."

"Dead? No . . . I just talked to him two days ago."

"We're looking into his death. I was hoping you could tell me about how he was acting when you last saw him."

"Didn't talk to him much. Just long enough to bemoan the lack of charters we were able to take because of that nor'easter and the incoming snowstorm."

"Anything unusual about your conversations?"

"No, I don't reckon there was. He was doing a lot of treasure hunting lately. Liked to talk about that a lot. Too much, some people would say."

His pulse spiked. "Treasure hunting?"

"That's what he called it. He liked to scour the shoreline here in Hatteras after storms."

Brody's hopes sank. For a moment, he'd thought he was onto something. "I see."

"After this last nor'easter, he told me he found something that I was going to want to see. He had to talk to someone about it first."

Brody's interested spiked again. "He didn't tell you what it was?"

"No, sir. But he sounded awfully excited about it."

"Did he scour the shoreline often?"

"He mostly looked for shells. He liked to sell them to a few local shops to pick up a few extra dollars. But he did mention some interesting things that had washed ashore after that ship overturned out in the ocean a few months ago. Bags of potato chips! No value, but we all know around here that storms can churn up the strangest things. I wondered what that last nor'easter might have uncovered."

A key, maybe? Brody wondered.

"Did he mention going anywhere?"

"The road leading to the island was washed away, so we've been stuck here. The only way to get off the island is by boat. When I didn't see his at the slip, I just assumed he'd taken it inland to ride out the storm."

"Thanks for the information. You've been very helpful."

Brody hung up and chewed on what he'd learned. Ivan must have found that key after the nor'easter. It very easily could have been washed up from the Beaufort area where Blackbeard's ship, the *Queen Anne's Revenge*, was found.

Had he then tried to get off the island? Was he running with the key? Trying to meet someone?

Brody didn't know. But more pieces were falling in place.

***

Brody hurried to the bathroom to splash some water on his face. As he returned, he saw the food cart leaving and knocked at Felicity's door.

"Come in," she called.

He stuck his head inside, surprised to see that Felicity wasn't eating. No, her eyes were fastened to her phone.

He'd seen the device lying beside her on the road when he found her and had grabbed it. Apparently, the snow had broken its fall. Otherwise, it wouldn't be working now.

"Anything interesting on that phone?" he asked,

knowing he sounded suspicious. But, at this moment, he wasn't exactly sure whom to trust. There seemed to be a lot of people with a stake in this.

"Yeah, I'd say so. Come look at this," she said, still staring at the screen.

He came around beside her and peered over her shoulder. As he did, the edge of her hospital gown cascaded down, exposing her shoulder. He looked away, willing his thoughts to remain pure.

She quickly scrambled to pull it back up, her cheeks flushing slightly.

"What did you want me to see?" His voice came out in more of a croak than he would have liked.

"What do you see here?" She held up the phone. It was a photo. Rather blurry. The background was dark bronze, and there were two letters smeared across the screen.

He squinted as he tried to determine what he was looking at. "Initials?"

"What initials?"

He squinted again, wishing it was a clearer picture. "I don't know. It looks like an E maybe. And there beside it . . . is that a T?"

A satisfied smile crossed her face. "That's what I thought also."

He straightened so he could see her face better. "What are you looking at?"

"I took a picture of the key because I saw a small engraving on the back of it and got curious. I wanted to take it to someone who could enlarge it and make it clearer, but I'm not going to have time to do that. I just used my phone instead."

"This is from the key that was in my pocket? That the man stole from you?" he clarified, things starting to click in his mind.

Felicity smiled again. "That's right."

"Edward Teach." Brody ran a hand through his hair. He'd thought Aunt Bonny's theory was just comic relief. What if she was on to something?

Her smile widened. "You got it. Otherwise known as Blackbeard."

Just like they'd talked about last night. He'd like to dismiss the theory, but it kept coming around again. However, he'd talked to his friend about the research project down there . . .

"Speaking of Blackbeard . . . I have some information that you'll find interesting." He filled her in with what he'd learned.

"So it's a researcher from Project Teach? That's so . . . unethical."

Brody nodded. "It sounds like this guy had dollar signs in his eyes. It's the only reason he'd take off and do something like this."

"We can't let him do that, Brody."

He raised an eyebrow as he pondered her words. "You mean, the *police* can't let him do that."

Her eyes lit with fire. "If this man finds anything of historical significance, he's going to sell it to the highest bidder. The public will never be able to appreciate what he's found. It will be like a piece of our country's past has been sold and forgotten."

"I think we're jumping ahead of ourselves here." He needed her to slow down. There was so much they still didn't know. So many pieces that still needed to fall in place.

She shook her head, her thoughts obviously racing ahead of this conversation. "I've got to find that treasure before he does."

He stared at her in the hospital gown, her hair tousled, her face without a trace of makeup. Even after being in the hospital overnight, after being left for dead in the cold, after being held at gunpoint, she still looked stunning.

And vulnerable. Her logic was obviously compromised.

"You're in no state to go find any treasure," he reminded her.

"The doctor said I could go home this morning." She glanced at the clock on the wall, which read nine a.m. "That should be happening soon."

"You don't have a car." He needed to get her to slow down, to think of her safety. To think this through, period. This was real life. It could be dangerous. And he didn't want to see her hurt.

She raised her chin. "I'll get a ride back to the house to get mine."

Talk some sense into her, Brody. "Where are you even going to start? It's going to be like a wild goose chase. All we know about is the key. We don't even know enough about the key to lead us anywhere."

She frowned. "And the maps. I saw the maps."

"But you don't have any of the maps."

Her frown deepened as determination raised her chin again. "I don't know yet. But I'll think of something."

He crossed his arms, knowing he had no right to tell her what to do. Yet he couldn't encourage her in this pursuit. She was only going to get hurt, and that was the last thing he wanted. "For the record, I want to state that I don't think this is a good idea."

She turned toward him, squirming as her IV caught. The moment quickly passed. "For the record, I understand. And, for the record, I'm not asking for your help."

Why was she pushing this so hard? It didn't make sense to him. Most people would have let this drop at the first sign of danger. Besides, the key didn't really have any significance to her. It just didn't make sense.

But she wasn't going to drop this, so he needed to change his tactics. "It's either I help you or you go at this alone," he finally said.

Confusion fluttered through her lovely brown eyes. "I don't know if you helping me is a good idea."

"If it means being a second set of eyes so you don't get yourself killed, then it's a great idea." He refused to break eye contact. She needed to know how serious this was.

She pressed her lips together before blurting, "Or I could get you killed! Neither is a great option."

"How about we focus on neither of us getting killed?"

She leaned back into her pillow, her hair fanning out around her. She offered a resolute nod. "It sounds like a plan."

He fought a frown. His gut was torn between adventure and safety. But he knew whether he was involved or not, Felicity was going after this treasure. He feared the repercussions of what would happen if this guy got his hands on her again.

"I'll help. But first we need a plan."

CHAPTER 17

Three hours later, Felicity stood in Brody's living room. He lived in a small cottage near the heart of town, yet away from the more expensive, historic homes along the river. The place was neat and well-kept with clean, white siding and a cozy-looking porch.

His house was tiny and old with small, boxy rooms. The decorating needed a woman's touch, but, since he was single, she didn't expect him to have that finesse. Instead he had a plain navy-blue couch, some mismatched end tables, and some pictures of the sea decorating the walls.

She could hear the water from the shower rushing through the pipes as Brody prepared for their trip. He'd insisted on stopping by his place first, and he'd insisted that she stay with him.

His surge of protectiveness sent her emotions into a tizzy. Part of her enjoyed and appreciated the gesture, while the other part fought to be independent. But she knew she'd have a better chance of doing this if Brody were with her. She was no soldier, although she had taken fencing lessons for several years in high school and college. She supposed that would only help her if she ended up in a sword battle with some pirate impersonators—unlikely to happen.

She walked over to the bookshelf and looked for pictures there. There was one of Brody with an older man and woman. Must be his parents, she guessed.

There were no pictures of him with a woman by his side, though.

Why wasn't someone like Brody snatched up and taken by now? It certainly wasn't because of his looks. Any woman would find him attractive. Felicity certainly did.

Her cheeks flushed at the thought.

So maybe it was his personality that kept him single. Was he too gruff? Too bossy? Married to his job?

"Hey, everything okay?" a deep voice said.

She looked over and spotted Brody standing there, a clean black T-shirt clinging to his still-damp chest, low-slung jeans hugging his hips, and bare feet. His hair was glistening and wet, and he had a small, white towel in his hands that he was using to rub it dry.

And he'd shaved.

She looked away. "Yeah . . . everything's . . . it's good. Just fine."

Great. Now she was stuttering and fumbling over her words.

All because he had to come out of the shower smelling so spicy and clean and looking so alluring. What was wrong with her? Would she ever learn her lesson?

"Just let me grab a few things. Do you want something to eat? Feel free to help yourself to anything in the fridge."

"Now that you mention it, I am kind of hungry."

She went into the kitchen and began putting together some sandwiches. It was better than thinking about Brody fresh from the shower. Way, way better.

Not really. But it was safer. Healthier.

No sooner had she put the food on the table than did Brody step into the room and sit down with her.

"Do you mind if I pray?" he asked.

"Knock yourself out."

She closed her eyes as he began. "Lord, please give us wisdom. Grant us safety. Bind any danger . . ."

His words eventually faded, but not before moisture warmed her eyes.

Her mom and dad had prayed like that. They'd had such a strong faith. And for what? For nothing. Her grandmother had also had a strong faith, and she'd been murdered. It didn't appear that God gave any favor at all to those who loved and served Him.

"Felicity?"

She jerked her head up and wiped away the moisture from beneath her eyes. She forced a smile, hoping he didn't ask questions. She didn't want to go into that now.

"Dig in," she said, hoping to divert the subject.

He cast one more glance at her before picking up his sandwich and taking a bite.

"So, where do you want to start?" he said. "I have ideas, but I'll hear yours first."

"Naturally, I think we should start by finding out more information on this guy with Project Teach. Maybe that will give us a clue as to where he's going now that he has the key."

"My thoughts exactly."

"So we'll head down to Beaufort. I don't think they got hit with snow as badly as we did here."

He glanced at his watch. "If we leave as soon as we're finished eating, we might make it there before they close today. It will be a couple hours' drive."

"I think that's what we should do." She nodded, a

139

fizz of excitement bubbling inside her. She hadn't felt this curious about something in a long time.

Could this really be her chance to prove herself? She didn't want the material wealth such a find would cause. No, she wanted to restore herself professionally.

She couldn't bring herself to mention that to Brody, though. He wouldn't understand.

Brody took his last bite. "Let's go."

***

"Felicity. Felicity!" Someone nudged her.

Her eyes popped open, and she sat up straight. She'd fallen asleep, she realized. The last thing she remembered was riding down a country road, heading to Beaufort with Brody. Everything must have caught up with her, and her body had needed rest.

She wiped her mouth, hoping against hope that she hadn't been drooling or anything else embarrassing.

"We're here," Brody said softly.

Thankfully, Brody had swung past her own house before they left. She'd also cleaned up and changed clothes, as well as packed a few things just in case they didn't make it back tonight. She had no idea where this adventure might end up taking them, but she wanted to be prepared.

She stared at the picturesque town in front of her. What seemed like endless docks stretched near the downtown area, where galleries, restaurants, and gift shops were located. In the summer, she could imagine boats out on the water, enjoying the miles and miles of blue. Small patches of snow still remained in the gutters and beneath trees, though the sun tried to melt them with its bright rays.

Brody turned off the main street, down a few more, and finally pulled to a stop in front of a large building. A sign out front read Project Teach.

"There are a few cars out here, so someone must be inside," she said.

"That's a good thing for us."

"What are we going to say? They're going to ask us why we're asking questions," Felicity said.

"I'll tell them I'm Coast Guard and we're investigating an attempted rescue out in the Perquimans that could be connected."

"But are you?"

He shrugged. "We turn investigations like this over to local police usually. But it's not unheard of that we might ask some questions ourselves."

"It sounds like a plan."

She was surprised at how badly her hands shook as she stepped out of the truck. She had never done anything like this before.

Don't think of it as deceit, she told herself. *You're not lying. Brody is Coast Guard, and you're both looking for information. That's the truth.*

When Brody put his hand on the small of her back to lead her inside the building, she nearly jumped out of her skin. It must be her nerves. It had nothing to do with the spark she felt at his touch. Nothing at all.

A young, blonde receptionist greeted them when they walked in, and Brody took the lead. As he approached the desk, Felicity soaked in the area. It was a gray, lifeless welcome to the building—from the carpet, to the walls, to the desk. The only thing in the room that gave any indication that they were researching the infamous pirate was a replica painting of him on his boat behind the receptionist.

"I'm with the Coast Guard, and I need to talk with someone about Archibald Campbell," Brody started.

In an instant, the woman's face went from cheery and polite to strained. "One second."

She rushed toward the back and emerged a moment later with a lanky man who had thinning hair, gold-rimmed glasses, and a coffee stain on his white shirt. The man couldn't be much older than Felicity. In fact, he almost looked like . . .

"Felicity French?" His eyes lit with recognition.

"Derek Peterson," she said.

"Long time no see." He grinned, instantly more relaxed as he stood in the area between reception and a back hallway.

She forced a smile. Derek had always been nice, but a little too nice. She'd suspected he liked her in college, and he hadn't been one to take a polite hint. "I had no idea you worked here."

"You know each other?" Brody's eyes lit with curiosity.

Felicity nodded. "Derek and I went to school together at UNC."

"You went to UNC?"

She nodded, realizing there was a lot Brody didn't know about her. If she were smart, she'd keep it that way. "I did. For undergraduate."

"Don't let her humility fool you," Derek said. "She was brilliant. One of the shining stars of our graduating class. Valedictorian. Fencing champion. Most likely to succeed."

"He's overstating it." Felicity had to change the subject. "How long have you been here, Derek?"

"Just a few years. It's really an exciting project. I mean, who wouldn't want to uncover this kind of history about our country? Pirates. Pirate ships. A lost part of our history. If we solve this, we can move on to the lost colony in Manteo next."

"I can imagine how excited you are," Felicity said. "All of this is an amazing task and accomplishment."

He glowed under her compliment, going as far as to glance at her hand.

He was looking for a wedding ring, she realized.

When he didn't see one, he turned to Brody, seeming to size him up before scowling.

She had to get a handle on this conversation before it went in an undesirable direction.

"We need your help," she blurted.

"What can I do for you? I heard you were here about Archibald." Any of his earlier ease disappeared. The subject of Archibald obviously made him uncomfortable.

"Can we speak in private?" Brody asked.

"Of course. Follow me to my office."

They wound down a short hallway and into a small corner room without windows. It was loaded with papers and books and coffee cups, but he cleared away enough of his research that they could find seats. Then he closed the door before sitting across from them. The space smelled like old Chinese food and Vicks VapoRub.

Derek sat behind a massive, cluttered desk and laced his fingers together. His gaze darted nervously from Brody to Felicity. "Do you know anything about Archibald?"

"Not really," Felicity said.

Derek's head went into his palm. "I think he's gone off the deep end."

Brody leaned toward him. "What can you tell us about Archibald?"

Derek leaned closer, even though no one was

around and the door was closed. "Is all this off the record? I don't want to lose my job for breaking some kind of confidentiality clause."

"It's all off the record," Brody said before lowering his voice. "It's important, Derek. We believe he may have killed someone."

"Killed someone?" His eyes widened before his forehead went back into his palm again. "This isn't good. It isn't good at all."

"Talk to us, Derek," Felicity said.

He raised his head and let out a long sigh before focusing. "As you probably know, any of the treasure from the *Queen Anne* belongs to the state. The state hired several historians and archeologists to examine any of the finds. They call us Project Teach."

"Keep going," Felicity encouraged.

"We brought Archibald onboard because he had an outstanding résumé and came with the highest recommendations. He was an outsider to our little community here, but that was okay. Someone with his experience couldn't be passed over. And he was brilliant. Brilliant."

"How so?" Brody shifted in his seat, his full attention on this conversation.

"He knew exactly how to handle these artifacts that we're getting from the *Queen Anne*. He's one of the best researchers we've got here. But there's always been something a little different about him, you know? He was so driven . . . but also secretive. I always felt like there were things he wasn't telling us."

"But you didn't know what?" Brody said.

Derek shook his head. "No, but he insisted on working strange hours. He'd be here at night by himself. He was almost obsessed with those maps."

"Did he ever show any dangerous tendencies?" Brody asked.

Derek shook his head. "I can't say he did. But he got this fire in his eyes sometimes. Usually it was if someone touched his stuff. I was always afraid he'd go off the deep end."

"When was the last time you saw him?" Felicity asked.

"He was here three days ago. He was working especially hard examining those maps. Like, obsessively. I'm not sure he left here for thirty-six hours straight."

"Why?" Brody asked.

"He didn't tell us. He said he wanted to do some research first."

Felicity's mind raced with possibilities. "He didn't even give you any hints?"

Derek shook his head again. "No hints even. We all just thought that he would tell us what it was as soon as he'd correctly preserved the paper. He said it was big. Then he disappeared."

"And the maps disappeared with him?" Felicity asked.

Derek nodded, his frown deepening. "Exactly. If I knew then what I know now, I would have done things differently. But he was brilliant, and I told myself that people like that want to do things their way."

"What do you think now?" Felicity asked.

"I think he found some kind of clue."

"Clue to what?" Brody asked, tensing beside her.

Derek hesitated a moment. "His main obsession was Blackbeard's treasure. He felt sure it was still out there. That was one of the reasons he wanted to work here. He thought this work could lead people to more answers. I just had no idea he would take it this far."

"You know anything about this key?" Felicity held up her phone.

Derek's eyes widened as he took her phone from her. "Yes. Yes. This looks like the keys used during Blackbeard's time. It's a classic style of that time period. At least, that's how it appears just from the picture. I've seen keys like this before when researching old castles in France."

"Does it go to a treasure chest, by chance?" Brody asked. He still wasn't 100 percent on board with this theory. It would be a stretch for anyone to believe.

"No, no. Of course not. It's too big. But it does go to a room."

"Could that be Blackbeard's key?" Felicity asked.

"It's hard to say without seeing it. I'd certainly say the style fits the time period, and given Blackbeard's proclivity to stealing things from French vessels—Spanish and British too, for that matter—I'd definitely say it could be linked to him. Where did you find this?"

Felicity licked her lips, deciding to dive right in. "A man actually found it. He died. Probably at the hands of the man who worked here, whom we believe was working under an alias."

Derek's face paled even more. "I see. He must think it's connected to his mission—no one stands in his way."

"The initials ET were on the back." Felicity watched his reaction carefully.

His eyes lit, as he seemed to realize the implications of the find. "Edward Teach. Of course! Do you realize what this means? We could be sitting on one of the most significant finds of this decade. People would go crazy because of this."

"It sounds to me like people *are* going crazy over this," Brody said. "Speaking of maps: where is Blackbeard's treasure generally thought to be hidden?"

"Three places, primarily. Either somewhere on Ocracoke Island, at a place called Teach's Oak in Oriental, or on Holiday Island up in the Neuse River."

"I'm assuming people have looked at all of those places." Brody tapped his chin with his index finger.

"Extensively," Derek said.

"And how have people drawn these conclusions exactly?" Brody asked.

"Mostly it's been handed down through word of mouth. Ocracoke, of course, is because that was where Blackbeard's last stand was."

"I see." Brody leaned closer. "What are your theories?"

Derek seemed surprised at the question. He fluttered around a moment before shrugging. "My theories? Well, I don't know. There are several ideas I'm fascinated with. You know that he lived as a common man here in North Carolina for a while, right? Not for very long. But most people believe he took a wife in the area. During that time, he could have easily scoped out places to hide his stash."

"Why would he even hide it?" Brody asked. "Why not just enjoy it?"

"Otherwise, people would steal it. He probably never thought he'd end up dead. He thought he'd escape with his fortune one day—and his favorite wife. Unfortunately, that never happened."

Brody shifted in the uncomfortable plastic seat. "And I guess he never bothered to tell anyone what he did with it?"

"Not to our knowledge. You would think it would have come out if one of his wives or colleagues knew where it was. They would have come into wealth, which would have made people ask questions and make assumptions." Just then, Derek's phone rang. "Excuse me a moment."

When he hung up, he turned to them. "I'm sorry, but there's someone here that I need to speak with. I've given you everything I know."

"If you think of anything else, give me a call." Brody put his card on the table.

"Will do."

CHAPTER 18

As they were leaving, the woman at the front desk called to them. Brody paused and walked back toward her as she waved them over. She was slightly overweight, with a doll-like face.

"I heard you say you were asking about Archibald," she whispered.

"That's correct. Any idea where he is?" Brody asked.

She looked from side to side as if to make sure no one was listening. "I probably shouldn't say this, but Archie was a sad excuse for a human. I overheard him on the phone the other night. I came back because I'd left my cell here, but he didn't know I came in."

"What was he saying?"

"It was something about a man named Winsome. I thought he said he was taking a bath, but that seemed really odd. He was whispering, like whatever he was saying was top secret. But it just struck me as strange."

"He talked about him taking a bath?" Brody's hands went to his hips, obviously skeptical.

"Or could he be talking about the town of Bath—notoriously known as the place where Blackbeard took up residence?" Felicity stared at Brody.

"I think you're right," he said. "Smart thinking."

"Did he say anything else?" Felicity turned back to the woman.

The receptionist shrugged. "He'd been acting strange lately. I tried to sneak into the room and see what he was working on, but I wasn't able to."

"Was there anything unique in the room?" Felicity asked.

"One of the cannons we recovered. It was only weird because his specialty was maps. That was his project. I wondered why he had the cannon in his office."

"What's your theory?" Brody asked.

"I think he discovered something. Something big. Something that he wants all for himself. He was that kind of guy. He thinks only about himself."

"You seem to feel pretty strongly about that," Felicity said.

"I've got good gut feelings."

"If you remember anything else, will you let us know?" Brody took out his card.

"Sure. I'd love to see him get what he has coming to him."

Brody waited until they'd stepped outside before saying anything to Felicity. "That was interesting."

"To say the least."

He wanted to ask how exactly she knew Derek, but he didn't. Derek had mentioned UNC. That she'd been respected. There was a lot he didn't know about Felicity, but they had other more pressing matters to discuss.

"Archibald definitely discovered something," Felicity said. "He wants the treasure for himself, and he's on his way to get it now."

"What do you say we go to Bath?"

"I think that's a great idea. We need to figure out

who this Winsome guy is."

"I just pray he's still alive."

Brody's words caused her heart to lurch. She hadn't thought of that. But she hoped the same thing.

***

As they drove to Bath, Felicity searched on her phone for anyone with the last name of Winsome. One person in town bore that surname, and his first name was Walter. She hoped he might have some answers. And that he was okay—that Archibald hadn't gotten to him first.

The trip from Beaufort to Bath took two hours, mostly on country roads. Brody turned on the radio, and a song by Daleigh McDermott came on. Felicity had heard a rumor that she lived in Hertford.

"You met her yet?" Brody asked.

She shook her head. "No. You?"

"Yeah, I know her husband. I had my truck towed to his shop."

"He's a mechanic?"

Brody nodded. "Daleigh's theory is that you should do what you love. That's what Ryan loves. They're a really down-to-earth couple. I think you'd like them."

"I doubt I'll have a chance to meet her. I won't be in town long enough."

"You plan on leaving soon?"

"Staying here was only a temporary stop. I knew that from the start."

"I see." He nodded slowly.

His reaction made Felicity wonder if he'd be happy when she was gone. After all, she'd caused him a headache in the short time she'd been around.

"What are you looking up now?"

"The man who grabbed me was wearing a class ring of some sort. I couldn't read what it said, but it was distinct with a star and sun on it. Plus, the man had an Australian accent. I want to see if I can identify a college Down Under that fits that description. I know it's a long shot, but . . ."

"It's worth a try."

She searched through several screens before stopping. "Ah ha! Here's something. I think this is the ring." She showed it to Brody.

"Southwestern University of Australia?" he said.

"Now I need to figure out distinguished relic hunters from the university." She typed in some new items on the search menu. A moment later, an article popped up on her screen. She enlarged the picture and showed it to Brody.

"Is that him? Archibald?"

His eyes widened. "It is."

A satisfied smile curled her lips. "His real name is Magnum Lewis."

She began reading the highlights aloud to Brody.

"Magnum Lewis is one of the leading relic hunters in the United States. Apparently, he made a name for himself after discovering a shipwreck up near Cape Cod. It made him millions—until the government claimed a majority of it." She scrolled down further. "His former colleagues call him ruthless. Those who admire him say he's brilliant and focused but disillusioned."

"Does it say anything about his history?"

She scrolled some more, looking for additional information. "Interestingly enough, he started as part of a documentary crew. He was one of the producers as they hunted for some old treasure left by Native Americans. Part of the treasure that was discovered disappeared, but the crime could never be linked directly to Magnum. However, everyone thought he was guilty."

"I guess charges were never pressed?"

"It doesn't appear they were. But shortly after that, Magnum left the production crew and he started his own relic-hunting operation. He hired a crew of . . . it looks like five or six people. Some have backgrounds in water salvage, another in construction. One works security mainly. They're profiled here in another article."

"They sound like quite the formidable team."

"Don't they? Magnum sounds like someone who won't let anyone get in his way. I suppose that's why he went undercover. There was something at Project Teach he wanted."

They pulled off the country highway, turning toward Bath. Felicity knew enough to know that Bath was North Carolina's first town and port. Its proximity to the Pamlico River had made it a much-desired area in its early days. It was incorporated in the early 1700s and even considered as a possibility for the state capital at one time.

"Turn here," she told Brody.

A few narrow, wooded lanes later, they pulled up to a white, clapboard-sided house located on several acres. A small garden peeked out from the back of the house, and a carport had an old, blue Crown Victoria parked beneath it.

Before stepping out, she observed an old cannon in the front yard, painted a glossy black and surrounded by neat red border stones. She imagined in the summertime there were probably cheerful flowers around it. An American flag hung proudly by the front door, right above a grass-green welcome mat.

"Let's do this," Brody said.

Felicity nodded, desperately hoping this trip wasn't

a total waste.

***

Felicity quickly pulled her long hair back into a neat bun and slipped on plastic framed glasses. She found people took her more seriously this way. If she'd had time, she would have worn some sensible khakis and a button-up top. Instead, she had to settle for her boot-cut jeans, thick-soled shoes, and a gray V-neck sweater beneath her black North Face jacket.

Felicity let her gaze wander as they approached the house. Was Magnum here? Was he waiting, ready to pounce from behind one of the trees at the edge of the property? Had he hidden inside, with a gun pointed to Walter's head?

Or had he already been here? Had he attacked Walter and left him for dead? After all, if he'd tortured and killed Ivan, who said he wouldn't do that to anyone who got in his way?

She hoped that wasn't the case. For the first time in a long time, she almost wanted to pray. This situation went way beyond her capabilities, and faith in a higher power would offer some comfort—something she desperately needed.

"You ready for this?" Brody's gaze fell on her for the first time since they'd left the truck, and his eyes widened when he saw her. She didn't have time to explain her transformation to him now.

She nodded resolutely. "Ready as I'll ever be."

As they stepped onto the front stoop, she saw the gun in the back of Brody's waistband. When they'd stopped by her house, Felicity had grabbed hers also, and she kept it stashed in her purse. They had no idea what they were walking into and had to take precautions.

To her surprise, a man answered the door on the first knock. He was an older gentleman, but he still looked solid. His six-foot-plus massive frame only helped that. He had a shock of white hair, a square face, and yellowed teeth.

It was his voice that sounded frail, like a direct contradiction to his large frame, as he said, "Can I help you?"

They had to play this carefully. For all they knew, this guy could be on Magnum's side. They didn't want to show their hand too easily.

"I'm Felicity, and I'm with Cupperdine University," she started. "I'm here with my assistant, Brody, doing some research on the rich history of this area."

"And that brought you to Bath?" he questioned.

She nodded. "It did. This region plays a vital role in North Carolina's history. I'm doing my PhD on that very subject."

"What's this have to do with me?"

"I heard through the grapevine that your family played an interesting role in this area, dating back as far as the early 1700s. I was hoping to ask you a few questions about that."

"Right now?"

"I know it's sudden, and I do apologize for that. Your name showed up in my research, however, and I knew I couldn't leave without stopping by here first."

He glanced behind him. "Okay, then. Come in for a few minutes. Can I fix you some iced tea?"

"That sounds great," Felicity said.

As he walked into the kitchen, she and Brody sat on the olive-green, plastic-covered couch complete with hand-stitched doilies on its arms. Brody leaned close enough that his breath tickled her cheek. "Slick move back there with the new look and cover story. You sure you've never done this before?"

"Positive. My insides are quivering so badly I'm not sure I'll be able to keep the tea down."

"You're doing great."

She hoped she didn't blush under his compliment. Truth was, if she'd had an assistant as handsome as Brody back at the university, she would have been in serious trouble.

Walter returned a moment later and set two glasses of tea on the table. Around here, it was always cold tea. And it was always sweet enough to rot your teeth just by looking at it.

She'd never lost her taste for it, even when she lived across the country.

"Now, what can I do for you?" Walter hiked up his pant legs before sitting in a stiff-looking chair across from them.

"How far back does your family's history in this area actually go?" Felicity started, knowing she needed to be careful. Otherwise, her whole cover story would be blown. She also needed some way of figuring out if Magnum had stopped by here earlier. Walter hadn't given any indications of other visitors.

"It goes back centuries. In fact, this has been my family's home for years. It's been built and rebuilt a couple of times. I could've moved, but I like staying in touch with my heritage."

"I'm particularly interested in Blackbeard and his role in this area. Did your family ever hand down any stories to you about him? I know two centuries is a considerable amount of time, but some stories have lasted longer."

He chuckled and leaned back. "Funny you ask that. Blackbeard stories were abundant in my family."

"Why's that?"

"Well, I don't know how true this is, but legend has it that I'm related to Jacob Winsome, the first mate of the infamous Edward Teach."

Felicity's eyebrows shot up. "Is that right? I thought his first mate was Israel Hands."

"He was. For a while. I realize that Jacob Winsome is not as well-known, but there are two separate documents that mention Jacob Winsome. He became an honest man after Blackbeard was beheaded, and he settled down right here in Bath. On this very property, in fact."

"Interesting."

"I'm not saying it's totally true, but it's made for some good stories. Would you like to see some of the items that have been handed down to me over the years?"

Felicity glanced at Brody. "We'd love to."

"Follow me then."

He shuffled toward a back bedroom. Her spine pinched as they walked. Was this a trap? Was she being too trusting, something that had gotten her in trouble on more than one occasion? At least Brody was here with her, in case things really went south.

When they stopped in a bedroom full of display cases and antique-looking trunks, she let out a breath. There was no one here. Just objects full of history and sentimental value.

Walter proceeded to show them old bullets and arrowheads and jewelry. There were glass dishes, a can of snuff, and an old porcelain bull. Most interesting to Felicity was an old gun—the same style that Blackbeard may have used. In fact, it may have even dated back to his time.

However, she saw no evidence that it would offer any answers or clues.

Most of the items he showed them, though interesting, didn't relate to this case at all.

What was she missing? Why had Magnum wanted to come here?

"Have you ever had any of this appraised?" Felicity asked, picking up a delicate-looking plate.

Walter shrugged. "Nah. I never want to sell it, so why do I care how much it's worth?"

"Good point." But she'd guess a lot of it was worth quite a bit. Not enough to gain Magnum's interest, however. "Most of this probably doesn't relate back to Blackbeard. I'd guess it to be Depression Era."

She let out a sigh. She didn't see anything that would lead her close to figuring out what Magnum might have wanted.

"My Annabeth used to love antiques." His eyes filled with tears. "She left me two years ago. A heart attack. Didn't even have a chance."

Compassion squeezed Felicity's heart. She reached toward Walter and clasped his hand. "I'm so sorry. I know how brutal grief can be."

He nodded, his eyes still wet. "At least there's the promise of heaven, right? Where we'll be reunited."

Her throat went dry. Wouldn't that reassurance be nice? What would it be like to believe in an afterlife? In a purpose for the pain? That this world wasn't our final stop?

She cleared her throat and squatted by one of the trunks. She looked at several of the items hoping something would click in her mind.

As she rocked back on her heels, the chest caught her eye. The details on it were extraordinary. Leather dome. Brass studs. Iron handles. French, if she had to guess from looking at the design.

"What do you know about this chest?" she asked.

Walter lowered himself into an antique chair. "It's been in the family for years."

"May I take everything out of this to examine it?" she asked.

Walter stared at her for several minutes before finally nodding. "I suppose. Just don't break anything."

With Brody's help, she carefully unloaded vases, plates, and old photos. When that was done, she stared at the empty box. It was lined with flowered-fabric panels that had probably been added within the past several decades.

She leaned closer and saw something sticking out from beneath one. "Walter, it looks like there's something under this panel at the bottom. Do you know what?"

"I don't have any idea what you're talking about." He leaned from his chair to examine it.

She rested her hand atop it. "Would you mind?"

"Can you put it back together?"

"I can. And if I can't, I know someone who can." She was fortunate to know some of the best in the business.

"I'll say yes, but only because I'm curious."

Carefully, she tugged the panel's bottom. Her chest tightened when she realized she could be destroying a potentially valuable antique. But there was something beneath it. She only hoped it wasn't simply a design feature.

A slight tremble captured her hands as she grasped the paper and pulled it away. Excitement tinged her blood as she flattened its creases.

As she spotted the text on the other side, her

hopes deflated. "It's just an old newspaper. It was a longshot, right?

"Look at this, Felicity." Brody pointed to something at the bottom of the chest. "The bottom isn't welded to the rest of the chest."

Her heart raced for another moment. "It's not?"

She peered into the chest. He was right. The bottom wasn't welded into the rest of the chest. "That's . . . amazing."

"I'll say," Walter said, looking over their shoulders.

Coincidence? Maybe. But it was worth checking out.

Brody pulled out a pocketknife and gently pried the bottom off. Beneath the metallic bottom was a paper. She pulled it out, careful not to rip the delicate parchment any further. There already appeared to be a tear on the right side.

Gently, she opened the folds.

Her pulse spiked when she saw the drawing on the other side. It was a map. An old map of North Carolina.

"Well, what do you know?" Walter clucked his tongue. "All these years, and I never knew it was there."

"Look at this—it's made of hand-laid paper," Felicity said, holding the map up to the light.

"What's that mean?" Walter asked.

"Back before 1800, paper was made by hand, not machine. Someone had to pour paper pulp into a wooden frame. The bottom had cross-hatched wire mesh, which left a pattern in the paper. You can see it here."

"Those close together thin lines that cross every inch or so?" Walter asked.

Felicity nodded. "They're called chain marks, and they look a little like the weave of a rug."

"So you're saying this is potentially two centuries

old?" Walter asked.

She nodded, her heart racing with excitement. "That's right. But it's only part of a map. I wonder where the rest is?"

"That's a good question."

Felicity looked at Walter. "Is there any way we could borrow this?"

"Borrow it? What would you want to do with an old map?"

"I think this could be very useful to my research. I'll even give you a one hundred dollar deposit. If we don't bring it back, the cash is all yours."

"I was going to give it to you for free," he muttered. "But I'll take one hundred dollars as a deposit. Seems reasonable."

Brody shifted beside her. "Walter, has anyone else stopped by looking for this?"

He shrugged. "I wouldn't know. I went to stay at my sister's house. I only got back ten minutes before you arrived."

CHAPTER 19

Brody's interest in this quest was growing by the moment. He hated to admit it, but it was true. There was something going on here—something that had captured his curiosity.

Felicity sat beside him in the truck as they bounced down the road. The map was in her hands, and she studied it with intensity. Her hair was still back in a bun and she wore her glasses. She looked smart—and adorable.

"The waterways have changed," she muttered. "Subtly. I mean, the shorelines around here are always shifting with storms, and maps back then weren't drawn using satellites like they are now. But this is fascinating."

"I'm glad you think so. Any idea what it means?"

"Not yet."

He glanced in his rearview mirror, and his spine stiffened. The same Jeep had been behind them for the past five minutes. Coincidence? Maybe. But he didn't think so.

He wouldn't tell Felicity about it yet. He wanted to be certain first.

He had to be careful anyway. The roads here were shaded, which meant the sun wasn't hitting the snow and melting the icy spots.

"Magnum must have thought this was somehow

connected with Blackbeard's treasure," Felicity muttered. "But how? There's no X marks the spot."

"Maybe you need the other half of the map to see that part."

She shook her head. "What if this really did belong to Blackbeard's lesser known first mate? That's a fascinating idea."

"I don't know about that. But I agree that it looks antique." He glanced in his mirror again. The Jeep was still there.

Spontaneously, he turned down a side street.

"What are you doing?"

"Taking a scenic byway," he muttered.

Felicity glanced behind her. "We're being followed, aren't we?"

His jaw flexed. "Maybe."

She looked behind her and gasped as she registered the vehicle. "What if it's Magnum or one of his men?"

"He wants this map." Her fingers visibly tightened on the map. "This is significant. There's something about this map that's valuable—in more ways than one."

"We have bigger issues at the moment than figuring out that map," Brody said. "He's gaining on us."

"He can't get this."

"Right now I'm going to focus on staying alive."

She nodded a little too quickly. "Good idea."

As Brody accelerated down the small two-lane road, Felicity pulled out her phone and began taking pictures of the map. "Just in case," she said. "I want to be able to study this."

"I don't plan on letting Magnum take it."

"All of this isn't worth risking anyone's life. I'm not sure Magnum feels the same way."

"Let's see what we can do here." He watched the speedometer climb higher. As he did, the vehicle behind him also accelerated. This could turn ugly. And dangerous. He prayed that neither of those came to fruition, but this whole scenario had already been set in motion.

The Jeep remained directly on their tail now. Any closer, and they'd collide.

If Brody went any faster, he could lose control of the truck. But it seemed the best of his options right now.

"Hold on," he muttered.

Felicity stashed the map beneath the seat and gripped the armrests. Her face had gone pale, but he didn't have time to dwell on that now. He needed to figure a way out of this situation.

"We're going to die," Felicity squealed.

"No one's going to die." But he needed a plan. And he needed it quickly.

He scanned the road ahead of him. As he did, the Jeep rammed him.

His truck veered toward the ditch on the other side of the road.

He gripped the wheel, desperate to remain in control. He managed to right the vehicle, but he knew time was of the essence.

A sharp curve loomed ahead. He had to use this for his advantage. He prayed it would work.

"What are you doing? We're going to hit that tree!" Felicity said.

"Trust me."

"Trust you? I hardly know you." She squeezed her eyes shut.

Just as she did, Brody jerked the wheel. The truck spun, the back swerving around in forward motion until they were facing the opposite direction.

The Jeep rushed past, unable to brake in time. It crashed into the ditch.

Brody hit the accelerator and sped away.

Magnum—or one of his men who was doing his dirty work—was going to have to tend to his own wounds.

Because stopping now would put Felicity's life on the line, and he wasn't willing to risk that.

***

Felicity's heart pounded in her ears. In her chest. In her throat.

Sweat sprinkled across her forehead, and her fingers wouldn't release themselves from the armrests.

Her life had flashed before her eyes, more than once.

Magnum was determined to get this map. To do whatever it took to get what he wanted. And that was a dangerous trait to have.

Her life was now on the line, as well as Brody's. How had all of this happened? She'd simply been minding her own business. Trying to escape her past. Recuperate from her failure.

And all of this trouble had crashed into her life.

"You okay?" Brody glanced at her from the driver's seat.

She nodded, though the action felt tight and unnatural. "I'm . . . fine. I think."

"We need to lie low. This isn't going to stop Magnum. I don't know what will"

She nodded, grateful to have Brody to lean on. She would have never survived that on her own. He'd been there for her more than once, and that fact hadn't gone unnoticed.

"What now?" she asked.

"A friend of mine has a hunting cabin near Belhaven," Brody said. "We can use that as a home base. That will buy us some time."

"Until what?" She glanced at his strong profile.

He shrugged. "Until we figure out our next move."

"Our?" His words surprised her. She figured he'd want to get rid of her as soon as possible.

He cast a side-glance at her. "I'm in this now, whether I want to be or not."

"I guess we both are. I didn't ask for any of this either."

"If you'd given the key to me . . ." he reminded her.

She frowned, guilt pounding at her. "You're right. I'm sorry. You can drop me off, and wash your hands of this. You've done enough. Maybe you should hide away a few days until this blows over."

"You really think I'm going to send you out on your own? You're crazy."

"You don't owe me anything. You don't even know me."

"I know enough." His voice sounded surprisingly raspy and sincere.

"What's that mean?" She hardly wanted to ask, especially since she felt hope growing inside her: hope of something more, hope for something deeper.

"I know you're determined. I know you're not going to let this drop. I know Magnum knows who you are, and he's going to keep coming after you."

"That all sounds like my problem, not yours."

He sighed. "Look, I have some time off. I wouldn't be able to live with myself if something happened to you. Besides, it's my job to help people."

"On the water. We're not on the water."

He rubbed his jaw before narrowing his eyes at her. "Are you really going to keep arguing with me?"

Her cheeks flushed. Why was she being so stubborn? She knew: Life was easier when you didn't rely on anyone but yourself. When no one could let you down or betray you.

"I just want to give you every opportunity to get out of this now while you can," she finally said.

"I think I've made it clear that I'm in. Whether you like it or not."

She nodded, her spine stiffening as stubborn instincts urged her to keep arguing. Deep inside, she knew there was no use. Besides, she needed Brody's help, whether she liked it or not, as Brody was so fond of saying. "Fine. Have it your way. But don't say I didn't give you the opportunity to bail."

***

Brody unlocked the small cabin using a key that was hidden under a rock by the front door. He stepped inside, and a musty smell enveloped him. No one had been here in a while, and the place had been sealed up. It wasn't ideal necessarily, but it would work.

Felicity walked in behind him, her arms drawn over her chest. She seemed uncomfortable. That was good. She shouldn't relax. There was too much on the line.

"I'd try to do the polite thing and offer you some sweet iced tea, but that's not going to happen right now. But you can have a seat if you'd like," Brody said.

Frowning, she lowered herself onto the couch with the map still clutched in one hand. Leaving her coat on, she held the map up and began studying it again, as if she might see something this time that she didn't before.

As she examined it, he went into the small kitchenette and found enough supplies to make some coffee. He started a pot, knowing the hot drink would help keep them warm. The temperatures would drop as the night continued to grow deeper and darker.

With the coffee percolating, he started a fire in the old stone-covered fireplace in the corner. Keeping himself busy gave Felicity some time to think. He didn't know her that well, but he sensed she liked space to process things, and he wanted to respect that.

With the fire warming the room, he poured two cups of coffee and set them on the table in front of Felicity. He sat beside her and studied the map.

He'd never been involved in a situation like this, and he needed to carefully consider his options.

Giving up and handing everything over made it seem like they'd be letting a bully win. Everything in him fought against that. But he had to think about Felicity's safety also. This couldn't be about winning. It had to be about being smart.

"We've got to find the other part of this map," Felicity announced, a wrinkle between her eyes. She slipped off her coat, then her glasses, and pulled her hair out of the bun.

His throat went dry at the sight. He imagined burying himself in that hair, tasting her lips, and feeling her soft skin. He shrugged his coat off also since the room was now heating up.

He shoved the thoughts aside, knowing they had more pressing issues at hand. The rush of attraction had thrown him off guard.

He tugged at his collar—suddenly hot. And it wasn't because of the gently roaring flames across from him. "How do you propose we do that?"

She shook her head. "I'm not sure yet. But that lady at the front desk of Project Teach mentioned that Magnum had a cannon in the office. How does that tie in?"

"I wish I knew. That puts us in a very precarious position."

Her gaze connected with his. "As long as we stay one step ahead of him, we're okay."

CHAPTER 20

He leveled his gaze. "Why is this so important to you?"

Her eyes widened, as if the question surprised her. "Wouldn't it be important to anyone? This could be a significant find."

"It's more than that to you. What's going on, Felicity? You can at least tell me that. I've risked everything to help get you this far."

She frowned and looked away. "I didn't ask you to do that."

"You didn't have to."

She didn't bother to argue. Instead, she leaned back and let out a resigned sigh. "You really want to know? Because it's not pretty. Or flattering. It's *really* not flattering."

"I really want to know." He leaned back and waited, resisting the urge to touch those silky-looking locks.

She sucked on her bottom lip a moment, and he could see the storm raging inside her. He waited, giving her the time and space she needed.

"I was working on my PhD in North Carolina history, but as I did that I also worked as an antiquarian," she started, rubbing the coffee mug in her hands but not taking a sip.

"A what?"

"An antiquarian. Basically, I'm an expert in antiquities, specializing in rare books. I'm able to appraise certain items, tell you the time period something was created and how much it could sell for at auction."

"Okay." He shifted, turning to face her as she told the rest of her story. He was more fascinated than ever.

"Long story short is this: I got a job working on a high-profile piece. It had even been featured on the national news as a significant historical find."

"That's good . . . right."

"It turned out to be forged."

He let that sink in. "I see. You took the fall for it?"

She nodded slowly, still rubbing the mug. "I'm the one who made the call. The forgery . . . it was impressive. From a trusted source." She sighed and abandoned her coffee in favor of running a hand through her hair.

He turned toward her, curiosity lighting his gaze. "Tell me about what you do."

"I worked part-time at the college as I worked on my PhD, and part-time for a firm that does appraisals on rare books."

"Sounds interesting."

"It is. It was. I'm not doing it any more." The reminder about how everything had crashed down around her hit her like a punch in the gut. She'd gone from living her dreams one moment to being totally discredited the next.

"What happened? If you don't mind me asking. I mean, we do have all night to talk as we wait here."

She sucked in a quick breath. Could she even open up? She hadn't spoken about it since she'd come back here. Her aunt only knew bits and pieces. "I'm afraid you'll think I'm a terrible fool."

"I could never think that."

He said that now . . . "You haven't heard my story yet. Not all of it, at least."

"Try me."

She heaved in a deep breath and sat back. As she did, Brody's hand brushed her back. Even through her thick sweater, the realization caused electricity to jolt down her spine—a totally irrational reaction. "I actually worked for Ricky. He was not only my boss—he was my boyfriend. My controlling boyfriend."

"You mentioned him before."

"He wasn't always a nice man. He was either charming or he was cruel. I was the one who usually saw his cruel side." She glanced at her hands, noticed how she was twisting them in her lap. She stopped herself, knowing that she was showing her nerves too much. "Anyway, I was doing pretty well. People were starting to request me. I was close to finishing my PhD. A TV show asked me to do an on-air interview about some documents that had been found that they believed were connected with the Titanic."

He twisted his head, as if impressed. "Interesting."

She nodded. "They really were. But I'm pretty sure Ricky didn't like the attention I was getting. We got a big-name client, and he assigned me to help with the evaluation and appraisal of the work."

"Okay."

"I went to work on it. There's a lot that goes into appraising a book and how old it is. One can never really tell how far it dates back, but we use varying clues about the writing style, the kind of paper used, the way people are addressed. If possible, we do send off a small sample of the paper for testing and sometimes that will reveal more facts to us."

"What happened next?"

She stared out the window a moment and took another sip of her coffee. "Well, there were some old letters that someone had apparently found in their basement. They appeared to have belonged to Thomas Jefferson."

"The former president? Founding father of the US?"

"That's right. They looked authentic. Like, really authentic. They would have made a significant historical impact."

"Why? Why did they say?"

"They were like his lost records. They had his ideology, and thoughts, and some personal facts. The letters were so fascinating. I spent months examining them."

"What were your conclusions?"

"They seemed authentic, but there were a couple of red flags. One of the letters—the handwriting—didn't quite match with other documents. And there was something about the paper that bugged me."

"I'm sure you researched it, right?"

She swallowed hard, knowing it was too late to stop the conversation now, no matter how tempting it might be. "I went to Ricky for his advice and expertise, and he was adamant that it was the real thing. His confirmation seemed to drive away my fears and hesitation. I mean, Ricky knows what he's doing."

Wrinkles formed at the corner of Brody's eyes. "What happened next?"

"I finally wrote up my thoughts and evaluation. I said it was worth a large amount of money, but that wasn't all. This was practically a national treasure. I went on TV to talk about my findings. Professionally, I thought I was on top of the world, and I felt so fortunate to have been handed the opportunity."

"I have a feeling there's a but in here somewhere."

She nodded. "Ricky had it all forged."

Brody flinched. "Really? Why would he risk ruining his company's reputation like that?"

"I guess it was worth it if he could bring me down. He made a big deal of firing me, and said he couldn't have me associated with his company any more."

"Did you break up then?"

She shook her head. "Not initially. I mean, at that point, I thought it truly was all my fault."

"How did you discover Ricky was behind it?"

"I went to talk to him at work one day. He wasn't there. I knew his parents had left him a small cabin by the lake nearby. I went there. He wasn't there either, but I found all the supplies that were needed to make the forgery. I had no doubts."

"Did you confront him?"

"Of course. He denied it. But I could see the truth in his eyes. He was behind all of it. His goal was simply to make me weak."

"That's pretty low—and extreme."

"That's Ricky for you. He never expected to be caught. I made a motion with the American Association of Historians to have his licensure revoked. That really made him mad. Until that happens, I can't really go forward with my story. I don't know if I will."

"But no one will hire you otherwise."

"Maybe it's time for a career change."

"I thought you enjoyed it?"

"I do. I've always loved books. And finding rare ones feels like finding a treasure. It's better than finding a chest full of gold even. But sometimes you just have to realize that your ship has sailed."

"Everyone makes mistakes. Certainly there's always redemption."

"Maybe."

"That's why you came to Hertford?"

She nodded. "Yeah, I had to get away."

"How did he take you leaving? You said he was controlling."

Her frown deepened. "Not well. He insisted I couldn't make it without him. Said I'd be crawling back. Said I'd ruined my life by faulty research."

Typical of someone who was controlling and manipulative. An abuser. Emotional abuse was still abuse.

"And?"

She raised her chin, starting at the window in front of her. "And I'm determined that my life isn't ruined. I'm embarrassed and slightly ashamed of myself for the traps I fell into. But I haven't given up."

"You see this Blackbeard thing as a way to redeem yourself."

Her head dropped again. "I suppose so."

"There's someone else who can offer redemption, you know."

She raised her eyes to meet his. "God?"

He nodded.

"Thanks for the sermonette, but you can stop now."

"You're not a believer?"

She shrugged. "I suppose not. My parents were. I grew up in church."

"I've heard it's hard to keep the faith while being immersed in academia."

"I suppose that's true. I don't really know when I

lost it. I suppose it was gradual."

"I guess mine is the opposite. Grew up in a family without any church or Bible. It wasn't until I hit rock bottom that I realized something was missing in my life."

She leaned back, her attention on him now. "What happened to you to make you hit rock bottom?"

Did he really want to share about this part of his life? Usually, he'd say no. But she'd just revealed a hard part of her past. Besides, something about Felicity beckoned him to trust her. "My girlfriend was abducted when she was walking home from high school."

Her eyes widened. "That sounds horrible. I'm so sorry."

He nodded as the memories hit him. "I was away at college. I came back to help search for her, but it was too late. Andrea was long gone."

Andrea Whitaker? Felicity remembered the huge case about the missing teenager. It had made national news. After years with no answers, her body had finally been recovered several months ago.

"I can only imagine what it was like living with the what ifs for so long," she said softly.

"I was supposed to come home that week too, but I had a paper I needed to write and a test to study for. I told her I'd try to make it home the next weekend instead. She understood. But I always wondered how things might have turned out differently if I'd been home."

"You couldn't have known." She squeezed his arm.

Her touch caused warmth to spread through his blood like a welcome fire after a cold day. "I know that now. But it's hard wondering."

Their gazes locked, and he wondered for a moment if there was something between them. What it would be like to kiss her. How it would feel to take her into his arms.

Before he could entertain the thought too long, Felicity's phone buzzed on the table. She released his arm, and he immediately missed her touch, wanted it back.

When she looked at the message on her phone, her face went pale.

"Brody, they've got my aunt."

CHAPTER 21

Panic exploded inside Felicity.

Magnum must have gotten her cell number from her Aunt Bonny. He'd sent a haunting picture of her dear aunt with a gag over her mouth and blank wall behind her. The message below the photo was clear: give him the map or she would die.

He knew about the map. How? Had he simply been watching them? Or had he roughed up Winsome?

She desperately hoped it wasn't the later.

"What am I going to do?" she whispered.

Brody squeezed her shoulder. His touch brought her panic down a notch. "We'll figure something out. I just need to think for a moment."

"What if they hurt her?" She pressed her eyes shut, unable to bear the thought. Her poor aunt . . . She didn't deserve any of this.

"Don't think like that. Believe me, I know what it's like."

She pinched the skin between her eyes, a sudden headache coming on. "I can't believe they grabbed my aunt. They have no mercy. She's old and frail and . . ."

Before she could say anything else, Brody pulled her into his arms. "It's going to be okay."

She surprised herself by not resisting. Instead, she folded into him, finding comfort in his strong, capable arms. "Everyone always says that . . . but what happens when it's not okay?"

He said nothing, only held her for another moment. Silence stretched between them until finally Brody spoke. "We don't have a choice, Felicity. We've got to do what he wants. Your aunt is more important than any of this."

She nodded, trying to pull herself together. In order to do that, she had to get away from Brody. His touch cast a tantalizing spell on her, one that was dangerous and threw her off balance. "You're right. Whatever it takes. Who cares about this stupid treasure or my professional reputation? Not when the lives of people you love are on the line."

"Text him back."

She sucked in a long, deep breath, knowing she had to draw on every ounce of her strength to get through this. "What do I say?"

"Tell him you'll meet him. You'll give him the map for your aunt. See what he says."

"Okay." She picked up her phone, but her hands shook so badly she wondered if she'd be able to text anything. Somehow she managed to type the words, after several mistakes and lots of backspacing.

"Now we wait." Brody placed his big, strong hand over hers.

Heat gushed through her again.

This was no time to be infatuated. But Brody just seemed to have that effect on her. Besides, he was only being polite by offering comfort and friendship. When this was over, they'd go their separate ways.

The minutes ticked by, and she stared at the phone, waiting for a response. But time dragged on and there was nothing.

"Listen, would you mind calling Walter? I need to know he's okay," Felicity said.

"Absolutely." Brody pulled out his phone and paced to the other side of the room.

Felicity could barely make out what was being said. Her anxiety ratcheted up with each passing moment as worst-case scenarios plagued her.

Finally, Brody joined her on the couch again. "He's okay. He said some men showed up right after we left, claiming you were a fraud and a thief. Really they were just looking for information, I think. They didn't perceive Walter as being a threat."

"So he's unharmed?"

Brody nodded. "He's unharmed."

"Thank goodness." Her hand went over her heart. She didn't want anyone else to get hurt because of this.

"That map is significant, Felicity, just as you thought," Brody finally said.

"I'm not sure how useful it is without the other half." She'd been over it a dozen times already.

"Where could the other half be, even? And does Magnum already have it?"

"Good questions. I wish I knew." She stared at the map, wishing something would pop out at her. "I just can't interpret what significance this has. There's nothing on here to indicate where Blackbeard buried his treasure."

He leaned over her and pointed to one area near what was now Oriental. "Teach's Oak?"

"It fell over years ago, and the ground all around it has been dug up over the years."

"Ocracoke?"

"Again, treasure hunters have scoured the place for the past two hundred years."

Just then, her phone buzzed. "It's him!"

Brody scooted in closer to read the message with her.

Meet me at 9 at the Green Forest Marina in Belhaven. Bring the police, your aunt dies.

***

Brody turned over in bed and pulled a dusty blanket closer around his shoulders. It was cold in here, but it only seemed right to offer Felicity the couch next to the fireplace. She'd looked pale as she lay down with an old pillow and ratty quilt. At least they had a safe place to stay.

The thought of her being so close did something strange to him. It stirred something inside him, a longing he'd thought was lost. He had the strange desire to be near her. To comfort her. To hold her.

He turned over, his back toward the door. He couldn't think like that. There was too much on the line here.

Instead, he focused on what seemed like less dangerous territory.

The map.

Just what was so special about that map? Magnum must believe there was a big payout waiting for him if he was going through all this trouble to find it. He'd killed a man, after all. That meant he probably wouldn't hesitate to kill or at least hurt either Felicity or her aunt. He'd been willing to run them off the road today in order to obtain the map for himself.

Brody hoped that, once the map was handed over, they could put this behind them. He'd be able to resume his vacation time and work around his house. He'd have dinner with his friends, go to church, go to Bible study. Felicity would become a distant memory . . . or would she?

Had she already taken up residence in his heart? Even if it was just a small place of residence, it still was beginning to feel semi-permanent. Which was ridiculous. He hardly knew her. She drove him crazy. She was stubborn and too smart for her own good. He'd be smart to evict her—now. Somehow that just didn't seem possible.

Finally, at five a.m., he threw the covers off and climbed out of bed. He stoked the fire then jumped in the shower, the warm water refreshing and invigorating.

Dear Lord, please be with us today. I don't want this to turn ugly.

As soon as he was dressed, he stepped into the living room. He was pleasantly surprised to see that Felicity was both up and had made some coffee. She sat underneath a blanket by the fire, sipping from a mug. She'd turned toward him when his door opened.

His throat went dry at the sight of her. Her hair was slightly tousled, her eyes still had that sleepy look, and she all-together looked cozy, warm, and inviting.

"Morning," she murmured. "There's more coffee in the pot."

"You been up long?" His feet thudded across the wooden floor until he reached the kitchen. Secret delight rushed through him when he realized Felicity had also set out a coffee mug for him.

He'd taken care of himself for so long that he didn't realize how nice it was to have someone look out for him—even if it was something as simple as coffee.

"I couldn't sleep last night," Felicity said, her hair hanging down around her face and a sleepy look in her eyes. "Too much on my mind."

"That's understandable." He poured his coffee before sitting across from her. Today was big. Important. He hadn't forgotten that. "We have a big day ahead of us."

She shook her head. "As soon as I get my aunt back, I'm dropping all this. I've been so foolish already. I should have never taken that key. I'm so sorry."

"You couldn't have known this would happen."

"I'm not a risk taker, Brody. I never do stuff like this. The one time I do, the results are disastrous. I should have stuck to what was expected of me."

"Don't beat yourself up," he said quietly. "It's not a fun place to be. The punches we throw at ourselves can hurt the worst."

Her gaze fluttered to him, and a moment of understanding passed. Andrea. He'd beat himself up for years over Andrea. He knew exactly how she was feeling. "I know."

She took another sip of her coffee and licked her lips. "I guess I should get ready to go. We're an hour or so away, so we'll want to leave early."

He nodded. "I'd say. We can grab something to eat on the way."

"I don't think I can keep anything down." Her gaze locked on his, and the air seemed to vibrate with tension around them. "What if things don't work out the way we want, Brody?"

Desperation strained her voice.

Brody opened his mouth to speak. But, before he could, he realized there was nothing he could say.

CHAPTER 22

Felicity's gaze scurried around the marina, looking for a sign of what was to come. She saw nothing—no hints as to where her aunt was. No Hummer. No Magnum.

"Where are they?" she whispered, pulling her arms over her chest with apprehension.

"We're early," Brody reminded her, standing entirely too close behind her. She wasn't arguing though. There was something about his presence that calmed her.

The marina was bustling as people launched boats to begin their fishing expeditions for the day. Several warehouses were scattered about the area where trucks came and went. Despite the cold, the scent of fish and seafood saturated the air.

The sun was rising, climbing higher in the sky, and patches of snow, mostly from where the parking area had been cleared, sat like miniature mountains in random places. The air felt brisk, but not nearly as brisk as it had been. In a few days, they would never be able to tell they'd had a snowstorm here, except for the salt plastered on road-weary cars and puddles that would muddy the landscape.

She grasped the map in her hand, trying not to press too hard and wrinkle it. Part of her didn't care if it got wrinkled, but another part feared that any misstep on her end would result in her aunt being harmed . . . or worse.

"We've got this," Brody whispered.

Just the feel of his breath on her ear sent another ripple of nerves through her. She wished she felt as confident as Brody sounded. All she could think about was everything that could go wrong.

Finally, a man stepped beyond a building in the distance. Felicity instantly recognized him. Magnum.

He looked just as slimy as she'd imagined. He had curly, sun-bleached blond hair that was slicked back from his sun-kissed face. Expensive sunglasses rested over his eyes. Each action seemed purposeful and arrogant.

But he was alone. Where was her aunt?

Brody's arm went to her waist, and he squeezed, as if to reassure her.

As Magnum stepped forward, they met him halfway.

"Where's my aunt?" Felicity blurted, her gaze darting behind him.

"One thing at a time." Malice saturated his voice. This man couldn't be trusted. Yet what choice did she have? He held all the power over her. "Where's the map?"

She raised it, her hand trembling. "Right here. But we're only doing this as an exchange."

"How do I know it's the real thing and not a fake one? We don't want any replays of the Jefferson Conspiracy." Satisfaction stretched in the half-curl of his lips.

Felicity felt her cheeks heat. "Don't bring that up."

His smirk deepened. "Embarrassing, huh?"

"Where's my aunt?" she repeated, not wanting to talk about this here.

He held out a hand. "I need to see the map. You're clever. You could have recreated it."

"In the twelve hours since you contacted me? You know I couldn't have done it that quickly."

His eyes narrowed. "The map. You're going to have to play by my rules."

"We need to see her aunt first." Brody stepped out in front of Felicity, his chest puffing out protectively. "Then you can see the map."

Magnum raised his hands. "Then the deal is off."

Felicity's eyes scrambled to meet Brody's as tension filled her. What was she going to do? She couldn't risk not getting her aunt back, and Magnum knew that.

"I can see you're not interested. I'll be going then." Magnum turned like he was going to walk away. "I'll give your regards to your aunt."

"No, wait!" Felicity could hardly breath. The situation slipped out of her control. It had always been out of her control, she supposed, but she felt it falling even further away. "Fine . . . you can see the map. Just don't hurt my aunt."

That same satisfied look washed over his face, and he snatched the map out of her hands. Felicity held her breath, waiting to see his reaction as he studied it. Finally, he nodded, seeming pleased.

"This was exactly what I wanted. There's only one problem." He paused. "I need the other half."

"We don't have the other half." Anger tinged Brody's voice as he bristled beside her.

Magnum's eyebrows darted up, like he didn't have a care in the world. "Then that's a problem."

"That wasn't a part of our deal." Felicity's voice rose with each word. He was changing the rules, and she didn't like it. Yet she was powerless to stop it.

He held up his phone. "All I have to do is press this button, make this phone call, and boom! Your aunt is dead. I instructed my men to pull the trigger as soon as they heard the phone ring."

"But you promised . . ." As Felicity's voice trailed off, she realized the futility of this conversation. Magnum wasn't going to compromise. He didn't have to.

The man chuckled, the sound causing nausea to form in her stomach. How could she have been so stupid? She wanted to put all this behind her, but that wasn't going to happen.

"I get what I want, Ms. French." Magnum still grasped the map. "And I use whatever means necessary."

"Why is this treasure so important to you?" she asked, desperate to understand what was really going on. Maybe if she just had a little insight . . .

"Certainly you've heard how much it's worth. Not millions. Billions. I can buy my own island and never have another worry in the world."

He was sadly mistaken if he thought buying an island would ease him of any trouble or bring fulfillment. But this wasn't the time to get philosophical. He needed a counselor for his delusions.

"Why do you think Blackbeard's treasure is still out there?" she asked.

"If you must know, I bought some journals at an auction. Almost impossible to read. But I managed to do it. It was a first-hand account of Blackbeard and his adventures here in the area. Said he'd hidden maps somewhere that led to the treasure. Said to look into his roots. I knew I had to get my hands on those recovered maps from *Queen Anne's Revenge*."

"So you used an alias to get hired at Project Teach," she mused aloud. "As soon as you could, you took the maps. Which doesn't make any sense since you already had access to them."

He flinched. She'd hit on some kind of nerve. But why? What? Did that cannon somehow tie in to all of this?

"I knew you were a smart one," Magnum growled. "But now you've distracted me from my original purpose. Getting the other half of the map."

"You're playing dirty," Brody muttered.

"Find the other half of the map, and you'll get your aunt back. Don't involve the police. You have three days."

"Three days?" Felicity screeched. "People have been searching for this treasure for years. You expect me to find this map in three days' time? You're crazy."

"If anyone can do it, it's you."

She paused before asking, "Why would you say that?"

He smirked. "You're Blackbeard's kin, aren't you? You've got pirate blood in you. Your aunt has been telling us all about it. I'm sure if you're desperate enough, you'll figure things out. You were smart enough to find this in one day. I've been searching for years."

"Your request is unreasonable," she finally said, unsure what else to say. There would be no convincing him. So it was either find this map or find her aunt. Otherwise, her aunt would be dead. Felicity would truly be alone in this world. The thought caused a hollowness to echo inside her.

"I'll be in touch."

As he started to walk away, Brody lunged, as if he might grab him. Felicity's arm shot out to stop him. She had to keep her aunt alive. This was all her fault.

"He's vile," Brody muttered, staring at Magnum's retreating figure.

"I know. What are we going to do, Brody?"

"We're going to find the other half of that map. We don't have any other choice."

***

Brody's mind raced as they sat in his truck in the parking lot of the marina. The engine gently hummed as heat gradually made its way through the vents and warmed them. The cracked leather seat beneath him suddenly felt as hard as an ice cube. Life continued on around them, as if nothing was wrong.

He knew that for Felicity, everything felt wrong.

He had to help her. He realized the task before them was nearly impossible. Yet they had no choice but to try. He had to, for Felicity's sake. For her aunt's sake.

He pulled his gaze from out the window and saw Felicity had buried her face in her hands. He sensed her tears without seeing them and placed a hand on her shoulder. He wished he could take away her pain. All he could do was try to help her find resolution to this. He hoped that would be enough.

"I know this is hard, but we don't have time to feel sorry for ourselves now," Brody started, keeping his voice gentle. "We've got to figure out a plan."

We. Why did he keep referring to this as if it was his problem as well? He knew: there was no way he was jumping ship and leaving Felicity to do this on her own. He wasn't that heartless.

Felicity raised her head high enough to shake it. She pulled her sleeves over her hands and sniffled. "How? I don't even know where to start. We've rehashed all of this already. I have no clue where the other half of the map could be."

He sat back and thought for several minutes,

praying for an answer to come to him. He reviewed everything he knew. Everything he thought he knew. Everything he wanted to know.

He straightened as an idea hit him. "Your aunt really believes Blackbeard's blood is in your family, right?"

Felicity nodded, drawing in a deep breath and glancing at him with red-rimmed eyes. "That's right. She's said that for years."

"Did anyone else in your family agree?"

"My grandma would just smile. She was the quieter of the two, and she took everything in stride. I always assumed she also thought Bonny was crazy."

"But she didn't deny it."

Felicity shrugged. "I guess not."

"Are there any family heirlooms left at your house, Felicity? Pirate or not?"

She was silent a moment, staring straight ahead. "There's that sword. I didn't pay it much mind until a couple of days ago. I realized it was old, but swords really aren't my thing. Books are."

"Any other heirlooms?"

She sighed and ran her hands across her cheeks. "My grandma left most of her things up in the attic of the house."

"Have you ever looked through them?"

She shook her head. "Honestly, it always seemed too hard for me. I assumed I would one day, but the pain always felt too fresh."

A pang of compassion pounded inside him. "The pain of losing her?"

"Yeah, I guess I'm the type who likes to stay busy rather than confront the things that hurt me. Even though I love anything of historical significance, I couldn't bring myself to look through her possessions. I wasn't going to come back—until I had to."

He squeezed her arm. "Why don't we go back to your grandma's place? Let's start there. Maybe—just maybe—there will be some kind of clue."

She glanced at him again, this time with her eyebrows raised. "A clue that I'm related to Blackbeard?"

He shrugged, knowing the idea sounded crazy. "I have no clue. But I don't have any other great ideas of where to start. You?"

She shook her head and drew in a deep breath. "No, I don't have any."

He put the truck into drive. "Then let's go."

CHAPTER 23

Felicity's stomach was in knots by the time they pulled up to the old plantation house. It was just after lunchtime—they'd grabbed a burger from a fast-food joint on the way, but Felicity had hardly tasted it. She was lucky to keep it down.

When Brody put the truck in park, Felicity stared at the house in front of her. For years, she'd been fascinated with this place and its history. But after her parents died, she just hadn't had the heart to look into her roots—to really look. It seemed to remind her of how much she'd lost, and she wasn't ready to face that yet.

Now she had no choice.

"When was this place built?" Brody asked, still sitting in the truck beside her.

She glanced at her grandma's place. The house looked lovely with the covering of melting snow as she stared out the windshield at it. "1802."

"Wow. You remembered that easily."

She shrugged like it was no big deal. "I've always been fascinated with old things. This is no different."

He let out a long sigh that caught her curiosity.

She shifted to face him better. "What was that for?"

He turned toward her, disappointment in his gaze. "The year 1802 was after Blackbeard's time. He was killed in 1718, I think."

Felicity felt her lungs deflate. "Of course. I'd forgotten that. So this could all be for naught."

"However, we don't have any other leads at this point. Let's go cross this off. If we don't find anything, we can move on."

They trudged out of the truck and climbed the rickety porch. Felicity's keys jangled against each other in her hands as she attempted to unlock the door. After several failed attempts—her hands were trembling too badly—Brody took the keys from her and slipped the correct one into the lock.

He pushed the door open, and an empty house stared back at them.

How could it be that her grandma was no longer here? How had a home once filled with so much joy been reduced to a shack, a shell of what it had once been? It seemed like a travesty.

She'd avoided that thought for so long.

"Why don't we start in the attic and see what's up there?" Brody said.

She nodded, drawing every last ounce of her strength. She led Brody upstairs and through the hallway where the bedrooms were located. She pushed open the door at the end, and a set of steps yawned at them. They were dark and haunting and had always made her throat go dry.

Brody reached beyond her and flicked the switch. "No light?"

She shrugged, a sudden chill washing over her. "I haven't been up here in years. I went once as a child, and I accidentally got locked in. My parents didn't realize I was there, and they were locking up the house before a trip. It took them fifteen minutes to find me—fifteen minutes that felt like hours. I've never liked this place since then."

"That's understandable." He looked back at her. "Got a flashlight?"

"No, but there are some lanterns in the bedrooms like the ones I pulled out during the storm. My grandma kept them all over the house. It's a Depression-Era thing, I think. They didn't throw anything away, just in case."

He slipped into the closest bedroom and emerged a moment later with a kerosene lantern. "This will work." He struck a match and lit the wick.

Brody started up the stairs first, and Felicity stayed close behind him, imaginary spiders crawling over her skin. She felt like this was a scene from one of those old mystery novels she used to read as a child. A dark room, a lantern, and a guy and girl exploring the unknown searching for clues.

It always seemed much more romantic in the books. Right now, it seemed intimidating. Scary. Overwhelming.

She held back a scream as a cobweb caught her face near the top of the stairs.

"You okay?" Brody paused long enough to glance at her.

She wiped at imaginary creepy-crawlies. "Yeah, I'm fine. Just jumpy."

"It is kind of spooky up here, if I do say so myself."

Against her better judgment, she grasped Brody's arm, desperate not to lose her connection with him. He didn't pull back or object. In fact, earlier she'd thought she'd seen a spark of attraction in his eyes. Had she been imagining things? And why did that idea fascinate her?

Finally, they reached the top of the steps. The

upstairs was cold—colder than the rest of the house. And it was so dark.

She stepped closer to Brody as her eyes adjusted to the dark space and the room came into view. Memories of being here alone captured her thoughts and made her trembles return. It had been a horrific day—especially when she'd remembered all of Aunt Bonny's stories.

"Where do we start up here?" Brody raised the lantern, casting its light throughout the room.

Her gaze scanned the place as she pushed her memories aside. Antique furniture—probably worth quite a bit—was covered with old sheets. Stacks of family portraits leaned against one wall. An entire shelf of knickknacks sat against another wall. An old filing cabinet rested in the corner.

"How about there?" She pointed to the filing cabinet.

"I suppose it's as good a place as any."

She remained close as they walked through the dark room. The cabinet itself was entirely too new to be an antique—it was probably thirty or forty years old. But her grandmother may have stored older documents inside.

Fanny Pasture hadn't been one for talking much. She did things quietly, when she wanted and for whatever reason she wanted.

I wish I had a chance to ask questions, Grandma. To listen to your stories. To reminisce with you.

But it was too late for that.

Brody handed her the lantern and opened the first drawer. It squeaked and squealed before begrudgingly stretching to full length. Swarms of dust escaped, and Felicity held back a sneeze.

"These look mostly like old tax returns and insurance policies." He feathered several pages.

"That sounds about right. Grandma was a bit of a packrat. I don't think she got rid of much. Again, it goes back to the Depression Era. When you have nothing, you hold on to whatever you can."

He closed the drawer and pulled open the next one. Based on the file-folder labels, it held more tax returns. How many years back did they go?

He also pulled out an old sash reading "Miss North Carolina." He raised his eyebrows at Felicity.

"My mom and grandmother were both beauty queens. I guess I didn't have that in my genes."

"I'd say you do," Brody said.

Her cheeks flushed at his words, and she wondered how to respond. Before she had the chance, Brody lowered the sash back into the drawer, shoved it shut, and opened the final drawer.

"I'm not sure how far we're going to get with this." Felicity felt her hope plummeting. She rocked back on the dusty floor.

"Maybe farther than we think." He pulled out a file folder labeled "Important documents." "Sounds promising."

They sat on an old loveseat, lantern between them, and opened the folder. Pages of old, old papers stared back at them. There were birth certificates, marriage licenses, and even social security cards.

"Wow. Look at this. This is my parents' marriage license," Felicity muttered, tears springing to her eyes.

"I know this is probably hard for you."

"I'll be fine." She was determined to pull herself together. This wasn't the time to break down, but she felt like she was on the brink. All this reminded her of how quickly life could change.

Brody squeezed her knee. "There's a lot of family

history up here."

She wiped the last trace of moisture from under her eyes. "I guess so. I shouldn't have been avoiding it all these years."

She stared at a picture of her mom and dad on their wedding day. She bet they would have never guessed how it all would end for them when they got married. A plane crash. At least they'd been together. For a long time, Felicity had wished she'd been with them. It seemed less painful than going on without them.

Brody reached the end of the folder. "It doesn't look like there was anything useful in here. I'm sorry, Felicity. We can take the drawers out, I suppose. See if anything fell behind them."

"Seems like an exercise in futility." She hated to sound so pouty, but that's how she felt. Like she'd been backed into a corner. Like her hope was disappearing on the horizon. Like she'd been forced to walk the plank.

"It might not be."

Something on the back of the photo caught her eye. "Wait. What's this?"

She pulled the yellowed, fragile paper off the back of the photo where it had been stuck. Carefully, she opened it. Just as she did, a breeze drifted through the room and snuffed out the lantern.

She practically jumped into Brody's lap as darkness enveloped them.

Brody's arm went around her waist. "It's okay. Just the drafty house."

She willed her muscles to relax, but it didn't work. They were still tightly wound. If only she could see something. Anything.

All the stupid tales her aunt had told her about Blackbeard's ghost haunting the place fluttered through her mind. If she heard footsteps, she was going to freak out.

As if to play into her fear, a creak sounded in the distance. Her heart nearly stopped before starting back up again at a dangerous speed.

"It's just the wind," Brody whispered.

He was doing something beside her. Fiddling with something. The lantern, she realized.

A moment later, light flared to life in the room.

Her heartbeat slowly went back to normal, and she breathed a sigh of relief.

Suddenly embarrassed, she slid off Brody's lap. "Sorry about that."

"Anytime." His voice held a teasing tone.

She glanced round the room. There was no one. No one visible, at least. Her spine remained clenched as she anticipated what might happen next.

She wanted to get out of here as soon as possible. She jolted into action and pulled the folds apart and stared at the text on the paper.

"What is it?" Brody's breath hit her cheek and sent her heart rate into the stratosphere again.

She desperately wished he didn't have that effect on her.

Her eyes widened as she read the text. "It's a deed. A land deed."

"To where?"

She scanned the document. "It appears to be a piece of property off the Perquimans River."

"Whose name is it in?"

"William Pasture. Loretta's husband. My great-great-great-great-great grandfather."

They exchanged a glance.

"I think I know where we should head next," Brody

said.

Felicity nodded, excitement zinging through her blood. "Let's go."

*   *   *

An hour later, they pulled up to the property listed on the deed.

There wasn't much there except an old cabin that was probably a hundred years old. Trees grew through its roof. Trees surrounded it, for that matter, until the building was almost invisible to the human eye.

Sure enough, a river ran beside it.

The sun was starting to sink lower, casting strange shadows on the place and promising that darkness would fall soon. The air felt cooler than before, and the snow, once beautiful, now looked ashen in places as it mingled with the dirt.

"You didn't know this was in your family? Certainly you got a tax bill every year," Brody told Felicity.

She pulled her North Face jacket up closer to her face, as if anticipating the cold they were about to experience. "I didn't take care of the family's estate. My aunt did. She was going to show me what I needed to do, in case of her absence . . ." Her voice cracked as she finished the sentence.

"This place doesn't look like much."

"We should check it out, I suppose," she said.

They climbed out, and Brody took her hand to help her over the high grasses. The snowfall made much of the landscape limp with dampness, and clumps of grass now slumped in large heaps. Their feet sank beneath it in mud and other gunk that it was better not to see, reminding him of the Alaskan tundra. Finally, they reached what used to be the front porch.

Brody gave the door a shove. It didn't open. He threw his shoulder into it—it panged from where he'd done the same after being locked in the closet. He ignored the pain, though. They needed to get inside the old shack.

On his second try, the door burst open.

The musty scent of a space that had been closed up for entirely too long filled their senses. Felicity had grabbed one of the old lanterns they'd brought with them. She quickly lit it and held it up.

The inside of the cabin came into view. There wasn't much to it, and the floor looked like it could give way at any minute. There were already holes there—and trees starting to poke through the roof. Soon, nature would claim this entirely.

"It looks like no one has lived here in years," Brody said.

"I can't even imagine why someone in my family owned this. Was it a hunting cabin or something?"

"Hard to say." He tipped a foot forward and tested the floor. "You should stay here. I don't want you getting hurt."

"I don't want you getting hurt."

He offered a grateful smile. He really did appreciate her concern. Though they'd gotten off to a rocky start, she'd continued to surprise him. The concern she'd shown when Walter talked about his wife had touched him. "I'll be okay."

Her wide eyes assessed him. "You were just rubbing your shoulder. That doesn't seem okay."

"It will be just fine. Just hold the lantern for me."

Hesitantly, carefully, he stepped onto the floor. It groaned beneath him.

One wrong move and, not only would he fall

through the floor, he'd have to battle whatever rodents probably lived under this house. The thought wasn't pleasant.

He took each step carefully. There wasn't much to look at, but an old bookcase stood along the far wall with a fireplace next to it. It appeared the place was a one-room living quarters and was built before the time of bathrooms or closets.

He reached the bookcase and moved it aside.

A mouse squeaked and darted away. But there was nothing behind it. And nothing on it. As he did that, Felicity crept across the room toward the fireplace and began tugging at the stones there. None of them moved.

The only furniture in the room was an old table and chairs, and something that looked like an old desk was in the opposite corner. He'd check those out next.

"You think one of your relatives owned this place?" He pulled out drawers and searched every crevice.

"I can only assume. Though I can't believe I've never heard about it before. I'll have to ask Aunt Bonny—" Her voice caught.

"You'll be able to ask her," Brody assured her. "I promise you that."

"I wish you could know that. But neither of us do."

"If it's the last thing I do, I'm going to track down this map and get your aunt back."

Felicity's grateful smile was all the thank you he needed. He pushed in the last drawer and stepped back. There was literally nowhere else to look. There was no bathroom. No kitchen. Nothing.

"I'm sorry, Felicity. This appears to be a dead end. Another one."

She stepped back toward the door and nodded slowly. "We gave it a shot, right? It seemed like a good possibility."

As a mouse skittered by her feet, Felicity yelped and twirled around.

As she did, something crashed beside her. A piece of the wooden wall had fallen off. With the section gone from the wall, the area beneath it was exposed.

Carved there were the words "Wait Until Dark."

CHAPTER 24

"What does that mean?" Felicity ran her fingers over the words. Someone had carved them right into the wood.

Wait until dark.

Brody stood behind her, his presence again sending tremors up and down her spine. He continued to have that effect on her, and she didn't like it, while at the same time, she craved more. "That's strange."

"It looks crude," she muttered, studying it.

"I agree. And old. But I'm not sure it has anything to do with this."

"Probably not. I mean, what could it mean? We don't even know if this property has anything to do with any of this. Everything is just a stab in the dark at this point."

"If anyone can figure this out, you can."

She felt her insides twist. She'd told him about her massive failure, and he still had confidence in her abilities. What if she let him down, just as she'd let herself down?

Instead of dwelling on that thought, she pulled out her phone and snapped a picture. Maybe it would come in handy. She doubted it, but maybe.

"Let's see if there's anything under this one," Brody reached around her, to a similar piece of the wall—a small square instead of the long, lean lines of wood that lined the rest of the house. With a little prying, Brody removed it.

Sure enough, words had been carved there also.

"The moonlight will be your guide," he read. "That's interesting."

"To say the least." Felicity snapped a picture of that also. "Are we supposed to wait until dark here and let the moonlight guide us? It's so vague. Why would someone leave that message?"

"It's either a clue of some sort, or someone got bored and wanted to mess with the minds of whoever found this."

"It's working. My mind is officially messed with."

Brody let out a sigh. He obviously knew the same thing she did: time was ticking away. "It's already getting late. Maybe we should grab a bite to eat and come back here. I think there's a full moon tonight. Maybe the timing will work out just as it's supposed to."

"If we're wrong, we're wasting a lot of time." She frowned when she thought about it. She hated the uncertainty of it all. "But you're right. Let's eat so we can keep up our energy. Then we can come back here and see if there's anything to discover."

***

The nearest place to get something to eat had been almost thirty minutes away from the out-in-the-middle-of-nowhere spot. Brody and Felicity had grabbed some fried herring from a local restaurant known for the specialty and eaten it mostly in silence. By the time they got back to the truck, the sun was beginning to set. They'd both ordered coffee to go, knowing they'd need it to stay awake tonight.

Brody wasn't sure where all of this would lead, but

they had to at least try. For Felicity's sake he had to do whatever it took. He had to admit that this all seemed like a wild goose chase. But they had no choice except to participate in it, at this point.

As Brody started to turn into the lane leading to the house, he paused and let his headlights shine on the grassy area.

"What is it?" Felicity asked.

He put the truck in park and hopped out. He squatted by something on the ground, examining it a moment.

Felicity joined him.

"Tread marks," he told her.

"From when we were here earlier?"

He shook his head. "No, if you look at them you can tell they're wider and deeper. Here are our tracks."

"Someone else was here," she whispered. "Magnum."

"I've wondered if he had someone keeping an eye on us. It appears he does."

"Do you think he's here now?"

"There's only one way to find out."

They climbed back in the truck. Brody still had his gun tucked away safely in his waistband. He'd use it if he had to. He only hoped he didn't have to.

Slowly, he eased the truck over the bumpy, overgrown road. As it cleared slightly at the end, the house came into sight. But no other vehicles.

"Wait here. Lock the door." Brody grabbed his gun.

"Be careful." Her eyes were wide with concern.

As soon as he climbed out, she pressed down the lock. Once Brody knew she was tucked in safe and sound, he ventured around the house, looking for a sign that anyone else was here.

He spotted more tire tracks. Magnum, in his oversized Hummer had been here. It appeared he was gone now, but Brody had to be certain. He didn't want to put Felicity's life on the line again.

He skirted the side of the house and spotted some footprints near the windows there. He had no doubt they'd been inside. Before he checked that out, he noticed the footprints ventured from the house and toward the river. He followed them.

The prints stopped by a large oak tree overlooking the river.

He squatted by the trunk.

A hole gaped beside it.

A hole . . .

Magnum thought the treasure was buried here, Brody realized. Perhaps he thought this was Teach's Oak.

Had Magnum found anything? Was that why he'd left so quickly? He and Felicity had only been gone two hours maximum. Was that enough time for him to find a buried treasure? Wouldn't he still be here if he had, looking for more?

Brody let out a sigh. He didn't know. He didn't have the answers yet. And, until he did, all he could do was try his best.

***

"Anything?" Felicity asked as Brody climbed back into the truck.

He shook his head as he sat down, bringing with him an earthy scent of dirt and leaves. His cheeks were ruddy from the cold, and he instantly reached for the coffee he'd left in the holder between the seats.

"Not really," he said before taking a sip.

"Someone's been here. They've been digging."

Her heart raced with anticipation. "Did they find anything?"

"That's the question of the hour." He held his hand in front of the blaring heat coming through the vents. "I didn't see any evidence that anything had been dragged out from the space. The dirt is so wet, there would have probably been proof if something large had been hauled out."

She stared out the windshield as she gathered her thoughts. A few cypress trees cut into flat landscape. Snow made everything seem peaceful, and a full moon was just starting to rise, adding a certain atmosphere to the moment.

"Magnum has been following us," she finally said with a shake of her head. "Any sign he's still here?"

Brody stretched an arm across the back of the seat, wishing he had better news. "Not that I can tell."

"He could have been just waiting, watching us—or having his men do it for him."

He cast a quick glance her way. "Kind of like the sentinels that Blackbeard was said to have left behind to guard over his treasure?"

She gave him a curious look, surprised at how much he knew about history and pirates. "You know about that?"

"Anyone who's ever loved Blackbeard does." He grinned, the moonlight illuminating his strong profile.

At once, she had the urge to run her fingers down his cheek, to feel the scruff of his beard, to inhale the scent of leather and spearmint that she associated with him.

Her cheeks heated as she realized her thoughts. She had to focus on their conversation. "Maybe that's true. But I think you secretly like to read."

He shrugged. "Maybe back in the day."

She shifted to better face him. "Why did you take leave from the Coast Guard, Brody?"

A shadow fell across his face. "I've been running for the past ten years, trying to keep myself busy. Trying to keep myself focused on my work and everything else, just so I would forget my guilt about what happened to Andrea. In another way, I was punishing myself, thinking maybe I could somehow make things right. I finally realized I couldn't go on like this, that I needed to deal with it. I know, ten years seems like a long time, but all that time, I was never really sure if she was alive or not."

"I get that." Pain overstayed its welcome all too often.

He rubbed his jaw. "As long as there was hope she was alive, I couldn't let it go, no matter how hard I tried."

"Has your time off helped?"

"I'd just started it when you found me nearly buried in the snow outside your home. But I know if I can focus on spending some more time in prayer that will be a good start."

Her heart panged with hope. "You really believe in prayer, don't you?"

He turned toward her. "Don't you?"

She shrugged. "I used to. My parents did. It was practically a Southern rite of passage to go to church, you know? But I've fallen away from it."

"And has life been better since then?"

She thought about it a moment before shaking her head. She thought about the pain she'd held onto so tightly. The sleepless nights. The ways she'd felt utterly alone. "No, it hasn't been. Not at all."

He didn't need to say anything else. His words

remained with her, echoing in her mind. Her life wasn't any better now. In fact, she felt emptier than ever.

"Maybe it's time for me to make some changes also," she whispered.

CHAPTER 25

Brody's hand, once across the back of the seat, now rested on the back of Felicity's neck. Their gazes caught, and, for a moment, she wondered if he was going to kiss her.

Before he could—or perhaps before he could think about it, she blurted, "How'd you get the bullet wound on your chest?"

Something hard crossed his gaze and he looked away. "By being destructive."

"What do you mean?"

He let out a small sigh. "I told you how I beat myself up after Andrea was abducted. I almost felt like I should punish myself. That meant volunteering for any missions that needed my help. The more dangerous, the better."

She waited for him to continue.

"We're under the Department of Homeland Security now, and sometimes we're called outside of what our expected areas are. I was asked to accompany some marines on a mission off the coast of Africa. Somalia, to be exact."

"I had no idea the Coast Guard did that."

His expression remained stony. "We do. Not very often. But there's an international group designed to help combat piracy in that area. The Coast Guard helps there when necessary. Usually, the military will do their job, and the Coast Guard will step in to collect evidence and act more as law enforcement.

"The mission went south when the pirates tried to completely take out our ship. I thought for a minute that the pirates were going to take us all as hostages."

"That really sounds scary."

"There was a gun battle. I got hit. But we won. In the end, that was what mattered."

"How bad was your wound?"

He frowned and stared out the window. "I was in the hospital for a week. They didn't know if I was going to pull through or not."

"Oh . . . wow. When was that?"

His eyes crinkled on the sides as he seemed lost in thought. "It was a year ago. Shortly after that, evidence resurfaced in Andrea's disappearance. All in all, it made me realize that something had to change. I wasn't handling her death in a healthy way. With the help of my friend Joshua, I started going to church and found a meaning deeper than myself."

"I see."

He turned to face her. "What happened with you? With your parents?"

She shivered. When she did, he reached behind the seat and found a blanket. Carefully, he draped it over her legs, and warmth began to spread through her, easing away some of the cold.

But the memories hit hard and fast. Sometimes the thoughts of that day felt so fresh, like everything had just happened yesterday. "A month before I was supposed to leave for college, my parents were killed in a plane crash."

"Oh, Felicity. I'm so sorry." He wiped some hair

away from her face.

She nodded, ignoring his touch. She had to if she was going to finish her story. "It was all over the news. You probably heard about it. Flight 237?"

He nodded. "I do remember that."

"It was hard, to say the least. I think I reacted the opposite of you. I didn't punish myself as much as I tried to stick my head in the sand and pretend everything hadn't happened. I went to college, as planned. I did everything I could to forget about what happened. I tried not to think about it. I never came home."

"But you still had your family's house, right? And what about holiday breaks?"

"My aunt volunteered to take care of the house for me. My parents and I were only there at that house for a few years anyway, so I wasn't terribly attached. I took anything I wanted before I left for college—a few pieces of jewelry, an old clock. Things like that. As far as holidays, I was always the first to volunteer to build houses for the poor or to move new students into the dorms between semesters. Whatever I could to avoid the hurt." She shrugged. "In some ways, I even became a different person."

"What do you mean?" He played with a piece of her hair again, twirling it, wiping it from her face.

His touch was becoming harder to ignore. "I used to be a free spirit. But, after my parents' death, I tried to control everything I could. That included my appearance and my actions. It was never really me. Nothing was—not my stuffy career. Not the way I worked on my PhD. They'd never been my goals. I just had to keep myself busy. Honestly, I always call my aunt Bonny crazy, but, the truth is, there's a part of me that's like her."

"What did you really want to do?"

She shrugged and stared at the moon as it hung higher in the sky. "I do love old things, and history fascinates me. But I'd love to work at a museum. Do something hands-on. I don't know."

"I see."

She turned toward him. "We've talked about faith and church a couple of times. All of this has made me realize I miss having faith in a higher power. Turning my back on God was my biggest mistake of all. I need to get back to my roots, to my faith."

Brody's hand cupped her cheek, and he gently wiped her tears away with his thumb. "That's great news."

Her heartbeat quickened when she glanced up and saw the look in his eyes. The desire. The longing.

Before she knew what was happening, their lips met. It was soft, at first. Tentative. Questioning.

But when neither hesitated, the kiss deepened. Their lips tugged at each other's. Searching. Prodding.

They pulled back—though barely. Their foreheads still touched.

That kiss had been unlike any that Felicity had ever experienced. Even with Ricky. When the two of them had kissed it seemed so formal. Just like their relationship.

Nothing about it had ever been comfortable, though she hadn't been able to see it at the time. Until this moment, for that matter.

"You surprise me, Felicity," Brody rasped.

"Is that good or bad?"

"It's good. Very good."

With that said, he reached under her. Swept her legs up. Pulled her over the console that separated them.

She let out a laugh. She didn't question him. No, she trusted him. Brody wouldn't hurt her.

Nestled snuggly against his chest, their lips found

each other's again, this time not as tentative. Her fingers grasped his neck, played with the curls of hair there, traced the edge of his slight beard.

His lips trailed down her neck, sending fireworks exploding through her.

They both seemed to sense they needed to stop and pulled back.

Brody looked just as breathless as she felt.

He pulled her hand to his lips and kissed her knuckles.

"I should probably move back to my side of the seat, huh?"

"I don't mind if you stay here." He grinned and his arms tightened around her waist.

She realized she was halfway on his lap. And, if she stayed here, they'd only want to kiss more. She'd never felt such a jolt of attraction and longing. It scared her. Thrilled her. Fascinated her.

Just then, a noise caught their ears. Both of them jerked their heads toward the sound. It came from the river.

It was a boat. Speeding by. No—it was slowing down. Near them.

They had to check it out.

***

"Stay behind me," Brody whispered as they trekked through the high grass.

He was careful to keep them in the shadows. The moon was already shining high in the sky, casting sufficient light for them to be spotted. That was the last thing he wanted.

Finally, they paused behind the old shack, just out

of sight.

The men on the boat yelled in the distance, though he couldn't make out any words. One voice stood out above the others. One with an Australian accent.

"Magnum," Felicity whispered beside him. "Is my aunt with them?"

Brody peered around the corner and spotted the boat on the water. They'd stopped on the shoreline, and it looked like they were throwing something overboard. He saw the silhouettes of three men, but that was it. "It doesn't look like it."

"Can you tell what they're doing?"

Brody squinted, wishing he could get close enough to hear without giving away their location. "Not really. Magnum must have seen that same message on the side of the cabin doors. I'm not sure why he'd come back in a boat, though."

"He's waiting for the moonlight to reveal something. But you're right—why by boat?"

"Your guess is as good as mine. Quite possibly."

Brody glanced around, hoping for some kind of clue to jump out at him.

Wait until dark. The moonlight will be your guide.

What if none of this had anything to do with Blackbeard? What if it was some kind of old fishing cliché that whoever had last used this cabin had carved?

Though the moon illuminated the area, its glow was spread evenly. Nothing was highlighted or spotlighted to offer any answers.

The men in the boat continued talking at the shoreline. They were doing something. Dropping something in the water.

But why?

He felt Felicity shiver beside him. The night was

biting cold, and damp to top it off. He knew if he tried to convince her to go back to the truck she would only refuse. Instead, he put an arm around her shoulders, trying to forget their kiss.

There was no way he'd forget about that any time soon.

But, right now, he had to focus.

He watched the men, trying to figure out what they were doing. Was there anything at the shoreline worth exploring?

"Was this area on the map?" Brody whispered.

Felicity glanced up at him, her eyes wide with questions. "I think so. Why?"

"The waterline is always changing. What was once land could now be under water."

Her jaw slackened with realization. "You think Magnum and his men are going to search the water? That maybe they think the treasure is now hidden there?"

He nodded. "Yeah, I think they might."

Just then a bullet sliced through the air.

"They know we're here!" Brody said, his hand on Felicity's back. "We've got to get back to the truck. Now!"

CHAPTER 26

Bullets continued to fly around them as they raced across the uneven terrain. Felicity's lungs burned as she gulped in the cold air. She had no choice but to continue. They had to get to safety.

Why would Magnum shoot at them? They'd never find the second half of that stupid map if they were dead.

She'd guess he didn't want to kill them. Maybe he just wanted to scare them away so he could search the area himself.

Certainly he'd known they were going to be here. He'd been following them, after all.

This was a power play. He wanted them to know he was still in charge.

She should recognize that easily enough after her encounters with Ricky over the past couple years.

She hated being manipulated or strong-armed. But right now she had to stay alive. She had no choice but to run.

She dove into the truck. Brody did the same, right behind her. He pulled out his keys and stuck them in the ignition, cranking the engine.

"I don't want to get into a gun battle right now," he said. "Not for no good reason. I say we get out of here."

She couldn't agree more.

He sat up just enough to put the truck into reverse and hit the accelerator. Just as they reached the street, a bullet shattered the back glass.

Brody muttered something indiscernible under his breath. He wondered if Joshua's insurance would cover such damage.

They were going to need to find this treasure themselves, just to pay for all the extra expenses they'd incurred. Felicity knew she should offer to help, but since she was out of work that would be a challenge.

She'd have time to worry about that later.

"They're ruthless," she said instead.

"You don't have to tell me."

"Where are we going?" she asked as the truck righted itself on the road and silence stretched around them. The contrast to the earlier scene was stark, so stark that her heart pounded in her ears at the sudden change.

"I say go back to your place. It's just as close as the cabin where we were. Plus, my guess is that Magnum won't try to track you down there. He's still holding out hope you'll find that map."

She crossed her arms and sighed. "I'm running out of ideas."

"Let's talk out the clues," Brody said. "What do we know?"

"We know that there's a key leading somewhere. A door, most likely, based on the size of the key itself. It's too big for a box."

"Okay."

She took a deep breath, trying to focus. "We know there's half of a map. I'd guess it's at least from the 1800s. Maybe older. Maybe Blackbeard's."

"Agreed."

"My ancestors also may have a connection with Blackbeard. We found a deed leading to that property. At that property, there were messages carved in the wood saying, 'Wait until dark' and 'The moonlight will be your guide.'"

"Right."

"I think that's all we've got."

"I say we search your attic more. Maybe pull out those file drawers. I don't know. Maybe there's something."

"For my aunt's sake, I guess we don't have a choice." She glanced at Brody. "I'm sorry I dragged you into this. I know I've said it before, but it bears repeating. Especially after everything that's happened."

"If the stakes weren't so high—if your aunt's life wasn't on the line and you hadn't almost been killed, I might say this was fun." His expression sobered. "But there's too much at stake."

Felicity nodded in agreement. "Aunt Bonny is a tough, old broad. I'll give her that. But I have no idea what kind of conditions they're keeping her in . . ."

He squeezed her hand. "Let's think the best. Okay?"

She clutched his hand and nodded. "Right."

"We're not going to give up hope yet."

For the first time in years, she closed her eyes and prayed, long and hard.

Lord, be with us. Lead us. Guide us. And protect my aunt.

***

Some time during the night, Felicity had drifted to sleep on the couch at her grandma's house. When she woke up, a blanket had been draped over her.

Brody, she realized.

When she thought about him, her cheeks warmed. Their kisses yesterday had been . . . amazing. More than amazing.

Brody had stirred something deep inside her. She couldn't believe he was real.

Even though she'd initially had her reservations and they'd butted heads, she'd come to respect his opinion, to look to him for his comfort and strength, to depend on his advice.

But her aunt was still being held captive.

She sat up and blinked as everything rushed back to her.

What time was it? When had she fallen asleep? How had she managed to rest with everything going on?

Her gaze finally found the clock on the mantel. She jetted up. It was almost noon.

What was she thinking? Her time was ticking away, and here she was sleeping.

She rubbed her eyes again and searched the room. She expected to see Brody sleeping on the other couch, but it was empty. He was gone.

She stood, the blanket dropping to the floor. Instantly, cold surrounded her.

The house was quiet—too quiet. An instant sense of uneasiness overtook her.

She wandered into the kitchen and saw a fresh pot of coffee brewing. She poured herself a cup, and her hands hugged it as she continued to wander the house.

When she walked into the dining room, she found Brody at a computer that had been shoved into the corner. He turned when he saw her, looking bright-eyed and wide-awake.

"Morning."

His grin caused another wave of heat to rise on her cheeks. "Morning."

Felicity stared at the screen, trying to figure out what he was doing. She padded closer, still trying to jostle her mind into action. Of all the places he might be searching, the computer was the last one she would have guessed.

"I've been trying to find anything I can online that could help us," he said.

"Any luck?"

He shook his head. "I wish. But, no, I haven't found anything."

"I guess we have no excuse then not to go search in the attic." She'd delayed doing it last night because it was so late and so dark when they arrived back. She'd hoped with a little sleep, she'd think more clearly.

"You want to eat first? I can make you something."

His gesture warmed her, but she shook her head. "The coffee will do. My stomach is churning too much to eat. Just let me get changed. I've got to wake up."

"I'll go on up there. You come up when you're ready."

She quickly showered and dressed. Her throat again felt dry as she headed up those attic stairs. She'd grabbed another lantern to light her way.

When she reached the top, she spotted Brody sitting in an old wooden chair in front of the filing cabinet. He'd pulled out all the drawers and was searching through papers.

"Any luck?"

He shook his head. "No, I wish I had better news. As you can see, I've gone through all of this. I figured it was our best option."

"I did also."

She let out a sigh. "I guess I could look behind some of these pictures and inside some of those old books."

Brody nodded. "Let's exhaust every possibility."

***

Four hours later, they'd exhausted every possibility. They'd found nothing except lots of dust and a few mice.

At the moment, they were back downstairs. Felicity plopped on the couch, fighting despair. She liked to believe—*wanted* to believe—there could be a decent outcome to this situation. But her hopes grew dimmer and dimmer with every failure and setback.

This couldn't end with her aunt being harmed . . . or worse. It just couldn't. Yet she felt helpless to do anything about it.

"Where did you say that sword came from?" Brody nodded toward the sword on the wall.

"According to my aunt, it's a hand-me-down from Blackbeard. I did see the initials ET on the handle, and many of the details match the style of that period in time. But it doesn't offer us any clues."

He stood and took it down. "Are you sure?"

"I can examine it again."

He sat beside her and handed her the sword. "Examine away."

She held it on her lap, the blade no longer sharp. The sword was heavy—so heavy that she had a hard time imagining having it strapped to her waist.

Carefully, she raised it toward her eyes and examined the intricate carving along the handle and guard. There were trees, and maybe an owl, maybe a skull. It was so hard to tell.

The handle was wrapped in leather, typical for the time period

The strange thing was, this sword didn't really look like it had ever been used. The thought seemed foreign. She'd seen this sword many times before—assuming it was mostly ornamental in the past. But normally the metal would have scrapes. The handles might have nicks. The leather would be more faded.

This one had none of those things.

"Well?" Brody asked.

She shook her head. "It's very interesting. The design is intricate—slightly faded. I like to imagine the history of the piece. Its origins, where it came from, who handled this. But we really have no way of knowing that."

"It's a shame."

She held the sword closer again, looking at the carving there. "You know. This looks slightly familiar, but I'm not sure from where. The design is rather common. Trees. A skull."

"Is there a moon?"

She squinted. "You know, now that you mention it, there is. It's a full moon hidden behind those trees."

"Coincidence?"

"It's hard to say." She touched the blade, felt its weight in her hand, and ran her finger down what was once a sharp edge. Did this have other clues that would help them? Next, her gaze traveled to that leather-wrapped handle. Was there something beneath the leather? Did she want to risk ruining the piece to find out?

Gently, she tugged at the handle. Holding the blade in one hand, and the handle in the other, she tugged harder.

"What are you doing?" Brody asked.

"Something about this sword feels off. Maybe it's

the weight of it. I don't know. The handle feels too thick."

"May I?" Brody extended his hand.

"Please do."

He held it, bouncing it in his hand for several minutes as if testing the weight himself.

"Do you know much about fencing?"

"Would you believe me if I told you I did?" She'd taken lessons all through college, feeling like sword fighting was a stress reliever.

"I agree that the handle feels thick. But I don't know anything about swords."

"Historically, people were smaller back in the eighteenth century. Based on that information, I'd assume their hands would be smaller."

"What are you thinking?" His eyes connected with hers.

"I know it sounds crazy . . ."

"We'll take anything at this point, right?"

She nodded. "Right. We're almost out of time."

As if on cue, her phone buzzed. She stole another glance at Brody before picking up her cell. "It's Magnum."

"Answer it." Brody moved closer.

The tremble in her hands began again as she accepted the call and put the phone to her ear. "Hello?"

"You don't appear to be looking very hard." Magnum's harsh voice came over the line, that familiar satisfaction in his tone.

It made Felicity want to leap through the phone line and smack him. "What do you mean?" she finally said.

"You're at your house. I thought you'd be out traipsing around, looking for that map. After all, your aunt's life depends on it."

Her back straightened with tension. "There is more than one way to look for something."

He grunted. "I suppose. But your time is running out."

"How do I know you didn't find the treasure last night when you followed us?" Tension pinched her spine as she remembered the way events had unfolded.

"I found a piece of gold. But there's more out there. A lot more. I want to know where it is."

Her heart leaped into her throat. Had she heard him correctly? "You found a piece of Blackbeard's gold?"

"Just a couple of pieces. We're searching for more in the river."

She stared at Brody a moment and saw the understanding in his gaze. "Why are you calling, Magnum?"

"As a reminder that I have your aunt."

"You better not have hurt her."

"Or what? Or you'll do a bad appraisal of my pirates' gold?" He let out a sardonic chuckle.

His words stung in ways they shouldn't. But he knew how to hit where it hurt.

"As a matter of fact, I talked to your ex. Ricky, right?"

Her throat tightened. "Why would you do that?"

"He's going to help me figure out the value of the treasures I find."

"*If* you find it."

She could hear his smirk across the phone line. "I'll find it."

"I want to talk to my aunt."

"She's fine."

"Prove it."

"Fine. Here she is. You have thirty seconds."

Rustling sounded in the background until her aunt's voice came on the line. "Felicity?"

"Aunt Bonny?" Tears sprang to her eyes. "Are you okay? Did they hurt you?"

"I'm fine. They've been feeding me crackers and water, so I guess that counts for food."

"They haven't hurt you?" She closed her eyes, praying for another confirmation.

"No, they haven't hurt me. They're mean men, though, Felicity. I wouldn't put anything past them."

She squeezed her eyes shut. "I know, Aunt Bonny. I'm doing everything I can."

"I know you are, dear. Just know, whatever happens, I'll be okay. I'm right with my Maker. Are you?"

"I . . ." She glanced at Brody. "I am. I am now."

Brody squeezed her knee.

"He's coming back," her aunt rushed. "But, Felicity, everything I told you is true."

"Everything you told me? What do you mean?"

Before her aunt could answer, Magnum came back on the line. "Your thirty seconds are up. If you're not careful, that will be the last time you speak with her. You have twenty-four more hours. And, whatever you do, don't involve the police. You do, your aunt dies."

The line went dead.

She nervously twisted the object in her lap.

As she did, the sword's handle popped off.

She let out a gasp before looking down. There, tucked into the hollow center of the blade, was a piece of parchment paper.

CHAPTER 27

Carefully, she pulled the paper from its sheath. Her heart raced, pounding in her ears, making her chest throb, making her lungs tighten.

Could this be what they were searching for?

Under normal circumstances, she'd use tweezers and other equipment to make sure the paper remained preserved. But she didn't have that luxury now. Time wasn't on her side.

The paper popped out, and she carefully unrolled it, still unable to breathe until her eyes were able to ascertain what was inside. As the images appeared, her heart raced even faster.

It was the other half of the map.

She glanced behind her. The curtains were still closed. Magnum and his men shouldn't be watching them right now.

"We found it." Brody's voice rose with excitement.

She nodded, feeling dumbfounded. "I can't believe it. Maybe I really will get my aunt back."

"What is it?" Brody studied her face a moment. He must have noticed something was wrong.

It was. Something nagged at the back of her mind, begging for her attention. What was it?

She shook her head. "I'm not sure. I mean, I vaguely remember the other map, and I'm mentally putting it together in my mind. The thing is: I'm not sure that this map will lead anyone closer to the treasure. It just looks like a common map. There's nothing marked here that's out of the ordinary."

"Magnum must not agree."

"But why? What's so special?"

"Is there a hidden message on the back that you need lemon juice and water to see?"

"That's a myth. People didn't really do that." She stood and walked toward the dining room.

"What are you thinking?"

"I took a picture of the other half of this map. It's on my phone camera."

"Okay . . ." He kept pace beside her as she hurried past the table.

"I want to put them together."

"You think that will help?"

"You never know." She sat at the computer and took a picture of the new map portion. It took several minutes, but she finally managed to manipulate the pieces until they fit together. She then printed out two copies so she could study them.

Brody remained quiet, giving her space to think, which she greatly appreciated and needed.

Her mind whirled—something internal begged for her attention. What was she missing? This map held some type of clue. She had to figure out what it was.

Adrenaline pumping, she grabbed a red marker from the desk drawer. "I know this is a long shot, but I've got to try. Teach's Oak was in Oriental, which was located about here." She pointed to one area of the map and marked the spot.

"Legend also said it was buried at Ocracoke," Brody said.

She nodded and found the approximate location of Ocracoke. She marked that spot with a red dot as well.

"And the final place was Holiday Island, which is in the Neuse River," she said.

"That would be right about here." Brody pointed to the area of the map where the river was now located.

Felicity marked that area as well. Then she held the map back and looked at it. It had a little triangle of three dots.

Her blood pumped with excitement. Could this really be it?

"What is it?" Brody asked.

"I'll show you." She got on the computer and searched through the images there until she found what she was looking for. "Here. Look at this."

"Blackbeard's flag?" Brody mumbled.

She nodded. "This is one version of it. There are several."

"Okay . . ."

"One minute, and I hope this will make sense." She kept scrolling until she found the one she wanted. She printed several different sizes, hoping one would work.

"I'm not following this."

"You see these three dots on the bottom of his flag?" She pointed to them.

"Can't miss them."

She held her breath, hoping this would work. Praying it would. "Watch this."

Her hands showed her nerves as she lowered the flag on top of the map. The first one didn't work. But the second appeared to be a perfect match.

She grabbed a thumbtack and poked a hole

through each of the dots.

When she pulled the papers apart, the dots lined up almost perfectly.

"His flag was a clue the whole time?" Brody said. "You're brilliant."

She let out a breath. "I don't know about that. I'm still not sure how much closer we are to finding answers."

"Put the flag back down on top of the map," Brody said.

She did.

"Do you see where the arrow of his spear is pointing?" He touched the area. "Could you put a pinprick there?"

"Why not?"

She did as he asked and, when she pulled the paper away, she studied the location of the new dot.

Brody put his hand on the mark. "Felicity, you realize where that spear was pointing, don't you?"

"No, where?" The truth was at the cusp of her mind.

Brody's eyes locked on hers. "It's pointing to this very house."

CHAPTER 28

"You really think the treasure is here?" Felicity asked, unable to believe a clue like that had been in front of them the whole time.

Brody leaned closer to examine the map. "Look at the map, Felicity. This river here is the river outside your house. It branches off here, a little bit farther downstream. Believe me. I study a lot of nautical charts."

"You're right. Has the treasure been here the whole time?" She shook her head, both flabbergasted and thrilled with the thought. "But where? We've searched the attic. There's nowhere else."

Brody leaned back and let out a long breath. "Does the phrase we saw yesterday mean anything to you?"

She recalled the crudely carved words on the wall of the old cabin. "Wait until dark; the moonlight will be your guide?"

"Yes, that's it."

She searched her memories for any of her aunt's old stories or family tales that might tie in but nothing registered. "I don't think so.

He squinted with thought before turning toward her. "The answers feel close."

"I agree." She stood. "I need to see that sword

again."

Brody followed her into the living room. She picked up the sword and studied the design on the hilt. The handle itself was rather plain, as was the guard. But the pommel was interesting with its intricate design. There was also the delicate symbol where the letters "ET" were. She turned it a different angle to examine it again.

"I know where I recognize this from," she whispered, the truth smacking her in the face. How had she not seen this before?

"Where?"

"There." She turned and pointed to the stained glass window atop the wall. It had been in front of her the whole time.

Brody glanced back and forth between the two. "You're right. It's a match. It's hard to tell, but it's the same."

Felicity stepped closer, something bugging her about all of this. "There's one thing I don't understand."

Brody appeared beside her. "What's that?"

"It's like we talked about earlier: this house wasn't built until 1802."

He turned away and studied the stained glass again. "You're right. That doesn't make sense. Yet the clues seem so obvious."

She wasn't ready to let this drop. The answers were here. She just had to find them. "Brody, do you know if the blueprints for this house would be on file as a matter of record?"

"I doubt they go back that far."

"But my grandma did have some work done on her bedroom before she died. Significant work. Maybe there's record of that."

He glanced at his watch. "I think the county clerk

works until five. We have about thirty minutes."

"You think we can make it?"

"I say we try."

***

Brody stood beside Felicity in an old, dusty room in the county clerk's office, pouring over old files. He rubbed her neck, sensing she was getting exhausted. As the saying went, this was like looking for a needle in a haystack. But they had to do everything they could to find answers.

Brody had gone to high school with the woman working the front desk, and he'd convinced her to let them take a look themselves. He was thankful she'd agreed to it because it made their task considerably easier.

As Brody stood and stretched, someone knocked at the door.

He tensed until he saw Joshua standing there. The police chief stepped into the room, a bag of supplies in his hands.

"Special delivery." He handed the bag to Brody and nodded a polite hello to Felicity. "Now, does someone want to tell me what's going on?"

Brody glanced at Felicity, and she gave him a nod of approval. He needed her permission first before starting. After all, this was her story, not his. She was the one with the stakes in this.

"A relic hunter named Magnum Lewis murdered the man you found dead in the snowstorm," Brody started, getting right to the point.

Joshua's eyebrows shot up. "Magnum Lewis, huh? There's an APB out for him. I just got it yesterday. He apparently stole some government property, among other things."

Good. At least that was in place. Maybe law enforcement would catch this man before he did anymore damage in his greedy pursuit.

"He's dangerous," Brody said. "Very dangerous."

Joshua's hand went to his hip, and his gaze flipped back and forth from Brody to Felicity. "I had that impression. How did you two get involved?"

"It's a long story." Felicity rubbed her lips together, anxiety written all over her features. They were pinched, and her voice cracked. "But it boils down to this: Magnum has my aunt."

Joshua straightened. "Your Aunt Bonny?"

She nodded a little too fast.

Joshua's gaze shot to Brody. "Why didn't you report this sooner?"

Accusation stained his voice. It was a good question. And complicated.

"Magnum said he'd kill Bonny if the police got involved. He wants Felicity to help him do something—"

"Something illegal?" Joshua's gaze fell on Felicity.

She shook her head. "No, not illegal. But almost impossible."

"There's no guarantee that once we hand over what he wants that he'll give Bonny back." Brody knew he was on borrowed time and he had to make this quick. But it was hard to succinctly summarize the past few days. "We may know where the treasure is."

"What treasure?" Joshua's shoulders raised. He looked like he thought both Brody and Felicity might be a little crazy. It was only going to get worse from here.

"Blackbeard's," Felicity said, looking up from the file she'd been studying.

Joshua shook his head, took a step back, and let out a faint chuckle. When no one else joined him, he narrowed his eyes again. "You're seriously telling me that this is all about a pirate's treasure?"

Felicity rubbed her hands on her jeans and nodded. "We know how insane it sounds. But people have been crazy about Blackbeard's treasure for centuries now. We have a lead, but we need to search the records here."

Joshua let out another chuckle filled with disbelief. "And what are you going to do if you find it? Magnum will still come after you."

Brody decided to step into the conversation before Felicity crumbled. He could see her emotions zigzagging back and forth, up and down. "We know. But we need to buy some time."

Joshua leaned against the wall and crossed his arms. "If you'd come to me earlier, I could have been searching for your aunt. I thought you would know better, Brody."

"It's a precarious situation, Joshua, with no easy answers." Brody's jaw hardened. He wanted to deny his words, but he knew there was a certain amount of truth there. Maybe Brody could have handled this differently.

Just like Andrea.

He should have handled that situation differently also. He should have come home that week. He should have looked harder. Maybe things would have turned out differently.

"You have no idea where they're holding her?" Joshua asked.

Brody shook his head. "No idea at this point."

"I'm still not sure I understand your game plan. You find the treasure. Magnum will try to steal it and maybe kill your aunt."

"I've got it!" Felicity stood, a paper in hand. "It makes sense now."

Joshua and Brody walked to her side of the table. Adrenaline rushed through Brody's blood. Was this really it?

"What makes sense?" Joshua asked.

She pointed to an area of the blueprint. "My grandma's house was built in 1802, just like they always told me. What I didn't realize was that there was an original house on the property that the new house was built around."

Brody squinted, trying to process that. "So you're saying that the remains of the old house are within the new house?"

"Kind of. If you look at this layout, you can see that part of the original house was preserved. Mostly the living room and a couple of bedrooms."

"Okay . . ."

"But there's this area here." She pointed to a square. "I can't figure it out for sure, but I think a couple of the original rooms are now tucked between the rooms of the current house."

"Why would someone do that?" Joshua asked.

Felicity shrugged. "It's hard to say for sure. But homes used to be built more solidly in olden days. Plus, if I'm right, this is the area around the fireplace. It may have been more economical to build around the fireplace instead of building a brand new one. Perhaps, at one time, these rooms were used for storage, but over the years, as the house grew in size, the need for storage wasn't as great."

"What do you suggest we do?" Brody asked.

Felicity's gaze met his. "We wait to see where the moonlight leads us. But I think we may have found the hiding place for Blackbeard's treasure."

CHAPTER 29

They grabbed some food at a local barbecue restaurant and ate it in the truck on the way back to Felicity's place. Her mind raced the entire time. The possibilities in front of them seemed endless. But her hopes rose and fell like the tide. There very well could be something hidden within the walls of her house. Or this could be nothing.

At least the police were aware of the situation now. That way if things went south, someone would know what was going on. Joshua had promised to keep his eyes open, but otherwise stay out of it until they asked for his help.

He'd probably only agreed to that at the request of Brody.

In her driveway, Brody hopped out and immediately squatted to the ground.

"What is it?" Felicity already knew the answer, but she asked anyway.

"Someone's been here."

Felicity shook her head with disgust. Magnum was going to do whatever it took to find this treasure. She only hoped her plan worked. Thankfully, she'd hidden everything before she left.

"Let's see if they did any damage inside," Brody

said.

With trepidation, she climbed the steps to her porch. The front door was unlocked. As Brody pushed it open, she held her breath.

When her living room came into view, she released the air from her lungs. Everything appeared to be in one piece. For now, at least.

"Stay here while I check things out," Brody said.

She didn't bother to argue. She watched as he pulled out his gun and checked the rest of the house. As he headed up the stairs, she held her breath.

She didn't hear any thumps or crashes. That was a good sign.

Dear Lord . . . please.

Finally, she heard footsteps. Just one set.

Brody appeared coming down the stairs.

"Someone was in the attic," he said. "It's torn apart. But, otherwise, everything seems fine."

"Oh, good." She finally exhaled, tired of this rollercoaster ride she'd been on for the past few days.

There was so much on the line here. Could they really pull this off?

They had no choice but to try.

"Let's get to work." Felicity gripped the bag Joshua had given them.

She went into the dining room. Thankfully, the curtains were still drawn, promising there was no one peeking inside. Privacy was of the utmost importance.

She pulled out some brown ink, a quill, some tea, and parchment paper, and set them on the table. Then she got busy.

The parchment paper was a good match and, with the right coloring, it could match the map. She'd taken a lot of pictures that she could work off of, and Joshua had brought them just the supplies they'd asked for.

She started by making some strong coffee. She took a paintbrush and slathered the coffee on the paper, which gave it a deeper brown color. As she did that, she heated the oven to 200 degrees. She slipped the paper inside but only for a few minutes. The crispness would help with the aging process.

Brody stood by idly. She knew he'd help, if there was something he could do. But right now if he could just keep an eye on the outside of the house that would be all the help she needed.

"Have you ever heard of mooncussers?" she asked as she waited.

"No, I can't say I have."

"Mooncussers would strap lights on nags—horses in modern day terms. This is where the beach town Nags Head on the Outer Banks got its name. Anyway, they would walk these nags up and down the sand dunes. At night, ships coming in from sea would see the lights bobbing in the distance and assume they were boats on the water and that the water was clear to sail through."

"Interesting."

She nodded and pulled the paper from the oven. It looked perfect. She didn't have any time to waste in adding the final details to the map. She carried it into the dining room to finish it. "What happened, of course, was that the ships would crash into the shore. When they did, these so-called land pirates would rob them of their treasure."

He crossed his arms, following her as she worked, his gaze constantly surveying the area for any signs of danger. "They were pretty clever."

"Weren't they? I kind of feel like we're giving Magnum a piece of his own medicine. We're making it appear that safety is ahead, but little does he know we're planning for a shipwreck."

"Nice." He fingered the paper. "You're pretty good at this."

"I went to school for this. Not counterfeiting, but . . ." She shrugged. "You know."

"I have faith in you."

She hardly heard him. "He's going to have Ricky evaluate this." Her muscles all seemed to tighten at that announcement.

"Your ex?"

She nodded and raised her quill. She could do this. She could imitate the marks on the maps. "I'm hoping we'll buy ourselves enough time in the process, though."

He glanced at his watch. "Speaking of time . . . you know we're running out, right?"

She nodded. "I think I've treated the paper enough for now. I just need to add the letters. The only thing I'm worried about is the tear line."

"What do you mean?"

"Tears are difficult. The paper is very detailed there. It will be easy to spot if the tear isn't consistent with the original. I think I can mimic it."

He squeezed her shoulder. "You can do it."

That didn't stop the anxiety from roiling in her stomach. Finally, she finished the last word and added the final dot. A dot that wasn't on the original. A dot that would send Magnum on a wild goose chase.

She stepped back and looked at it. Looked at printouts of the original. Finally, she nodded.

"I think I'm done. I just need to add a little more heat and then roll it up."

"You think he'll question it?"

"Magnum is the type who will question everything.

But this will buy us time. He'll give us Aunt Bonny back, and we'll get her hidden away. Hopefully, the real treasure will end up in the hands of someone who will truly appreciate it and not some money-hungry relic hunter."

But as she said the words, doubt began to creep in. She prayed she could pull this off.

***

Brody sat beside Felicity on the couch. The lights were turned off, and they both waited to see where the moon would shine. There was no TV on. Nothing but silence.

He could feel the jitters of excitement and nerves in Felicity as she sat beside him. Under other circumstances, he might be tempted to pull her into his arms, but now wasn't the time. He hoped he would have time for that when all this was over. Time to explore what a relationship between them might look like. What a chance at love might feel like. What letting go of the past might mean.

He held his own cup of coffee and slowly raised it to his lips. The waiting was the hardest part.

Felicity looked up at the stained-glass window above the front door. Could it really be the key? Was it in front of them the whole time?

The way she'd put everything together was just short of amazing.

"I hope all this works," she whispered beside him.

He squeezed her knee. "Me too."

"Thanks for being here through it all."

"Thanks for not chasing me off."

"I tried a few times," she reminded him.

He grinned. "Thankfully, I'm stubborn."

"Thankfully."

The sun had long since set. The moon was rising in the sky. But it wasn't aligned right yet.

Felicity got up and paced toward the door. She peered out the window.

"It's almost time," she told him. "It's getting closer."

He tried to imagine what might play out over the next hour. Over the next day. Over the next few days. It could be amazing. Or it could be horrible.

He prayed for the prior.

He glanced around the house. "By the way, what are you going to do with the place?"

She turned swiftly toward him. "This house?"

"That's right."

She shrugged. "I haven't thought about it."

"It would be beautiful if it was restored."

Her gaze fluttered around the place. "You're right. It would be. But I'm afraid I don't have the funds to do that. It would take so much time and money."

"Restoring this place seems right up your alley."

She nodded. "It is. I love old things and history. But I also realize my limitations."

"Any thoughts of going back to Raleigh?"

"It's hard to say. We'll have to see if anything keeps me here." Her gaze fluttered up to him.

He scooted closer. "I could work on that."

"I bet you could."

Just as he leaned in, she stepped back and drew in a sharp breath.

"Brody, there it is! It's an X. A real-life X marks the spot."

He looked over. Sure enough, the lines from the stained glass had formed an X on the wall above the fireplace.

That was where the treasure was. Located in one of the house's original rooms. Near the attic.

"Let's get to work," he said.

***

Against her wishes, Felicity found herself back in the attic with a lantern in hand. She knew they had to be careful. The chances were that Magnum and his men were still watching them. Though they couldn't see inside the house, any loud noises might alert them that something was going on.

Brody stared at the boards in from of him. "I'm going to start taking these down. Let's see if there's anything to this theory."

"Let's go."

Another ripple of excitement rushed through her. This all seemed surreal. But what if there really was something on the other side?

Using an old hammer, Brody pried the first board away. Blackness stared back. He took down another and another. They came down easily since the wood and nails were old. Incredibly old.

Finally, a two-foot section had been removed. The blackness only grew, and a cold, damp breeze floated out.

Maybe this was why it always seemed so drafty up here. In fact, her lantern had gone out the first time she and Brody came up here. Could it be because there was a room beyond these walls?

"Let's see that lantern." Brody reached for it.

She stepped closer, dreading being away from the light. Brody seemed to sense that and snaked an arm around her waist. Then he thrust the light into the opening.

Her eyes widened at what she saw there.

It was a room. A small room. Across from the section of wall they'd taken down was a door.

Felicity grabbed the lantern and stepped inside. She knelt down until she was eye level with the keyhole.

"This is it, Brody. This is it."

CHAPTER 30

Felicity stared at the door, gave it a nudge, examined the hinges. There was no way they could open this, not unless they had the right tools. It was solid and thick and held together with some kind of mortar, unlike anything she'd seen before.

"I can't believe it." Brody ran his hand over the wood. "This is crazy."

"To say the least."

Could this really be where Blackbeard's treasure was stored? Was it right here under her nose all these years?

Her throat went dry. She hadn't thought they'd actually be able to find the treasure. She'd worked so hard to make a forgery of that map to give to Magnum and buy herself some time.

But now that she'd found the treasure, maybe she should just hand it over. Get her aunt back. End all of this.

After all, none of this was worth her aunt's life. Without her aunt, she'd have no one.

Except Brody. But what did they really have? Was he interested in seeing where their relationship went? Or had they simply shared a few kisses?

She couldn't mess this up. She'd messed up too

much in her life already.

"Brody, I've got to tell Magnum," Felicity muttered.

She had to tell him now. That meant she had to get out of this attic and make the call.

She rushed toward the stairway before Brody could stop her.

Brody followed behind her. "Tell Magnum? You made him the map."

She didn't slow her steps as she rushed down the stairs. "What other choice do I have? It's the only way I can ensure my aunt's safety. We don't need the map anymore."

As they reached the hallway, Brody's hand went to her shoulder, slowing her down. "I'm not sure Magnum is the most trustworthy person, Felicity."

She turned toward him, her pulse racing out of control. She didn't have time to carefully weigh her options. She had to make a decision—now. Her heart told her this was the best way to keep her aunt alive.

"I've done everything he's asked. He has no reason not to cooperate." She took out her phone, her mind still racing. "I'm going to call him now."

"Felicity . . ." He reached for her, but she stepped out of his grasp.

"Yes?"

His face looked pensive. "I have a bad feeling in my gut."

She swallowed hard, questioning herself a moment. What if she was wrong? What if this backfired?

No, she couldn't think like that. This was still her best option.

She licked her lips, wishing her nerves would go away. "I've got to do this, Brody. And I've got to do it Magnum's way. He said if we involve the police that he'd kill my aunt. I can't risk that."

He nodded stiffly. "Okay then."

Felicity's fingers trembled as she dialed Magnum's number. He answered on the first ring.

"I was hoping to hear from you," he crooned.

"We found it." Felicity's words sounded unbelievable, even to her own ears. They'd really found it. They'd *found* it!

Brody stepped closer to hear the conversation, his touch sending another wave of shivers up her spine.

"You found the other half of the map?" Magnum said.

"We did better than that. We found the treasure."

"I underestimated just how good you were. Too bad circumstances aren't different. I'd make you a part of my team."

"I'll never be on your side.

He grunted. "Have it your way. Now, where are you?"

Felicity would bet anything Magnum knew exactly where they were. "I'm at my house. We found a secret room."

"Is that right? You think the treasure is there?"

She swallowed hard, starting to question herself again. The treasure had to be in that room . . . right? "I'm not sure. But there's a room. We can't get in without a key. I think . . . I think this is it."

He paused a moment, not saying anything, before growling, "You better be correct. We'll be right there."

"Bring my aunt," Felicity said, a little bit of gusto coming back into her voice.

He paused for just long enough to make her uncomfortable. "Of course."

Felicity hung up and rubbed her hands against her

jeans. This was happening. She'd get her aunt back. Magnum would get his treasure. This would all end.

"It's done." She looked up at Brody, halfway afraid to meet his eyes. She knew she'd see emotions there she'd rather ignore. She pushed aside those feelings. "Within a matter of time, my aunt should be safe."

"I . . . I hope so."

She couldn't look at him anymore. She couldn't stand to see the doubt in his eyes.

"You know what? I'm going to go get some water. I feel like I can't breathe."

Brody nodded. "You go do that. I'll be down in a second."

***

Brody paced away from the stairway leading to the first floor.

An impending feeling of doom pressed on his shoulders.

This had been Felicity's call. She was the one with the most at stake. But everything in him screamed that this was a bad idea.

Magnum wasn't going to release her aunt. He'd most likely kill both Felicity and Brody and then grab the treasure for himself.

His throat tightened as he tried to figure out the best plan of action.

He couldn't just sit by and watch everything blow up. He couldn't do it. Nor could he protect Felicity on his own.

He pulled out his phone and stared at it a moment.

Emotions clashed in his gut. Felicity might never forgive him if he did what he was about to do. But, if he didn't, she could end up dead.

She could end up like Andrea.

He couldn't let that happen.

At the thought of his first love, he dialed Joshua's number. His friend answered on the first ring. "What's going on?"

"Magnum is on his way here."

"Magnum Lewis?" Joshua repeated.

"That's right. He says he's bringing Bonny Pasture with him, but I'm not so sure about that."

"Why not?"

"He can't be trusted. Felicity doesn't want me to involve you, but . . . I don't know, Joshua. I'm trying to trust my judgment on this."

"What's your gut telling you?"

He squeezed his eyes shut, not wanting to voice the thought aloud. "That he's going to get what he wants and kill everyone here."

"I'm on my way. It will take me a few minutes to get there. There was an accident on 17 that has the road nearly closed."

"Thanks."

Just as he hung up, he heard a footstep behind him.

***

Felicity paused in the hallway and sucked in a breath.

Who was Brody speaking to?

She froze where she was as part of the conversation caught her ear. "Magnum is on his way . . ."

Betrayal stabbed through her heart.

Brody didn't think she was competent enough to make her own choices either—just like Ricky. He'd gone behind her back and . . . made her look foolish.

Shame filled her.

How could she have thought Brody was different? He was just as arrogant as Ricky. He cared nothing about her. Didn't respect her. Didn't think she was capable.

Maybe he even delighted in making her look stupid in front of others.

At that moment, Brody turned around.

His eyes flashed with guilt. He knew he'd been caught.

He started to reach for her. "Felicity, it's not what you think."

She jerked away, nearly spilling her water. "Then what is it?"

"Felicity, I'm afraid things are going to go south. I fear for your safety. I had to call Joshua—"

"You called the police?" Her mouth gaped open. "You know what Magnum said he would do. He's going to kill my aunt. Why couldn't you have just let me call the shots?"

He didn't break his gaze. "I was only trying to look out for you."

She threw one of her hands in the air, her voice rising with it. "By making me feel like an idiot?"

Brody shook his head and again started to reach for her. He seemed to realize the futility of the motion and dropped his hand. "That's not how I meant it. Felicity, I care about you—"

She wasn't falling for this again. "You care enough to stab me in the back."

"I care enough to not want a repeat of what happened to Andrea." His voice sounded still, solemn.

But she couldn't be weak again. "So you're just interested in saving your own reputation. That sounds familiar."

"It's not like that—"

Before he could finish his statement, a deep, accented voice cut through the air behind her. "Sorry to interrupt this love spat, but I believe you have something I want to see."

Felicity turned and spotted Magnum standing at the base of the stairway. He really must have positioned right outside her house to get here this quickly. And he'd come inside without making so much as a sound.

Her eyes immediately went to the gun he bobbed in his hands as he climbed the steps.

She looked beyond him but only saw two men following him.

Felicity forgot about how much she despised Brody for a moment as her spine stiffened. "Where's Aunt Bonny?"

Magnum clucked his tongue and his eyebrow twitched, as if this whole situation amused him. "First things first. Where's this room?"

She raised her chin, tired of other people trying to take control of her life. "I won't tell you until you show me my aunt."

He cleared the stairway and stared at her a moment before letting out a low chuckle. "I know it would be nice to call the shots, but that's my job, not yours."

"Then I won't tell you." She raised her chin higher.

"We can do this the hard way." All of the humor left his voice, and he sounded menacing instead.

His men rushed up the stairs and surrounded her and Brody. There were five of them including Magnum. No way they'd ever be able to take on that many men.

Magnum raised his gun. "Now, where is it?"

She knew she was outnumbered. If she didn't tell

him, these men would just tie her and Brody up and leave them to die. She may as well play along for as long as she could. "It's upstairs. In the attic."

He nodded to his men, and they scrambled up the stairs.

"Try anything stupid, and there will be consequences," Magnum warned, aiming his gun at her.

Panic raced through her. When the police showed up, her aunt was going to die. That was all there was to it.

"Now move." Magnum pointed with his gun toward the attic.

Felicity didn't argue. She started up the steps, Brody behind her, and Magnum bringing up the rear. At the top, Magnum tasked one of his men with watching them while Magnum did the honor of inserting the key into the lock.

She held her breath as she waited to see what would happen.

The lock turned. The door opened. Blackness yawned from the other side.

She'd seen too many movies, and half-expected bats to fly out. Or some kind of curse to begin wreaking havoc on everyone in the room.

Instead, there was silence.

Magnum motioned for one of his men to go in first.

The chosen one raised a lantern and stepped inside.

Felicity's eyes went dry. She hardly wanted to blink and miss anything. What was on the other side of that wall?

CHAPTER 31

A moment later, the man emerged from the room, a scowl on his face. "It's a chest. But it's locked."

"There's a chest?" Magnum grabbed the lantern and ducked into the room himself. When he stepped back out, he muttered curses under his breath.

"I thought you'd be happy," Felicity muttered.

"It's locked."

"You're going to let that stop you?" she asked.

Magnum narrowed his eyes. "It's not that easy. It's too heavy to carry, and those kinds of locks can't be jimmied like the new ones. We have to find the other half of this." He held something up.

Felicity squinted, trying to get a better look at it. It almost looked like a half key. "What exactly is that?"

Magnum crossed the room in a few strides until he was face-to-face with her. "It's half of a key. I need the other half in order to open that chest and find my treasure."

"Half of a key? Who makes half a key?" she asked.

He narrowed his eyes again. "Someone with a twisted sense of humor. Someone who wants to protect what he's plundered. Someone like . . ."

"Blackbeard," she finished. "Where'd you find that

half?"

His eyes darkened. "In the cannon exhumed from the *Queen Anne's Revenge.* It was hidden away in a compartment near the base. I knew it was there somewhere, but it took me forever to find it."

Facts started to click in her mind. "That's why you were really there working for Project Teach. How you managed to do that amazes me."

His eyes brightened this time. The man fed on admiration. "It's not that hard to fake credentials. I set up a few bogus websites. Made some dummy landing pages for articles written about me. Falsified a résumé. That was the easy part of my job."

"I still don't understand how you tracked all of this down to my house."

"Since we're being chatty now, I guess I can tell you this much. A man contacted Project Teach about a key. I just happened to get the email. He wanted to sell it to us. Said he'd found it washed up on shore in Cape Hatteras. I responded and went to meet him. I knew when I first saw it that it was the real thing."

"What happened then?" Felicity asked.

"I offered to buy it from him, but he didn't want to accept the amount I offered. I knew I had to have that key."

"So he tried to get away, but you stopped him," Felicity said.

Magnum shrugged. "Something like that. One of my men roughed him up, but the man was scrawny and managed to get away. He left the island as it was starting to snow, and we went after him. He got to land, but sent his boat out into the water to throw us off. That's when this guy came in." He nodded at Brody. "He picked the man up on the side of the road. We couldn't let him get away. I had to have that key."

"How did that man—he had a name, by the way, Ivan—know about Felicity's connection to this?" Brody asked.

"He must have overheard my guys talking." Magnum scowled again. "Turns out he was a smart old man. He scoped us out while we were eating at a restaurant in Hatteras. He must have heard too much."

"What made you so certain the key belonged with Blackbeard's treasure?" Felicity asked.

Satisfaction flashed in his eyes. "Simple. I acquired some journals at an auction. The entries contained a firsthand account of Blackbeard."

Felicity's heart rate spiked at the news. "Whose journals were they?"

"A banker named Charles Smith. Apparently, Blackbeard paid him off for his silence, but he had to tell someone. So he kept a journal."

"Why would Blackbeard befriend a banker?" Felicity tried to think it through, wondering what kind of connection they could have possibly had.

"This Charles Smith apparently couldn't stand the governor of Virginia, who'd offered a reward for Blackbeard's death," Magnum said. "The governor had taken some land that Charles thought rightfully belonged to him. As a result, he wanted revenge. What better revenge than to help the very man the governor loathed?"

"And that somehow led here?"

That all too familiar satisfaction filled Magnum's gaze again. "One of the entries mentioned that Edward Teach had taken a wife in Hertford. Someone named Loretta. I did my research, and it led me here. I figured there might be a clue at this house. I just never figured the treasure was here."

Felicity shook her head. "It doesn't make sense. Back then, this house was small, which would indicate Loretta Pasture didn't have much money. If the treasure was here, why didn't she use it?"

"From everything I've read, she died before she could ever enjoy it."

Brody bristled beside her. "Since you seem to have all the answers, then answer this: If Blackbeard left the treasure here for his bride, then why plant clues for others to find it?"

"I believe Blackbeard, in the event of his or Loretta's death, instructed his first mate to leave the clues in hopes that his children or his children's children would find it. But your guess is as good as mine." He held the gun up again. "Now, let's get downstairs and discuss this further."

Panic caused her heart to race. "I want to see my aunt. I need to know that she's okay."

A smug, arrogant expression captured Magnum's face. "You have nothing of value to me anymore, Felicity. I should just kill you now."

Brody bristled beside her. "Keep your hands off her."

"Lover boy is getting a little protective, isn't he? That's . . . sweet. The greatest stories of our time involve those of a man and woman falling in love. I'm only sorry you won't be able to see this little relationship to completion."

His announcement made Felicity's muscles knot with anxiety. "What are you going to do with us?"

"I haven't decided yet. As an ode to Blackbeard, I thought maybe it should be creative. Now, let's go." He shoved the gun toward them, then gestured to the stairway.

As they pounded down the steps, Felicity glanced around her. There were too many men surrounding her. She'd never be able to make a getaway.

Her muscles tensed at the thought. Brody had been right. Her decision to call Magnum instead of the police could very well get them killed. She should have listened to him. Maybe all of this could have been avoided if she had.

As Felicity stepped off the bottom step, a crash sounded behind her.

She twirled around and saw that Brody had tackled one of the men.

Brody! Her throat went dry.

She couldn't let him get hurt because of her.

Her gaze darted around the room. She needed something. Anything to help protect her.

She grabbed a lamp and, before she could second-guess herself, she swung it, hitting another man square over the head. He sank to the floor.

But Magnum. He had a gun.

Just as the thought crossed her mind, she saw him raise his weapon toward Brody.

She let out a scream. "Brody! No!"

***

Felicity's scream distracted Magnum just enough that Brody was able to kick Magnum's gun out of his hand and onto the floor. This was going to be a fair fight. Man against man. Fist against fist.

As he swung a fist toward Magnum's smug, little face, Brody couldn't get the look Felicity had given him out of his mind. She was terrified. Rightfully so.

They'd be lucky to get out of this alive.

They'd managed to take two men down, but there were still two more to go, not including Magnum.

Another man rushed toward Felicity. Brody's gaze remained on her, watching as she grabbed the lit candle from the table and flung the hot wax onto the man's face.

He howled with pain.

"I'm so sorry." Her hand slapped over her mouth, and her eyes were wide with apology.

As the last man came after her from behind, Brody struck a blow to Magnum's face. He'd have a black eye from that one. The punch was enough to divert Magnum's attention for a moment.

"Felicity, watch out!" Brody's voice pulled her back to the moment.

Where was Magnum's gun? He scanned the room. The pistol lay only a few feet from Felicity.

"Felicity—the gun!"

She glanced down and grabbed it. Her hands trembled as she raised it.

The attacker snarled. As he did, she fired. A bullet hit him in the shoulder and sent him crashing.

Knowing Felicity was safe, Brody turned his full attention on Magnum. The man was a beast. Solid all the way around.

Magnum threw a punch and hit Brody in the jaw. Pain radiated through him.

He couldn't let that stop him, though. He had to keep fighting. For Felicity's sake.

Before he could retaliate, Magnum caught him in a headlock. The airflow to Brody's lungs ceased. He jammed his elbow back. Swung his leg. Gripped Magnum's arm.

Nothing worked.

He was going to pass out if he didn't get any air.

"Stop right there!" Felicity yelled, holding up the

gun. Her voice trembled.

A strange smile crossed Magnum's face, and he backed away for a moment. "It's not that easy, sweetie."

What did that mean?

"Let him go, or I'll pull the trigger," she said.

"Go ahead."

Confusion crossed her features. "I mean it. I'll do it."

"You did manage to do quite a number on my men, so I have no doubt."

Where was Chief Haven? He should be here by now if Brody had called him.

"Shoot me," Magnum taunted.

"Why do you want me to shoot you?" The gun trembled in Felicity's hands.

Magnum's eyes sparkled. "Because I do."

"I'll only do it if I have to." Her voice cracked as a weight formed on her chest.

"Like if I threaten to kill your little boyfriend?" At that, he grabbed Brody and put a knife to his throat.

What had Brody been thinking? Where had the knife even come from?

Brody had been distracted by Felicity, by the whole situation. He'd let down his guard for a moment. Fatal mistake.

He could feel the blade prick his skin, and he froze.

"Shoot me, or I'll kill him," Magnum taunted.

Tears welled in Felicity's eyes. "Let him go."

"No."

Brody pulled at Magnum's arm. The brute had him in just the right position that he couldn't get away. He kicked and pulled and tugged. But nothing happened.

The knife remained right where it was.

"All I have to do is pull this blade and he's dead,"

Magnum said.

Felicity's eyes widened. Her breaths came quicker. Sweat sprinkled across her forehead.

Her gaze went to Brody, and she seemed to be sending him silent messages. He understood exactly what she was saying.

She was sorry. She forgave him. She cared.

As the blade pricked him again, he cringed. He felt the blood running down his neck, wetting his shirt.

"Felicity . . . you don't have to do this," he said, careful not to let his throat touch the knife. If her gunshot somehow killed Magnum, she'd have to live with the burden of taking another life. That was exactly what Magnum wanted.

Her eyes met his again. Wide. Scared. Confused.

"What's it going to be?" Magnum taunted.

In a split second, her eyes narrowed. "Fine. You win."

She pulled the trigger.

The gun clicked. But where was the bang? The flash of a bullet being discharged?

The gun was out of ammunition. Brody should have known. That was the game Magnum was playing.

Before he could think of his next move, Magnum rammed something down on his head, and Brody plunged into darkness.

***

Felicity gasped as she saw Brody crumple.

No! Not Brody!

She threw the gun down and stared at Magnum. It was just the two of them now.

How was she going to get out of this?

Something in her peripheral vision caught her eye. The sword. She could use the sword.

Before Magnum could realize what was happening, she reached up and grabbed it. She had no idea how sharp it was, but she had been a fencing champion in college. That had to mean something . . . right?

"A good, old-fashioned sword fight." Magnum chuckled. "Poetic, I'd say. I like it. But it's not fair if I'm unarmed."

With that, he plucked another sword from the wall. *This is ending in swordplay. Really?*

Felicity faced off with him, ready to fight for her life. To fight for Brody's life. For her aunt.

They stared at each other, pacing in a circle, neither breaking eye contact. Felicity would have to learn his style, anticipate his moves while advancing her own. She swallowed hard. It had been a long time since she'd done this. Too long.

Magnum advanced first. Felicity parried, and their swords clanked against each other until ending in a coupe.

"You're not going to win this one," Felicity muttered under her breath, still holding her sword steady.

"I wouldn't be so sure about that." Magnum forced her sword in the opposite direction before lunging toward her stomach.

She jumped back just in time. Her heart raced as she realized how deadly this could be. The swords may not be as sharp as they once had been, but they could still cause damage.

But she would do this for Brody. For her aunt.

Felicity lunged this time. Magnum blocked her.

They stared off for a moment. Felicity braced her legs in position, anticipating his next move, planning for his attack.

"Admit it: you're weak," Magnum said.

Her arm muscles burned. "I was the one who found the treasure, wasn't I?"

His eyes narrowed. "Luck."

"I wouldn't be so sure about that." With one last burst of strength, she knocked the sword from his hand and held her blade to his throat.

Sweat beaded on his forehead, and he let out a weak laugh. "I have to admit. You got me. I didn't give you enough credit."

"That's going to change."

Just then, men rushed into the house. The police, she realized.

Maybe this nightmare would end.

CHAPTER 32

Brody opened his eyes and saw Felicity staring at him. She almost looked like an angel leaning down over him.

"You're okay . . ." he said, his voice raspy and his throat sore.

She nodded, tears glimmering in her eyes. "I am. Thanks to you. I almost got us killed."

He glanced around. "Where am I?"

"You're still at my house. The paramedics are on the way."

Brody tried to sit up, but Felicity pushed him back down to the hard wooden floor. He reached for his throat and felt a cloth there.

"It's just a temporary fix until the EMTs get here," she explained. "Magnum only pricked your skin. What knocked you out was when he rammed his knife handle down on your head."

That must be why his head throbbed.

Everything rushed back to him. Felicity with the gun that didn't fire. The fear he'd seen in her eyes. Then blackness.

"What happened?" he asked.

Felicity filled him in on the swordfight, the police arriving, and Magnum being arrested.

"Impressive," he muttered.

She shrugged. "I don't know about that."

"I do. You were brave." He cupped her cheek, and his eyes grew misty as he remembered his betrayal and the hurt he'd seen in her eyes. "I'm sorry, Felicity. I shouldn't have gone behind your back and called Joshua. I was just so worried for you—"

She shook her head. "No, it's a good thing you did. We'd probably all be dead by now if you hadn't."

"I don't know about that." Joshua stepped toward them. "Sounds like she had some fancy sword-fighting moves back there. I caught a glimpse of a few of them as I walked in."

Felicity straightened as Joshua stood by them. "Did you find my aunt, Chief Haven?"

"That's what I was coming to tell you. We did. She was at a cabin about twenty minutes from here. The state police are with her now, and she's fine. She's apparently telling stories. Lots of stories."

Felicity's shoulders slumped with relief. "That's my aunt for you. You're sure she's unharmed?"

"Bonny is unharmed."

She let out a whoosh of air. "Thank God."

"They're taking her to the hospital to be checked out, just to be safe. We arrested Magnum and all of his men. We're taking some of them down to the police station now. Others we'll take to the hospital."

"What about the treasure chest? Were you able to get into it?" Brody tried to sit up again. His head ached like crazy, but he was just happy to be alive.

Felicity seemed to realize that trying to stop him was futile, and she slipped her arm around his back to support him. Her touch felt good; it felt right. He never wanted to be without it.

"I checked it out, but couldn't get into it," Joshua said. "It seems to be reinforced with some kind of steel or metal."

"That sounds fascinating."

"You have to have the key to get into it," Felicity muttered. "Magnum had half of an interlocking key. Without the other half, it's going to be a real chore to get that chest open."

At that moment, paramedics rushed in. As two approached him, Brody shooed them away for a moment. He wanted to finish this conversation. "How did your great-great-great-great-great-grandfather not realize that there was a treasure in his house? That's what I want to know. Certainly he'd known there was a room like that in his house when he got back from his trips out to sea."

Felicity shook her head. "I'm not sure. I don't know that we'll ever know."

Joshua nodded to Brody. "Listen, more state troopers just arrived, so I'll give you two some time."

With Joshua gone, Brody turned to Felicity. Regret panged in his heart. Had Felicity really forgiven him? "I know I already said this, but it's worth repeating. I'm so sorry I betrayed you."

She traced his jaw with her finger. "No, please don't apologize. I'm sorry. I wish I had a do-over. It was a bad decision on my part not to involve the police. My parents always accused me of being a little headstrong."

"Maybe we can have a do-over. I like that idea."

She smiled. "Thank you for everything, Brody."

"No, thank you. You made me believe in love again. I . . . I didn't think it was possible after Andrea."

"I know the feeling. When I thought I was going to lose you . . ." Her voice caught.

"I want to take you out on a real date when all this

is over. How's that sound?"

"It sounds amazing."

He smiled. "I can't wait."

***

"So, it all ended with this sword." Aunt Bonny picked up the sword and raised it in the air. "I told you that you had pirate blood in you."

Felicity smiled. "Yes, you did. I'm so glad you're okay, Aunt Bonny. I'm glad you're back with me now."

Not even twenty-four hours had passed since the bad guys were hauled off, and her aunt was already back at the house with them. A team with Project Teach was coming up the next day to examine the chest in the attic, and Felicity had picked up most of the house after the debacle the night before.

"I'm glad I'm back with you too," Aunt Bonny said. "It's taken me forever to catch up on all this. Can you explain it to me one more time?"

Felicity glanced at Brody, who sat snuggly beside her on the couch with his arm around her waist. "Those rooms around the fireplace were a part of the original house. The current house was built around them. We were able to read some of those journals that Magnum found, and they answered several of our questions."

"Like what?" Aunt Bonny sat down, the sword still in her hands.

"My great-great-great-great-great-grandmother may not have cheated on her husband at all," Felicity said. "We believe Blackbeard took the name William Pasture when he was in town here."

Aunt Bonny paused. "What?"

Brody nodded. He'd been over all of this with

Felicity several times. "That's what the journals made it sound like. So he had that room built and sealed. As soon as he returned, he and Loretta were going to escape together. But that didn't happen. After she heard Blackbeard had been killed, she died of a broken heart."

"A broken heart? Really?" Bonny blinked, as if this was just her kind of story. She'd be telling it around town and around the assisted-living facility for months to come.

Felicity nodded. "That's what the journal said. Now, I have a few questions for you as well. Did you know about that other property?"

"Well, yes, child. Of course, I did."

"Why didn't you ever mention it?"

Aunt Bonny shrugged. "I didn't think you'd care about an old hunting cabin. Men in our family used it for fishing trips up until about twenty years ago. It was rustic back then, but it worked for what they needed it for."

"Really? How about my father?"

"He used it too. He'd sneak away on weekend trips sometimes."

Felicity shook her head, wondering why she'd never heard about it before. If only she could go back in time and ask her mom and dad questions about her history, about their interests, about their dreams for her. "I never knew."

"There's a lot I could tell you."

"I'm sure there is."

"Maybe you could teach me some of your fancy sword-fighting moves." She swung the sword again and then threw it to Felicity. "Catch!"

Felicity jolted into action, barely grabbing the sword before it hit the couch. She gave her aunt a warning glance. "That wasn't a good idea."

Aunt Bonny remained unfazed. "You caught it.

Good job."

Felicity let out a long breath and glanced at the sword. "I think the handle got cracked when I was fighting with Magnum."

Brody leaned over her. "Yeah, it sure did." He tugged at something. "Look at this."

The pommel pulled away from the handle. Something was attached to the end of it. It was a . . . a key.

"I can't believe it," Felicity muttered.

"I can't either." Brody stared at the half-key. "This is it. This is what we've been looking for."

"We've got to see if this works," Felicity said. "Do you think Joshua will bring the other half over?" Felicity asked.

"Let's ask." Brody picked up his phone.

***

Joshua arrived an hour later, and all four of them went into the attic, into the hidden room, and gathered around the massive chest. A lantern sat in the corner, lighting the space around them.

The room wasn't large. Maybe six feet wide all together. But they all managed to fit.

Joshua handed her the other half of the key. "Felicity, I think you should do the honors."

She nodded and took the key from him. A surge of excitement welled in her.

This could really be it.

She could be making history here.

Her hands trembled as she fit the two pieces of the key together.

"Edward Teach—if he did all this—was brilliant," she muttered.

Her throat tightened as she leaned toward the lock. *Please work.*

She slid the key into the lock and twisted. It clicked.

The key worked!

Felicity turned it.

Everyone in the room seemed to hold their breath. With Brody's help, she lifted the top of the chest.

Something glimmered inside.

Felicity reached her hand in and pulled up . . . gold.

Bonny gasped. "Is it . . . ?"

Felicity nodded. "It is. It's a treasure chest. A real one."

Joshua reached for a coin. "Well, I'll be . . ."

Felicity held the gold piece close to the light, desperate to make out details. It had a crest in the middle with an "MJ" on one side and "VIII" on the other. The words around the edge read "PHILIPP V." A date at the bottom read "1715."

She gasped. "I can't believe this."

"What?" Brody asked.

"I can't be sure, but I think this is one of the tricentennial royal coins. They were made for Spain's King Philip V, really more as a presentation piece. Last I heard, there were only six pieces known to exist."

"So it's valuable?" Bonny asked.

Felicity nodded. "About a half-million dollars valuable. The last time one was found it was at a shipwreck down in Florida in 2015, off Fort Pierce. Blackbeard could have stolen loot from a Spanish ship."

"There are a lot of those coins here." Brody held up a handful. "They all look the same to me."

"The historical significance of this . . ." Felicity shook her head. "It's impressive. It completes a story in history. It's just amazing."

"I say we call Project Teach and see if they can get up here now," Joshua said. "You'll have to hire someone to figure out the financial claims you can make with this. I know nothing about that."

Felicity nodded. "I'm not overly concerned with that. I just want to see that this is handled properly."

"We'll also need to put some men on patrol around here. As soon as word of this leaks, you'll be a target."

"Understood."

Brody pulled her toward him. "You're amazing. More amazing than any treasure."

She grinned. "Thanks, Brody. I feel the same about you."

He pulled her toward him and planted a kiss on her lips. "I feel like things are turning around. Like good things are in store for both of our futures."

She held up a coin. "Because of this?"

He shook his head. "No, because of you."

EPILOGUE

Six months later

"Felicity French, you look gorgeous!" Aunt Bonny held her great-niece at arm's length, her face beaming. "Your parents would have been so proud."

Felicity held back tears as she realized the enormity of this moment—and the joy and waves of grief that accompanied it. "Thanks, Aunt Bonny. That means a lot."

"I've never seen a more beautiful bride." She patted Felicity's face a little too hard.

But that was okay.

Felicity turned away from her aunt and glanced in the bedroom mirror, where she was getting ready. She sucked in a breath at her reflection.

Was that really her? Had she been transformed into the woman in the mirror?

As she'd planned the wedding, Felicity had tried to decide between formal or relaxed. She'd gone with relaxed. Good choice.

Instead of having her hair neatly pulled back into a twist, she'd chosen to let her curls hang wild and free. She wore a simple white gown with a veil clipped at the back of her hair. Her makeup was light and natural–looking, with peachy cheeks and a light gloss on her lips.

"Brody's going to go crazy."

Felicity turned to the new voice in the room. She smiled when she saw Charity standing there. Charity was engaged to Joshua Haven. The two women had become good friends in recent months.

"Isn't he, though?" Aunt Bonny agreed, ruffling Felicity's veil.

"Thanks, you two."

Charity stared at her reflection in the mirror. "Are you nervous?"

Felicity rubbed her lips together. "Not really. Just jittery. The good kind of jitters. The I'm-going-to-be-in-front-of-people kind."

"Well, everything looks beautiful out there. Daleigh is warming up now. The lanterns are lit along the aisle, which reminds me of a fairytale. And there are daisies. Lots and lots of daisies."

Felicity smiled. Daleigh McDermott had agreed to sing and arrange the music for the wedding. Felicity couldn't be happier. She'd gotten to know Daleigh, and Brody was correct—the woman couldn't be more down-to-earth.

Felicity had decided to utilize all of her grandma's old lanterns. Since the wedding was taking place at dusk, she thought the final look would be magical. Apparently, she was right. And daisies had always been her favorite flowers, as well as her mother's.

Felicity and Brody were getting married outside at her grandma's house, now officially known as the Pasture Plantation. It was August, but it wasn't too hot. The sun was setting and should be casting its magnificent colors over the river. The yard had been landscaped and looked lovely, especially with the white chairs set up.

"Who would have thought six months ago that any

of this would be possible?" Aunt Bonny powdered her nose before borrowing Felicity's lip gloss.

Her words rang true. The state had given Felicity a portion of the treasure. It was enough that she'd been able to restore her grandma's house to its original glory. Felicity wasn't going to be living here, however. Instead, she'd opened it up for tours. She'd hired the area's best tour guide—Aunt Bonny—who'd been wowing guests since it opened a month ago.

She and Brody were in the process of building a house on another piece of property down the road, right on the river. They'd be living at Brody's place until then. When they moved, Aunt Bonny could live with them in a special place they'd designed downstairs for her.

Meanwhile, Magnum and his men were going to be in jail for a long time. They'd been unable to claim any part of the treasure. Project Teach was preparing most of the treasure for display at the museum in Beaufort.

About a month after the treasure had been discovered, Ricky had called and apologized. He'd asked to get back together. Felicity had no greater delight than telling him no.

"I think I hear the music starting. You ready?" Charity asked.

Felicity glanced at herself in the mirror one more time before nodding. "I'm ready. Let's go."

Charity adjusted her gown—she was her only bridesmaid—and then stepped out of the room. Felicity followed behind her, through the house, and onto the back porch.

The sounds of Daleigh's angelic voice drifted through the air as a refreshing breeze ruffled her dress. She smiled when she saw that all the seats were full. She'd gotten to know a lot of people in town through the church and Bible study and working with the historical society.

She'd started her own business doing historical appraisals, and she was working to finish her PhD. She wanted to use her experience to help restore homes in eastern North Carolina. Now that she had the money her ancestor had left her, she would be able to do a lot of good with it.

And Brody would be by her side the whole time.

She felt like her life couldn't be better.

She looped her hand through Bonny's arm. Her aunt would be escorting her down the aisle.

Together, they started down the aisle.

When Felicity looked up, she spotted Brody standing at the end. Her heart raced with anticipation. She couldn't wait to spend the rest of her life with him.

He wore black pants with a white button-up shirt. The scruff that she loved so much was trimmed and neat. But the smile on his face said it all.

He was just as excited as she was.

He'd never looked as gorgeous.

Aunt Bonny gave her away, and Felicity kissed her cheek before helping her aunt to a seat. Then she joined Brody on the stage.

As she took his hands into hers, joy filled her heart. Before the pastor even started, Brody leaned toward her.

"I love you, Felicity French," he whispered.

Her cheeks heated with delight. "I love you too, Brody Joyner."

His eyes sparkled. "This is the best day of my life."

A smile stretched across her face. "Mine too. Mine too."

And, she knew without a doubt, that it was.

###

Dear Reader,

As a child, I remember driving from our home in Virginia down to North Carolina, where both of my parents were raised. Back then, I didn't have to wear a seatbelt, so I'd pop my head between the two front seats and ask my parents endless questions about their childhoods.

Some of my favorite stories they told me were about my dad's hometown of Bath, NC. My parents would explain that Blackbeard used to live there, how buildings remained where he'd once dwelled, and how some people believed his treasure was still buried in North Carolina.

Then they'd tell me about summers spent picking cotton and collards. They'd drive me past my dad's old house, which was long overgrown with underbrush and vegetation. We'd eat eastern NC-style barbecue sandwiches. My mom would order fried herring when it was in season. We'd drink sweet iced tea on the back patio with friends while looking over fields of crops and battling mosquitoes.

I remember saying, "One day I'm going to write a book about Blackbeard and Bath. I'm going to write a book about all of this. About your hometowns. About life in North Carolina."

Wait Until Dark is that book.

I started this book fifteen years ago. Yes, fifteen years ago, long before I ever got my first book contract. Every few years, I'd pick it back up again and rework parts of it and then put it aside as other projects arose.

Earlier in 2016, I had my *ah ha!* moment when I figured out the direction I wanted this book to go. I came back to it, knowing that this was the time I had to finish it.

I hope you enjoy not only Felicity's and Brody's stories, but I also hope you enjoy this virtual visit to eastern NC and all it has to offer.

Until next time,
Christy Barritt
www.christybarritt.com

If you enjoyed this book, you may also enjoy these books in the Carolina Moon series:

Home Before Dark (Book 1)
Nothing good ever happens after dark. Country singer Daleigh McDermott's father often repeated those words. Now, her father is dead. As she's about to flee back to Nashville, she finds his hidden journal with hints that his death was no accident. Mechanic Ryan Shields is the only one who seems to believe Daleigh. Her father trusted the man, but her attraction to Ryan scares her. She knows her life and career are back in Nashville and her time in the sleepy North Carolina town is only temporary. As Daleigh and Ryan work to unravel the mystery, it becomes obvious that someone wants them dead. They must rely on each other—and on God—if they hope to make it home before the darkness swallows them.

Gone By Dark (Book 2)
Charity White can't forget what happened ten years earlier when she and her best friend, Andrea, cut through the woods on their way home from school. A man abducted Andrea, who hasn't been seen since. Charity has tried to outrun the memories and guilt. What if they hadn't taken that shortcut? Why wasn't Charity kidnapped instead of Andrea? And why weren't the police able to track down the bad guy? When Charity receives a mysterious letter that promises answers, she returns to North Carolina in search of closure and the peace that has eluded her. With the help of her new neighbor, Police Officer Joshua Haven, Charity begins to track down mysterious clues. They soon discover that they must work together or both of them will be swallowed by the looming darkness.

Other Books by Christy Barritt:

Squeaky Clean Mysteries

Hazardous Duty (Book 1)

On her way to completing a degree in forensic science, Gabby St. Claire drops out of school and starts her own crime-scene cleaning business. When a routine cleaning job uncovers a murder weapon the police overlooked, she realizes that the wrong person is in jail. But the owner of the weapon is a powerful foe . . . and willing to do anything to keep Gabby quiet. With the help of her new neighbor, Riley Thomas, a man whose life and faith fascinate her, Gabby seeks to find the killer before another murder occurs.

Suspicious Minds (Book 2)

In this smart and suspenseful sequel to *Hazardous Duty*, crime-scene cleaner Gabby St. Claire finds herself stuck doing mold remediation to pay the bills. Her first day on the job, she uncovers a surprise in the crawlspace of a dilapidated home: Elvis, dead as a doornail and still wearing his blue-suede shoes. How could she possibly keep her nose out of a case like this?

It Came Upon a Midnight Crime (Book 2.5, a Novella)

Someone is intent on destroying the true meaning of Christmas—at least, destroying anything that hints of it. All around crime-scene cleaner Gabby St. Claire's hometown, anything pointing to Jesus as "the reason for the season" is being sabotaged. The crimes become more twisted as dismembered body parts are found at the vandalisms. Someone is determined to destroy Christmas . . . but Gabby is just as determined to find the Grinch and let peace on earth and goodwill prevail.

Organized Grime (Book 3)

Gabby St. Claire knows her best friend, Sierra, isn't guilty of killing three people in what appears to be an eco-terrorist attack. But Sierra has disappeared, her only contact a frantic phone call to Gabby proclaiming she's being hunted. Gabby is determined to prove her friend is innocent and to keep Sierra alive. While trying to track down the real perpetrator, Gabby notices a disturbing trend at the crime scenes she's cleaning, one that ties random crimes together—and points to Sierra as the guilty party. Just what has her friend gotten herself involved in?

Dirty Deeds (Book 4)

"Promise me one thing. No snooping. Just for one week." Gabby St. Claire knows that her fiancé's request is a simple one she should be able to honor. After all, Riley's law school reunion and attorneys' conference at a posh resort is a chance for them to get away from the mysteries Gabby often finds herself involved in as a crime-scene cleaner. Then an old friend of Riley's goes missing. Gabby suspects one of Riley's buddies might be behind the disappearance. When the missing woman's mom asks Gabby for help, how can she say no?

The Scum of All Fears (Book 5)

Gabby St. Claire is back to crime-scene cleaning and needs help after a weekend killing spree fills her work docket. A serial killer her fiancé put behind bars has escaped. His last words to Riley were: *I'll get out, and I'll get even.* Pictures of Gabby are found in the man's prison cell, messages are left for Gabby at crime scenes, someone keeps slipping in and out of her apartment, and her temporary assistant disappears. The search for answers becomes darker when Gabby realizes she's dealing with a criminal who is truly the scum of the earth. He will do anything to make Gabby's and Riley's lives a living nightmare.

To Love, Honor, and Perish (Book 6)

Just when Gabby St. Claire's life is on the right track, the unthinkable happens. Her fiancé, Riley Thomas, is shot and in life-threatening condition only a week before their wedding. Gabby is determined to figure out who pulled the trigger, even if investigating puts her own life at risk. As she digs deeper into the case, she discovers secrets better left alone. Doubts arise in her mind, and the one man with answers lies on death's doorstep. Then an old foe returns and tests everything Gabby is made of—physically, mentally, and spiritually. Will all she's worked for be destroyed?

Mucky Streak (Book 7)
Gabby St. Claire feels her life is smeared with the stain of tragedy. She takes a short-term gig as a private investigator—a cold case that's eluded detectives for ten years. The mass murder of a wealthy family seems impossible to solve, but Gabby brings more clues to light. Add to the mix a flirtatious client, travels to an exciting new city, and some quirky—albeit temporary—new sidekicks, and things get complicated. With every new development, Gabby prays that her "mucky streak" will end and the future will become clear. Yet every answer she uncovers leads her closer to danger—both for her life and for her heart.

Foul Play (Book 8)
Gabby St. Claire is crying "foul play" in every sense of the phrase. When the crime-scene cleaner agrees to go undercover at a local community theater, she discovers more than backstage bickering, atrocious acting, and rotten writing. The female lead is dead, and an old classmate who has staked everything on the musical production's success is about to go under. In her dual role of investigator and star of the show, Gabby finds the stakes rising faster than the opening-night curtain. She must face her past and make monumental decisions, not just about the play but also concerning her future relationships and career. Will Gabby find the killer before the curtain goes down—not only on the play, but also on life as she knows it?

Broom and Gloom (Book 9)

Gabby St. Claire is determined to get back in the saddle again. While in Oklahoma for a forensic conference, she meets her soon-to-be stepbrother, Trace Ryan, an up-and-coming country singer. A woman he was dating has disappeared, and he suspects a crazy fan may be behind it. Gabby agrees to investigate, as she tries to juggle her conference, navigate being alone in a new place, and locate a woman who may not want to be found. She discovers that sometimes taking life by the horns means staring danger in the face, no matter the consequences.

Dust and Obey (Book 10)

When Gabby St. Claire's ex-fiancé, Riley Thomas, asks for her help in investigating a possible murder at a couples retreat, she knows she should say no. She knows she should run far, far away from the danger of both being around Riley and the crime. But her nosy instincts and determination take precedence over her logic. Gabby and Riley must work together to find the killer. In the process, they have to confront demons from their past and deal with their present relationship.

Thrill Squeaker (Book 11)

An abandoned theme park. An unsolved murder. A decision that will change Gabby's life forever. Restoring an old amusement park and turning it into a destination resort seems like a fun idea for former crime-scene cleaner Gabby St. Claire. The side job gives her the chance to spend time with her friends, something she's missed since beginning a new career. The job turns out to be more than Gabby bargained for when she finds a dead body on her first day. Add to the mix legends of Bigfoot, creepy clowns, and ghostlike remnants of happier times at the park, and her stay begins to feel like a rollercoaster ride. Someone doesn't want the decrepit Mythical Falls to open again, but just how far is this person willing to go to ensure this venture fails? As the stakes rise and danger creeps closer, will Gabby be able to restore things in her own life that time has destroyed—including broken relationships? Or is her future closer to the fate of the doomed Mythical Falls?

Cunning Attractions (Book 12)
Coming soon

While You Were Sweeping, a Riley Thomas Novella
Riley Thomas is trying to come to terms with life after a traumatic brain injury turned his world upside down. Away from everything familiar—including his crime-scene-cleaning former fiancée and his career as a social-rights attorney—he's determined to prove himself and regain his old life. But when he claims he witnessed his neighbor shoot and kill someone, everyone thinks he's crazy. When all evidence of the crime disappears, even Riley has to wonder if he's losing his mind.

Note: *While You Were Sweeping* is a spin-off mystery written in conjunction with the Squeaky Clean series featuring crime-scene cleaner Gabby St. Claire.

The Sierra Files

Pounced (Book 1)

Animal-rights activist Sierra Nakamura never expected to stumble upon the dead body of a coworker while filming a project nor get involved in the investigation. But when someone threatens to kill her cats unless she hands over the "information," she becomes more bristly than an angry feline. Making matters worse is the fact that her cats—and the investigation—are driving a wedge between her and her boyfriend, Chad. With every answer she uncovers, old hurts rise to the surface and test her beliefs. Saving her cats might mean ruining everything else in her life. In the fight for survival, one thing is certain: either pounce or be pounced.

Hunted (Book 2)

Who knew a stray dog could cause so much trouble? Newlywed animal-rights activist Sierra Nakamura Davis must face her worst nightmare: breaking the news she eloped with Chad to her ultra-opinionated tiger mom. Her perfectionist parents have planned a vow-renewal ceremony at Sierra's lush childhood home, but a neighborhood dog ruins the rehearsal dinner when it shows up toting what appears to be a fresh human bone. While dealing with the dog, a nosy neighbor, and an old flame turning up at the wrong times, Sierra hunts for answers. Her journey of discovery leads to more than just who committed the crime.

Pranced (Book 2.5, a Christmas novella)

Sierra Nakamura Davis thinks spending Christmas with her husband's relatives will be a real Yuletide treat. But when the animal-rights activist learns his family has a reindeer farm, she begins to feel more like the Grinch. Even worse, when Sierra arrives, she discovers the reindeer are missing. Sierra fears the animals might be suffering a worse fate than being used for entertainment purposes. Can Sierra set aside her dogmatic opinions to help get the reindeer home in time for the holidays? Or will secrets tear the family apart and ruin Sierra's dream of the perfect Christmas?

Rattled (Book 3)

"What do you mean a thirteen-foot lavender albino ball python is missing?" Tough-as-nails Sierra Nakamura Davis isn't one to get flustered. But trying to balance being a wife and a new mom with her crusade to help animals is proving harder than she imagined. Add a missing python, a high maintenance intern, and a dead body to the mix, and Sierra becomes the definition of rattled. Can she balance it all—and solve a possible murder—without losing her mind?

Holly Anna Paladin Mysteries

Random Acts of Murder (Book 1)
When Holly Anna Paladin is given a year to live, she embraces her final days doing what she loves most—random acts of kindness. But one of her extreme good deeds goes horribly wrong, implicating her in a string of murders. Holly is suddenly thrust into a different kind of fight for her life. Could it also be random that the detective assigned to the case is her old high school crush and present-day nemesis? Will Holly find the killer before he ruins what is left of her life? Or will she spend her final days alone and behind bars?

Random Acts of Deceit (Book 2)
"Break up with Chase Dexter, or I'll kill him." Holly Anna Paladin never expected such a gut-wrenching ultimatum. With home invasions, hidden cameras, and bomb threats, Holly must make some serious choices. Whatever she decides, the consequences will either break her heart or break her soul. She tries to match wits with the Shadow Man, but the more she fights, the deeper she's drawn into the perilous situation. With her sister's wedding problems and the riots in the city, Holly has nearly reached her breaking point. She must stop this mystery man before someone she loves dies. But the deceit is threatening to pull her under . . . six feet under.

Random Acts of Murder (Book 3)
When Holly Anna Paladin's boyfriend, police detective Chase Dexter, says he's leaving for two weeks and can't give any details, she wants to trust him. But when she discovers Chase may be involved in some unwise and dangerous pursuits, she's compelled to intervene. Holly gets a run for her money as she's swept into the world of horseracing. The stakes turn deadly when a dead body surfaces and suspicion is cast on Chase. At every turn, more trouble emerges, making Holly question what she holds true about her relationship and her future. Just when

she thinks she's on the homestretch, a dark horse arises. Holly might lose everything in a nail-biting fight to the finish.

Random Acts of Scrooge (Book 3.5)

Christmas is supposed to be the most wonderful time of the year, but a real-life Scrooge is threatening to ruin the season's good will. Holly Anna Paladin can't wait to celebrate Christmas with family and friends. She loves everything about the season—celebrating the birth of Jesus, singing carols, and baking Christmas treats, just to name a few. But when a local family needs help, how can she say no? Holly's community has come together to help raise funds to save the home of Greg and Babette Sullivan, but a Bah-Humburgler has snatched the canisters of cash. Holly and her boyfriend, police detective Chase Dexter, team up to catch the Christmas crook. Will they succeed in collecting enough cash to cover the Sullivans' overdue bills? Or will someone succeed in ruining Christmas for all those involved?

Random Acts of Guilt (Book 4)

Coming soon

Other Books by Christy Barritt:

Cape Thomas Series:

Dubiosity (Book 1)

Savannah Harris vowed to leave behind her old life as an investigative reporter. But when two migrant workers go missing, her curiosity spikes. As more eerie incidents begin afflicting the area, each works to draw Savannah out of her seclusion and raise the stakes—for her and the surrounding community. Even as Savannah's new boarder, Clive Miller, makes her feel things she thought long forgotten, she suspects he's hiding something too, and he's not the only one. As secrets emerge and danger closes in, Savannah must choose between faith and uncertainty. One wrong decision might spell the end . . . not just for her but for everyone around her. Will she unravel the mystery in time, or will doubt get the best of her?

Disillusioned (Book 2)

Nikki Wright is desperate to help her brother, Bobby, who hasn't been the same since escaping from a detainment camp run by terrorists in Colombia. Rumor has it that he betrayed his navy brothers and conspired with those who held him hostage, and both the press and the military are hounding him for answers. All Nikki wants is to shield her brother so he has time to recover and heal. But soon they realize the paparazzi are the least of their worries. When a group of men try to abduct Nikki and her brother, Bobby insists that Kade Wheaton, another former SEAL, can keep them out of harm's way. But can Nikki trust Kade? After all, the man who broke her heart eight years ago is anything but safe... Hiding out in a farmhouse on the Chesapeake Bay, Nikki finds her loyalties—and the remnants of her long-held faith—tested as she and Kade put aside their differences to keep Bobby's increasingly erratic behavior under wraps. But when Bobby disappears, Nikki will have to trust Kade completely if she wants to uncover the truth about a rumored conspiracy. Nikki's life—and the fate of the nation—depends on it.

The Good Girl

Tara Lancaster can sing "Amazing Grace" in three harmonies, two languages, and interpret it for the hearing impaired. She can list the Bible canon backward, forward, and alphabetized. The only time she ever missed church was when she had pneumonia and her mom made her stay home. Then her life shatters and her reputation is left in ruins. She flees halfway across the country to dog-sit, but the quiet anonymity she needs isn't waiting at her sister's house. Instead, she finds a knife with a threatening message, a fame-hungry friend, a too-hunky neighbor, and evidence of . . . a ghost? Following all the rules has gotten her nowhere. And nothing she learned in Sunday School can tell her where to go from there.

Death of the Couch Potato's Wife (Suburban Sleuth Mysteries)

You haven't seen desperate until you've met Laura Berry, a career-oriented city slicker turned suburbanite housewife. Well-trained in the big-city commandment, "mind your own business," Laura is persuaded by her spunky seventy-year-old neighbor, Babe, to check on another neighbor who hasn't been seen in days. She finds Candace Flynn, wife of the infamous "Couch King," dead, and at last has a reason to get up in the morning. Someone is determined to stop her from digging deeper into the death of her neighbor, but Laura is just as determined to figure out who is behind the death-by-poisoned-pork-rinds.

Imperfect

Since the death of her fiancé two years ago, novelist Morgan Blake's life has been in a holding pattern. She has a major case of writer's block, and a book signing in the mountain town of Perfect sounds as perfect as its name. Her trip takes a wrong turn when she's involved in a hit-and-run: She hit a man, and he ran from the scene. Before fleeing, he mouthed the word

"Help." First she must find him. In Perfect, she finds a small town that offers all she ever wanted. But is something sinister going on behind its cheery exterior? Was she invited as a guest of honor simply to do a book signing? Or was she lured to town for another purpose—a deadly purpose?

The Gabby St. Claire Diaries
(a tween mystery series)

The Curtain Call Caper (Book 1)
Is a ghost haunting the Oceanside Middle School auditorium? What else could explain the disasters surrounding the play—everything from missing scripts to a falling spotlight and damaged props? Seventh-grader Gabby St. Claire has dreamed about being part of her school's musical, but a series of unfortunate events threatens to shut down the production. While trying to uncover the culprit and save her fifteen minutes of fame, she also has to manage impossible teachers, cliques, her dysfunctional family, and a secret she can't tell even her best friend. Will Gabby figure out who or what is sabotaging the show . . . or will it be curtains for her and the rest of the cast?

The Disappearing Dog Dilemma (Book 2)
Why are dogs disappearing around town? When two friends ask seventh-grader Gabby St. Claire for her help in finding their missing canines, Gabby decides to unleash her sleuthing skills to sniff out whoever is behind the act. But time management and relationships get tricky as worrisome weather, a part-time job, and a new crush interfere with Gabby's investigation. Will her determination crack the case? Or will shadowy villains, a penchant for overcommitting, and even her own heart put her in the doghouse?

The Bungled Bike Burglaries (Book 3)
Stolen bikes and a long-forgotten time capsule leave one amateur sleuth baffled and busy. Seventh-grader Gabby St. Claire is determined to bring a bike burglar to justice—and not just because mean girl Donabell Bullock is strong-arming her. But each new clue brings its own set of trouble. As if that's not enough, Gabby finds evidence of a decades-old murder within the contents of the time capsule, but no one seems to take her seriously. As her investigation heats up, will Gabby's knack for

being in the wrong place at the wrong time with the wrong people crack the case? Or will it prove hazardous to her health?

Complete Book List

Squeaky Clean Mysteries:
#1 Hazardous Duty
#2 Suspicious Minds
#2.5 It Came Upon a Midnight Crime
#3 Organized Grime
#4 Dirty Deeds
#5 The Scum of All Fears
#6 To Love, Honor, and Perish
#7 Mucky Streak
#8 Foul Play
#9 Broom and Gloom
#10 Dust and Obey
#11 Thrill Squeaker
#12 Cunning Attractions (coming soon)

Squeaky Clean Companion Novella:
While You Were Sweeping

The Sierra Files:
#1 Pounced
#2 Hunted
#2.5 Pranced (a Christmas novella)
#3 Rattled

The Gabby St. Claire Diaries (a Tween Mystery series):
#1 The Curtain Call Caper
#2 The Disappearing Dog Dilemma
#3 The Bungled Bike Burglaries

Holly Anna Paladin Mysteries:
#1 Random Acts of Murder
#2 Random Acts of Deceit
#3 Random Acts of Malice
#3.5 Random Acts of Scrooge

#4 Random Acts of Guilt (coming soon)

Carolina Moon Series:
Home Before Dark
Gone By Dark
Wait Until Dark

Suburban Sleuth Mysteries:
#1 Death of the Couch Potato's Wife

Stand-alone Romantic-Suspense:
Keeping Guard
The Last Target
Race Against Time
Ricochet
Key Witness
Lifeline
High-Stakes Holiday Reunion
Desperate Measures
Hidden Agenda
Mountain Hideaway
Dark Harbor

Cape Thomas Mysteries:
Dubiosity
Disillusioned (coming soon)

Standalone Romantic Mystery:
The Good Girl

Suspense:
Imperfect

Nonfiction:
Changed: True Stories of Finding God through Christian Music
The Novel in Me: The Beginner's Guide to Writing and
Publishing a Novel

About the Author:

USA Today has called Christy Barritt's books "scary, funny, passionate, and quirky."

Christy writes both mystery and romantic suspense novels that are clean with underlying messages of faith. Her books have won the Daphne du Maurier Award for Excellence in Suspense and Mystery, have been twice nominated for the Romantic Times Reviewers' Choice Award, and have finaled for both a Carol Award and Foreword Magazine's Book of the Year.

She is married to her Prince Charming, a man who thinks she's hilarious—but only when she's not trying to be. Christy is a self-proclaimed klutz, an avid music lover who's known for spontaneously bursting into song, and a road trip aficionado. When she's not working or spending time with her family, she enjoys singing, playing the guitar, and exploring small, unsuspecting towns where people have no idea how accident-prone she is.

Find Christy online at:
www.christybarritt.com
www.facebook.com/christybarritt
www.twitter.com/cbarritt

Sign up for Christy's newsletter to get information on all of her latest releases here: **www.christybarritt.com/newsletter-sign-up/**

If you enjoyed this book, please consider leaving a review.

Made in the USA
Monee, IL
08 September 2020

41839489R00171